The Lightkeeper's Secret

Book Two of The Sea Crest

Lighthouse Series

Carolyn Court

Carolyn
Court

Enjoy!

Dedicated to my sister,
Betty Lynn Courtright

Thanks for your encouragement to write Maggie and James' story for The Lightkeeper's Secret.
Thanks again for all the times; it was never too late at night and
You were never too busy to hear my latest twists and turns of my manuscript for
The Lightkeeper's Secret
Book 2 of The Sea Crest Lighthouse Series.

Cover design by: Consuelo Parra
Model: Aquilina-das.deviantart

Chapter 1

Her pounding heart echoed as her clicking heels slowed and came to rest outside her attorney's office. She hesitated to enter as she contemplated, *What's the worst thing that can happen?*

She took a shaky, heart-rendering breath while the answer rang in her head. *My whole life could change forever.*

Bravely she turned the doorknob and stepped inside. Her eyes immediately met the smiling face of her longtime friend and attorney, Joe Lawrence, as he cheerfully crossed the lobby to meet her. "Hello, Maggie. Are you ready to finally hear their decision?"

That was precisely what she had been trying to figure out for weeks, and she wasn't sure how to answer him, as she continued to ponder the dilemma. *Today is the day I will finally find out what the Chambers brothers have decided. Will I inherit the Sea Crest beach house according to their grandmother's wishes? After all, it had been the summer home of their grandparents for many years.*

She responded, "Yes, I'm generally at peace with the various possible decisions they might make. However, their answer will surely impact my life, and I have no part in the outcome."

"That's not entirely true," Joe answered. "I think you did the right thing when you gave Michael and James some choices and stated that you would honor their wishes."

"Well, that didn't mean I didn't want it or need it," she sighed. "Of course, I was still hoping that I'd be able to go forward with my plans for the house," explained Maggie. "However, I refuse to take advantage of other people to get ahead, especially when they have just lost a loved one. I have to live with the consequences of what I do."

"That attitude may have made all the difference in the world to them. The brothers needed to hear how you felt and how genuine you were. After all, from what I could see, James had a shocking first impression of you, and it wasn't very good, either." Joe shook his head and then smiled and chuckled as he continued, "I mean, throwing him in jail and calling him the prime suspect. Maggie, you were something else!"

"Well, I was angry. I thought James and his brother were responsible for the disappearance of my best friend, Kate. I did not know what they had done to her, but they were going to pay for it. What was I supposed to do?"

"All the time, Kate was with his brother Michael. In spite of themselves, they were falling in love," Joe reminded her as they proceeded down the corridor to his boardroom. "None of us saw that coming." Joe shook his head in wonderment. "When we did find them, stranded, locked inside the Sea Crest Lighthouse, they asked for a Coast Guard Chaplain to marry them."

"Well, the following morning, they read their grandmother's letter explaining everything," said Maggie. "James was the only one who even knew about the will and about her giving the Sea Crest beach house to me. Michael didn't know anything about it or about me for that matter."

"Yeah, Grace told me what happened," said Joe. "It's incredible, isn't it?"

"Yes," Maggie responded. The whole chain of events is unbelievable. Even now, looking back on it, I'm shocked that I even had a chance to inherit the Chambers' beach house. By now, I'm sure they've had a few weeks to let everything sink in. Although Kate and Michael were on their honeymoon for two of those weeks, and I doubt he spent much time sorting out the beach house questions." Maggie smiled in spite of herself. "You know Joe, I've known Kate my entire life, and I've never seen her in love before. It's downright amazing to witness.

"I honestly don't have a clue what they've decided to do with their grandmother's beach house," she continued. "However, I'm sure you know what their decision is, or we wouldn't be having this official meeting."

They had just arrived in the conference room, and Joe thought he had better warn her. "Well, the brothers wanted to come here, in person, to explain their decision."

This news was unwelcome. "Don't you mean to soften the blow?" asked Maggie. She had not counted on seeing either of them today, but the thought of seeing James today had an unsettling effect on her.

"Maggie, they're trying to put their best foot forward, and I, for one, am glad they are already here," said Joe as he opened the door and gently guided her into the boardroom.

She wasn't ready for this. That's when she saw HIM. She had not seen James for three weeks. Well, granted, she hadn't seen him in real life, but she had seen him plenty during countless sleepless nights.

Both Michael and James stood up to welcome Maggie as she approached them. Michael was smiling as he took her hand and hugged her as he said, "Hello." She had seen him and Kate several times during the past week.

James, however, had a sudden feeling of anxiety. The red flags of his brain immediately started the warning, *Do NOT look directly into her eyes!* He took a deep breath as he silently pledged, *Well, I certainly don't intend to, that's for sure.*

"Hello Maggie," he said in a hoarse voice as he successfully avoided eye contact with her. He glanced at her with a mix of apprehension and quiet excitement as he took her hand.

"Hello," she quietly mumbled, but her voice broke as she felt a mild electrical charge surge through her at the touch of his hand. *What on earth was that?* she marveled. *I couldn't have felt more stunned if he'd had one of those prank toy buzzers, which gave an electric shock, attached to his hand.*

James must have felt something too because he quickly let go of her hand like it was a hot potato. *Well, this isn't going very well,* he thought as he sank back down into the comfortable leather chair.

Maggie faltered as she stepped over to the soft leather club chair, which Joe was holding for her, and sat down.

Joe had noticed the reaction that James and Maggie had to each other and almost laughed out loud. He couldn't resist as he opened, "Well, James and Maggie, I'm very proud of both of you, for your new-found tolerance of each other. This is the very first time I've seen you two even approach civility. Don't tell me the martial arts competitions have come to an end. By the way, you guys owe me for one broken lamp and a plant. The next time you two want to roll around on the floor together, use your own place."

Maggie and James were flabbergasted as they fumbled around, trying to respond to this unexpected evaluation of their behavior. They had been, hoping against hope, Joe had forgotten.

Joe watched in amusement at their embarrassment as they both apologized profusely.

Michael was shocked as he practically exploded, "You've got to be kidding. James, did you really fight with Maggie, an FBI Special Agent? What on earth is wrong with you?"

"It's a long story that I'll tell you later. But believe me, SHE started it!" was James' lame defense.

Michael just stared at his older brother in disbelief. He couldn't understand his outlandish behavior, which seemed to suddenly appear and take over James every time that Maggie was around him. He had never seen anything like it.

When Michael turned to look at Maggie, her blushing face proved - guilty as charged. She was, however, wishing that the floor would open up and she could just disappear. Her apprehension deepened when she noticed that Michael was here without Kate. *What did this mean?*

In so far as James was concerned, he had left to go to his home in New York City immediately after they had read their grandmother's letter about her desire to leave her beach house to Maggie. She had heard nothing from him or about him in the past three weeks. *What was about to happen?*

Joe calmly offered a nearby assortment of various pastries, fruit, drinks, and coffee, laying out a buffet sideboard. They all helped themselves and got seated around the large mahogany table. Now that Joe had broken the ice between everyone present, he took this opening to start the discussion regarding the beach house.

"Well, Maggie," Joe explained, "James and Michael have come up with some ideas that might work well for all of you. Nothing is set in stone unless you agree 100%. This meeting is a sort of planning session to satisfy their grandmother's wishes.

"James and Michael are grateful to your dad and agree wholeheartedly to join in their grandmother's effort to honor and thank your dad and let her last will stand as written."

Michael added, "The Sea Crest beach house is scarcely enough in comparison to the priceless gift that your father has given us."

James agreed, "It was an honor to meet your dad on my last visit here. I owe my life to him. It seems like the terrible feeling that I remembered about the Sea Crest area has been lifted."

James finished the thought to himself, *Of course, that may be because I was preoccupied with thoughts of that outlandish Irish red-head sitting across the table from me, right now.*

Joe stepped in to continue his explanation further, "So, regardless of what else they have in mind, this fact will remain unchallenged. They gratefully agree to give the Sea Crest beach house to you."

"Wow," Maggie gasp in surprise. She could hardly wrap her mind around it as she thought, *This is what I hoped for, but it is certainly not what I was expecting. Over the past few weeks, my mind has most often dwelt on what an ordinary person would do when faced with a situation of an unknown stranger, inheriting something of immense value, instead of the rightful heirs.*

However, realistically, I had not even entertained the possibility that they would let their grandmother's will stand as written. She looked at the brothers in confusion as she wondered, *Why had Michael and James done this?*

Maggie was so amazed that she couldn't even react for a second or two. When it finally sunk in, she was so touched that her legs were weak as she stood to thank them. First, she turned and hugged Michael as she choked up but somehow got out a grateful, "Thank you."

Strangely, however, when she turned to James, her entire demeanor seemed to undergo a painful change. She avoided his eyes as she reached to thank him. The touch of his hand sent a solitary droplet rolling down her cheek. She wasn't sure what was happening to her as she drew her teary eyes up to his.

James met Maggie's beautiful emerald eyes, and he was a goner. She was his arch-enemy, but he just could not resist her as he gently touched her moist cheek and whispered, "It's okay. Everything's going to be all right, Maggie."

Yikes! I almost kissed her! James realized in alarm! He promptly released her with a jolt so unexpected that she lost her balance and stumbled backward.

His brother Michael immediately sprang to his feet, caught her arm, and steadied her as he yelled, "Gee. James, why did you do that? Maggie nearly fell!"

Joe, her attorney, thought with delight*, Oh James and Maggie. Tsk, Tsk. That line in the sand, between love and hate, is so blurry, isn't it?*

Michael helplessly turned to Maggie and Joe and tried to apologize, "I'm so sorry for my brother's behavior. I don't know what came over him."

Joe chimed in, "Tell me about it! I've had to step in and separate the two of them more than once. They're something else."

Joe was delighted to see their emotions bubbling over for all to see. He knowingly thought, *I've seen first-hand the passion with which these two have provoked each other. However, when we discovered Kate and Michael, unharmed, and the reason for the anger and outrage was removed, all that pent-up energy crashed together, and the objects helplessly collided. At this point, total indifference is hard to achieve. It's the simple law of attraction vs. repulsion or something like that.*

Meanwhile, Michael was silently trying to figure out why his brother had displayed such appalling behavior towards Maggie. *How well do I truly know my brother?* he asked himself. *Maggie is not only my new wife's best friend, but she seems like such a talented professional. What on earth is going on?*

With that last question, a realization was slowly dawning on Michael. *I cannot believe anyone could seriously; get through to my brother. Although I also acknowledged that neither my brother nor I have ever known any women like Maggie or my Kate, an accomplished Coast Guard Search and Rescue (SAR) pilot.*

Joe cleared his throat and said, "With your permission, I'd like to continue with a couple of other issues that have developed as a result of the will."

"Yes, please continue," said Michael as James and Maggie strangely nodded their unspoken agreement.

"I contacted the Chambers' attorney, Jeffrey Williams, in New York City. We both agree that in the interest of fair play, Michael and James should retain the rights of first refusal in the case of Maggie selling the property now or in the future."

"Of course," agreed Maggie, "I think we should certainly do that."

The brothers nodded in agreement.

Joe said, "Fine. Both Jeff and I drew up this simple contract. It covers the rights of first refusal agreement in the event of a sale of the Sea Crest beach house." He passed the document around the table, and they each signed it.

"Thank you. I'll have copies made for each of you," said Joe.

"The next issue we need to handle is connected to the generous gift that Michael and James have offered to Sea Crest and The Sea Crest Lighthouse. Michael is drawing up the plans for the lighthouse repairs. These include the jetty and walkway, plus the lighthouse. His company will be doing the work as a way to help the community."

Maggie smiled as she responded, "I'm very interested to hear all the details about the repairs to be done to the lighthouse. I know Michael is in charge of the design, and his company is planning to handle the whole project. Kate has been on cloud nine all week due to his generous support and gift."

She looked over at James and wondered: *Why would he be included in this conversation? I have not heard anything regarding his part in any of this. In fact, he's been in New York City for the past three weeks. He hasn't just fallen in love with one of the leading women of Sea Crest, so precisely what does James have to do with any of this?*

Well, she was about to find out.

In an effort to get James on his merry way, Maggie helpfully volunteered, "Joe, since James and I aren't part of this next conversation, maybe we should just leave."

Joe was quick to answer, "Oh, I beg to differ with you. If you wait, I'll explain what the brothers have come up with and how it will all play out."

James remembered what a know-it-all Maggie was, as he smiled and secretly thought, *I'm delighted that she doesn't know anything that is going to happen next. We'll see how calm, cool, and collected you are then.*

Joe continued as he turned to Maggie, "I've had a few interesting conversations with Jeff. He seems to know exactly how their grandmother felt about Sea Crest and also about both you and Kate."

What on earth are you getting at? wondered Maggie.

"Well, I've been in touch with James, quite a bit, over the past three weeks and also with Michael since he returned from his honeymoon. They both agree that part of their grandmother's money that she left to them should be used to set up the beach house as an entirely usable headquarters for all your projects."

Maggie looked at the brothers in utter astonishment as she struggled with this incredible news. "What are you talking about? I wouldn't expect that in a million years."

James loved to see how uncomfortable she was. He silently anticipated, *If you thought you were squirming now, wait until you hear the rest of our plan, Baby.* James felt immediately guilty about the level of jeering satisfaction he felt at her expense.

Joe was continuing with what they all hoped would make their grandmother proud of them. "Michael has offered to draw up all architectural plans for changes made to the house. Both James and Michael have a limited understanding of what you might envision as you set up the beach house for future FBI surveillance of the coastline. James has agreed to handle the financing of the project. He'll be on hand to work with the project manager to make sure the work progresses well. Neither James nor Michael has visited the house in years, so they do not know what changes you need, but they want to help in any way possible."

"I don't understand," said Maggie. "I would never expect that. The FBI will be footing part of the bill for what I'll need."

"We'll explain that in a few minutes. First, we have one more thing to settle," explained Joe, "and this next part is on the table for preliminary negotiations. We'd like to come to a meeting of the minds concerning the future Sea Crest Lighthouse Museum."

Joe smiled as he added, "I've also spoken with Grace Cook about the value of some of the things from the Chambers' storage unit contents. She informed me that many items are priceless, in her opinion."

"Of course," exclaimed Maggie. "As the Sea Crest Historian, she's an ideal choice for museum curator and inventory expert.

The fact that she's a close friend of both Kate and myself gives us complete trust in her. What a wonderful idea."

Maggie was taken aback when Joe immediately stepped back in to further expound on her sterling credentials, just in case the two Chambers brothers didn't understand how brilliant she is. "Grace is well qualified on many levels. Her extensive educational background is incredible in both history and ancestry. She recently obtained a grant to research the history of Sea Crest after a storm destroyed the town hall with most of the land and historical records. She has been investigating any leads that would help document and reconstruct the lost information, including items from storage units, estate sales and newspaper articles, etc."

Joe paused for a moment when he realized he had gotten a little off track. He cleared his throat and continued, "Well, to get back to the matter at hand, the Town of Sea Crest does not have the funds needed to obtain any of these precious things from the Chambers' family. James and Michael would certainly like to retain their grandmother's belongings, so they are currently offering the bulk of the items to be 'on loan' to the Sea Crest Lighthouse Museum."

Maggie clasps her hands together in joy as she expressed her heartfelt gratefulness to the two brothers. "Wow! That's so generous. Thank you, both."

"Well, that's not all we're counting on," said Michael. "James and I were hoping you would also loan some items from the Sea Crest beach house to the museum, although we have no idea what might be in the attic."

"Of course, that sounds like a splendid idea," agreed Maggie. "I have no clue what's in the beach house either, but that's the least I can do."

"Well, not quite," explained Michael. "In fact, you might be sorry; you agreed so quickly. The next part of the plan might be a problem for you."

"Well, I certainly can't believe that," answered Maggie, solemnly. "Anything you need to make this work is okay with me."

"I'm getting to that," said Joe. "Now that we can count on historical items from both the storage unit contents and the attic, here is the next issue."

James was on the edge of his seat, waiting to see the famous Maggie Meltdown with this next idea. *She will never go along with this,* he thought with great anticipation. He had, after all, had three weeks to get used to the idea, and he now actually relished the thought. *On the other hand, Maggie would probably feel like the rug was pulled right out from under her.*

Joe began, "The Chambers' beach house has a separate wing that is equivalent to a guest house. It has a master suite with an en-suite bathroom, a sitting room with a big stone fireplace, and a small kitchen area. That's where the brothers used to stay when they visited."

"Wow, that's a pleasant surprise," smiled Maggie.

Wait for it, wait for it, thought James. His anticipation of Maggie's upcoming reaction was overwhelming.

"James needs to be in Sea Crest while the house is under construction, to oversee the work," explained Joe. "He certainly doesn't want to stay at the Sea Crest Inn during these visits. What better place for him to stay than the guest wing?"

Maggie was utterly unnerved as she thought to herself, in a near panic; *You've got to be kidding. And while we're at it, what exactly did they mean by that, anyway?*

She struggled to think it through without exploding. *Did they expect James and I could live under the same roof?* She remembered the past three weeks. She had been extremely conflicted as she agonized over James. *Yes, it was easier when I hated him.* For the very first time in her life, she was speechless.

Joe had arranged his whole presentation to make it impossible for Maggie to object. He silently regarded her as he speculated, *I've known you for many years, and nobody has ever gotten to you, my dear, or affected you as intensely as James has. I'll bet this arrangement will do you both a world of good.* He chuckled to himself with satisfaction - k*ind of like shock treatment.*

Well, he was not going to give Maggie one more second to say anything. Joe announced, in a very matter of fact manner, "So, in light of this agreement of all parties, and without further ado, we'll go forward with our evolving strategy. We'll respect and fulfill their grandmother's will, as well as honor her wishes.

"The brothers, James, and Michael Jensen are offering the following:

Michael, as the architect, will design the repairs for the Sea Crest Lighthouse. His company will handle all construction work at no cost to the Town of Sea Crest.

Michael will also develop and construct the Sea Crest Lighthouse Museum.

Michael will prepare the reconfiguration of the beach house to suit Maggie's needs.

As the Financial Manager, James will oversee all projects' financial side, including the beach house's build-out, from their inheritance left by their grandmother Chambers.

James will help Maggie with all things concerning the beach house to build as she wishes.

James, Michael, and Maggie will work together with Grace to place items of value in the Sea Crest Lighthouse Museum, with a legal status of *on loan from the owner*."

"Everybody Wins!" said Michael as he gave high fives to everyone.

Maggie was bewildered as she mechanically raised her hand to Michael's celebration.

Chapter 2

"Think of the good things. Many wonderful things had happened and are going to keep unfolding over the next few months." Maggie had been repeating that mantra to her Great Dane, Misha, for the past two hours.

The huge dog pranced along behind Maggie, following her through the house, wondering what was upsetting her new owner.

"Now, as Kate's maid of honor, I'm going to help Kate make her plans for her Wedding Celebration that's coming up," she said as she flounced her way into the kitchen. She opened the china cabinet doors and took out a dog biscuit. "Well, guess who's going to be there?"

Misha did not like to see Maggie upset. However, she did like Kate a lot, and she loved the dog biscuits and treats that she usually brought. Misha was sure hoping that Kate was going to come over.

Maggie dialed the number for the pizza delivery. "Yes, we want the regular order, large pepperoni pizza. I understand that our regular delivery person is no longer working for you. Okay, could you please let him know that we have a Great Dane? We don't want anyone else falling off the porch," she laughed.

The Mah Jongg Club was holding an emergency meeting. They each knew that Maggie had met with her attorney, Joe

Lawrence, to discuss James and Michael's decision concerning the Sea Crest beach house.

The Mah Jongg Club was more than a chance for these four friends to get together to play their favorite fun and fiercely competitive game. This meeting time also served as a secret cover for the women to plan their many 'anonymous acts of kindness.' The whole Sea Crest Community was abuzz with the mysterious phenomenon of all the beneficial surprises that kept happening to people. No one could figure out where all these benefits were coming from.

Maggie walked over to the china hutch and opened the beautiful, beveled glass double doors. The inside of each one was a delicately gathered French lace curtain panel, which shielded secret information from view.

As the elegant doors opened, it revealed their hidden display of various detailed plans for the 'anonymous acts of kindness' they envisioned for the Sea Crest community. Many of these ideas were in progress. A few even had add-on benefits that worked as a domino effect to generate multiple benefits to others. This comprehensive display inside the china hutch kept track of what they had in the works and planning for the future.

Kate rang the doorbell and excitedly let herself into the house. She was Maggie's cousin and her best friend and was eager to talk to her before the others arrived. Misha eagerly met her near the door. The Great Dane thoroughly enjoyed the extra attention, and Kate always brought something good to eat.

Maggie tried to look calm as she greeted her, "Hi."

"Well, what was their decision? Michael wouldn't tell me a thing," complained Kate. They had only been married for two weeks, but he held his ground against telling her.

"They are honoring their grandmother's wishes, and they are making a very generous offering of their own to build out the beach house suitable for all our various projects."

"You don't seem very happy. What happened?"

That's when the other two women arrived and came rushing into the kitchen.

Grace held her hands together and looked up to the heavens, "Oh, please tell us that you can either lease or buy the beach house."

Mary Beth, the Realtor, followed up with, "I hope they didn't make it out of reach for you. I gave them the prices for comparable properties. The same figures that I had worked up for you, Maggie."

"I'll explain everything to you in a few minutes. The pizza delivery guy is here. We better set up the Mah Jongg game and look like we're playing," Maggie said as she tried to explain to herself why she was so apprehensive about sharing her news.

They all looked at her with sympathy, assuming that she'd lost any hope of using the beach house.

Kate was the most alarmed by her behavior as she pondered what was going on. *After all, Maggie had hoped and prayed that she'd be able to use the beach house's ideal location for her FBI surveillance, even if she had the option to rent, lease it. She wasn't expecting to actually have the Chambers brothers let their grandmother's will stand, so what on earth was the problem?*

The doorbell rang, and Maggie held onto Misha's collar while Kate answered the door. The new pizza delivery boy introduced himself, "Hi, I'm Charlie. Alex recommended me for his old job as the pizza delivery guy. He has a new opportunity to work with a botanist here in town. It worked out terrific for both of us. He told me about your Great Dane."

"Of course," said Maggie, as she brought him forward into the great room. "Her name is Misha."

Kate accepted the pizza and handed off a dog treat to Charlie.

"Boy, I've never seen a dog like this before," he said as he gave Misha the dog biscuit.

Misha happily responded with friendly nuzzling; they were instant friends. "Wow, Alex told us she was something special. He also said that someone must have dropped her off and abandoned her. That's terrible. Are you going to train her to do FBI work too?"

"Not at present, but she's brilliant, and she's already been trained to do some amazing things."

"That's super. I remember you visiting the animal shelter. If you need a sitter for her, please let me know."

"Thanks. That would be splendid."

Her friends could hardly wait for Charlie to leave so Maggie could continue her saga involving the outcome of this morning's meeting.

Maggie took her time as she paid him for the pizza and jotted down his cell number. "That worked out nicely," she said as he left and climbed into his vehicle. "Once again, our first 'anonymous act of kindness' with Alex keeps on generating and multiplying separate acts of kindness. It seems to have taken on a life of its own."

They all sat silently, staring at Maggie.

Kate couldn't stand the suspense a minute longer, and she was the first to speak. "Okay, what happened this morning?"

Chapter 3

Maggie turned to her friends, "I've got great news, but there are a few strings attached." They all looked anxiously towards her as she continued, "I met with Joe today to hear what the Chambers grandsons have decided to do with the beach house. My first surprise was that both the brothers were there."

Kate joined in with, "Hurry up. Tell us what happened. Michael wouldn't tell me anything about what they were going to do."

Maggie answered, "Well, the good news is incredible. They're going along with their grandmother's wishes 100%. They are allowing me to inherit the beach house property, uncontested."

Everyone congratulated Maggie and was very excited about this unexpected good fortune.

After accepting their celebrations and noting how amazing it all was, Maggie continued. "We also discussed and agreed on what was fair and ethical as our lives played out further down the line. We all signed the contract stating that both James and Michael will have 'first rights of refusal,' when and if I ever sell the property. In effect, it would go back to the Chambers' family heirs. That feels good and sounds fair to me."

Mary Beth agreed, "Yes, I'm familiar with that. Is that one of the strings you were talking about?"

"Goodness no. That agreement is fine and shouldn't affect any projects we have for our 'anonymous acts of kindness' or my FBI surveillance plans for the beach house."

Now she hesitated while she wondered how to put this. Maggie carefully looked at Kate as she started. "Well, apparently, Kate knows more about the project than we do. She's been married to Michael for two and a half weeks now."

"That's right, seventeen days and twenty hours," Kate smiled dreamily, as she held out her hand to display her wedding ring and batted her eyelashes to show off.

It's an understatement to say that these four friends, who had grown up with her, had never seen her so carefree and happy. Her job as a Coast Guard Search and Rescue helicopter pilot was extremely dangerous and often ended tragically. She was also responsible for teaching and organizing the water safety programs and Red Cross CPR training at the Sea Crest Beach. They were very thankful and delighted that Michael had swept her off her feet and brought such heartwarming joy into her life.

"Okay, okay, we know you're in love," replied Maggie with a laugh. "Well, apparently, Michael is a world-renowned architect. He has worked on bridges and lighthouses all over the world. He has offered to have his company repair the Sea Crest Lighthouse and rebuild the jetty out to the lighthouse. This will include the graceful wrought-iron railing that runs along the top of the walkway between the beach and the Sea Crest Lighthouse."

"The plans are magnificent," Kate added proudly. "Tourists will come from all over to take pictures of the whole area."

Maggie was stalling for time as she turned to the storyboard display, full of sticky notes and paper clipped writings. There were even newspaper pictures of the damaged walkway and railing of the jetty. The structure had been mainly washed away after the hurricane-force winds came ashore. "It looks like we won't have to go forward with all these fundraising plans," she said as she quickly took them off.

"Hey Maggie, quit wasting time! What strings are attached to the beach house?" asked Kate.

"How bad can it be?" asked Grace. "They seem like such nice guys. What could they possibly do that would be the bad news?"

"Did James say something to upset you?" Kate asked with sympathy. They all looked at her in astonishment.

"Where did that come from?" asked Mary Beth.

"Well," Kate answered. "Michael said his brother acted very strange and frustrated around Maggie. It was extremely unusual, and unlike anything, he'd ever seen before. He couldn't believe how rude he was."

Now they all looked at Maggie in alarm.

"What did he do?" demanded Mary Beth.

Maggie was so flustered she didn't know exactly what to say.

Grace spoke up, "Oh, I think Joe and I came up with an explanation that fits the crime." She laughed as she asked Maggie, "Do you want to tell them? Or shall I?"

Maggie turned red as a beet as she stammered, "I don't even know what you're referring to, but rest assured, you and Joe are way off base."

"Does this have anything to do with you calling him the prime suspect when you thought I had disappeared, and you thought I was kidnapped or hurt or dead?" asked Kate.

"Yeah, that's it. James didn't like it," replied Maggie with relief.

"I'll bet he hated it when you threw him in jail. Isn't that right?" asked Mary Beth.

"Yeah, that didn't help either," she replied. Maggie thought, "Boy, I'm going to have to change the subject fast."

"Okay," she continued, "enough of this ridiculous talk. Let's get back to business."

They all tried to act serious and look very obedient, until Kate innocently asked, "How did James like it when you tried your karate moves on him?" Everyone burst out laughing.

Poor Misha didn't know what was happening as she watched everyone acting so silly and outlandish. Mary Beth and Maggie were holding their stomachs from laughing, while Kate was laughing so hard, she had tears in her eyes. What was wrong with these women?

Maggie tried, to no avail, to get out her last response, but with her rasping breath, she could only sob, "Well, he wouldn't tell me where you were or what his brother had done with you. He made me furious!"

"Well, Gee, Maggie, after all that, we have no idea why James would act so frustrated and strange around you," Kate declared between peals of laughter. "We just can't figure it out." she continued sarcastically. "Can you?"

"The only possibility I can think of would be the fact that I explained to him what would happen when the local police had finished questioning him. Maybe it was because I pointed out in detail that the FBI had a whole different set of interrogation techniques at our disposal, to make him talk."

She paused for just a second and then whispered innocently, "For some reason, he turned as white as a sheet."

"Oh, No!" cried Grace. "I can't believe you told him that. Now everything makes perfect sense. Remember how rude he acted towards you when we saw you the morning after the wedding?"

"Yes," Maggie answered cautiously.

"Well," explained Kate. "I initially thought the reason he acted so outlandishly was that he liked you. But now I know it was because he can't stand you."

Everyone continued to laugh. However, Maggie was only laughing on the outside. She couldn't think about that right now. She wanted to change the subject, so she said, "We've got to stop fooling around and get a couple of things settled."

"Mainly," she continued, "The Sea Crest beach house will be inherited by me very soon. Michael will be very involved in the repair and build-out of both the Sea Crest Lighthouse and the Sea Crest Museum. The potential problem is that the brothers will be using a portion of their inheritance to redesign the beach house to handle our many projects. This threatens to shed light on all of our secret projects within our Mah Jongg Club.

Kate said, "I didn't say a word to Michael revealing that our purpose for the Mah Jongg Club is to provide cover for our 'anonymous acts of kindness,' as well as play the game we love."

The ladies were mulling over how they should handle this situation when Maggie suddenly blurted out, "Well, that's not the worst part."

Everyone stared at her as she disclosed, "Their plan is that during this entire build-out time, James seems to think he will be staying in the guest wing of the beach house. They don't appear to think there is anything strange about this arrangement at all."

There was dead silence in the room.

"Whatever you do, please, do not kill each other," whispered Mary Beth.

The Mah Jongg members stole solemn looks at each other, right before they collapsed into fits of hilarity.

Chapter 4

James could not get the memory of this afternoon out of his mind. *I met Maggie's beautiful eyes, and I was a goner. She is my arch-enemy, after all. In my defense, I could not resist her as I saw the tear roll down her cheek. I think I even whispered something to the effect that, "It's okay. Everything's going to be all right, Maggie."*

Yikes. I almost kissed her! James realized in alarm for the hundredth time today. *To make matters worse, I dropped her so quickly that she almost fell.*

That night, as the moon rose in the sky, Maggie lay desolately in her bed. Her insides still had an excruciating ache that took her breath away.

This unexpected sadness and melancholy feeling seemed to permeate her whole being.

The remarks expressed by my friends today mark the first time I've ever experienced a reaction of any kind, triggered by hearing that a man couldn't stand me. In fact, I have interrogated many men and a few women, and none of them have liked me.

At the sound of the phone, she sat upright in bed. "Hello, Special Agent O'Hara speaking," she automatically said.

Upon hearing her voice, he hesitated and actually thought of hanging up.

"Hello!" she stated a little louder.

"Maggie? This is James," said the tentative voice on the other end.

"Oh..., James," Maggie managed to get out.

"Did I wake you? I didn't realize it was that late. I'm sorry, I'll call you tomorrow."

"No. No, that's okay. What do you need?"

"Well, I've been thinking about something all day, and I wanted to know... if you're okay."

"What does that mean? Am I okay?"

With a profound sadness that surprised both of them, James replied quietly, "You just... don't seem at all like I remember you."

Maggie sniffed with a little quiver that caught in her throat as she said, "Good night, James," like her heart was going to break.

James was thoroughly unnerved by this response, and on top of that, it sounded like she was crying. He had to do something quickly. "Wait, hold on, please don't hang up!" he practically yelled.

She had almost ended the connection, but when she heard his urgent plea not to, she hesitated just a second too long. Then against her better judgment, she shakily asked, "Why?"

"*Wow*," he thought. "*This cannot possibly be happening. I remember the tear that had rolled down Maggie's cheek this morning. Yes, I had almost kissed her. I had seemed strangely unaware that I was standing in Joe's office, and my brother was right there watching. The only thing in my universe at that moment had been Maggie*."

Out of near desperation, to say something, anything to get her not to hang up, he said, "Well, I guess I wanted to apologize to you."

Maggie was so taken aback by this that her only response was another small sniff, a sigh, and timid, "apologize... for what?"

James was again alarmed by this behavior. *"The Maggie I remember, the one I've had on my mind for three whole weeks, was not like this at all."*

He had never imagined her like this over the entire time he had known her. *I've spent many hours trying to set her up to infuriate her and pay her back for the numerous ways she has gotten the better of me. In fact, I've enjoyed thinking of ways to turn the tables and get even with her. Yet, this Maggie seems strangely vulnerable.* He felt the absurd need to protect her.

Well, this is all James could come up with, as he said, "I can't explain what happened, but I guess I almost dropped you this morning."

"I felt a little unsteady today. I'm sure it wasn't your fault," Maggie murmured.

"Well, I let go of you too quickly, and I'm very sorry. I didn't mean to do that," James said.

Maggie responded, "Thank you for your kind concern. Please don't give it another thought."

"Well, I guess I'll be seeing you tomorrow at the planning luncheon for the friends and family of Kate and Michael. We're are getting together to discuss the Wedding Celebration."

"Oh yeah, sure. I didn't even think you'd be in town," Maggie said.

"I'm down here until after the Wedding Celebration. It sounds like they've been organizing a pretty big deal," he continued.

Maggie thought, *James will be coming, and as the best man, he will be expected to take part in the celebration. No doubt, he'll give a toast to the happy couple, have a dance with the bride and probably the maid of honor, etc.*

James has mixed feelings as to what he thinks about this. *I can't stand the very thought of being around Maggie. However, on the other hand, I can't wait to see what crazy stunt she's going to pull next,"* he smiled as he expanded on this theme.

"After all, I'm convinced the reason I find her so surprising and shocking is that I never had a sister around, growing up. Exactly what that would be like is so contrary to how Maggie acts that it's hard to reconcile the two expectations into a believable image."

Meanwhile, Maggie responded to the preparations for the celebration, "Yes, I'd say it's almost as big as a wedding would be."

After a moment, she continued, "By the way, do you have any Scottish customs that we could include? I think it would mean a great deal to Michael to include his Scottish family traditions as much as possible. After all, you'll be inundated with the Irish side of the celebration, including the guest list. Any ideas you could give us to even things out would be welcome."

"I didn't even think about that. Michael and I could invite our father. That would be an important addition."

"Oh, I'm so glad you mentioned him. I have no idea if they've already asked him, but of course, he should be here. That would be great."

"This Wedding Celebration will be very dressy and about as formal as most weddings in Sea Crest," she added.

"Well, we'll all be wearing our kilts. They are reserved for 'dress attire only' occasions. Michael and I have the Chambers Clan plaid kilts that I brought down from New York City yesterday. Our dad has the Jensen Clan tartan kilt, and since it was hanging in the same wardrobe bag with ours, I ended up bringing his also."

Maggie suddenly couldn't resist asking, "By the way, did you drive the Bentley down?" The Bentley is the vehicle that James drove down previously when he thought something had happened to Michael. At that time, Maggie thought he was involved in Kate's disappearance.

James said, “Boy, if you’d had the FBI take that apart like you threatened to do, you’d be in big trouble.”

“Ha! Like what would YOU do?”

“Well, they would still be looking for your body, sister. What do you think of that?” demanded James with a laugh.

Maggie started to laugh at the very thought of him doing anything to her.

That’s when James thought, *“Now this is the Maggie I know and, - What? Now, wait just a minute. That’s going entirely too far. I just better calm down and be thankful that Maggie’s not still crying.”*

“Well, I’ll see you tomorrow,” said James as he abruptly hung up.

James sat there foolishly looking at the phone, muttering, *“That wasn’t my fault. I mean, for the second time in one day, she cried. I didn’t even know she could do that!”*

Maggie lay there for quite a while, wondering what was happening to her.

Chapter 5

The next day the Wedding Celebration planners were scheduled to meet for lunch at the Sea Crest Restaurant. Kate and Michael's wedding had taken place on top of the Sea Crest Lighthouse, under extraordinary and very spontaneous conditions. Only James and Maggie had been able to attend. Plus, of course, the Chaplain.

Now, this celebration would be an attempt to include everyone near and dear to them.

Maggie was one of the first to arrive at the luncheon. She watched Kate happily sailing between the tables, adjusting the flowers, and tweaking the table settings without a care in the world.

Maggie hugged Kate with excitement and joy. "It feels unbelievable that my best friend in the whole world is married. It all happened so quickly."

"Tell me about it! I can hardly believe how lucky and blessed I am," Kate bubbled over with unbridled happiness. "I love Michael so much!"

"Well, this celebration is a wonderful opportunity for the rest of us to get to know him better."

"Oh Maggie, I have something special you've just got to see!" Kate pleaded. She glanced around and then pulled her back into the restaurant and down to the chef's office. She hurried to the cabinet and opened it.

"Maggie, you just won't believe it!" Kate implored with her eyes absolutely shinning with anticipation as she withdrew her stuff. "Now, what do you think I have in here?"

"I'm sure I have No Idea," laughed her best friend. "However, I'm guessing it's pretty terrific."

"Great! Now that you brought up that challenge, you can have three guesses. I'm positive you'll never get it."

"Okay. Is my first clue, the fact that it fits in your briefcase?"

"Yes, and No," Kate teased. "In fact, I won't even make you use a guess on that clue. The first one will be: We have both loved and enjoyed it for years, but never knew how it was prepared."

After a moment, Maggie nodded thoughtfully and whispered, "All right, I might be on the wrong track with this, but - are the plans for how they make it located in your briefcase?"

"Yes! Your second hint will be, nobody in the whole Town of Sea Crest knows it except the person who gave this to me," Kate declared with glee.

"Well, I'm going to assume that you didn't come by this valuable information by any illegal extortion methods that you developed while on your honeymoon with Michael ..., Did you?"

Kate burst out laughing, "Truth be told, it has something to do with him. In fact, it's for him. However, if you're nice, he'll probably give you some."

Maggie spoke aloud, trying to piece her way through to the answer. "Let's see, who would have a well-guarded secret to something everyone loves? Might it have anything to do with your wedding? Why were *you* given special access to it anyway?"

This line of thought brought Maggie to a sudden memory. "Okay, Kate, for my third clue, I want an answer to this question."

"Fine," smiled Kate.

"I might have it. I want to know if you've done something truly great for this person. Something that's of significant value? Something of life or death magnitude?"

Kate nodded, yes, each time. Now her eyes were tearing up as Maggie asked, "Last summer on a Coast Guard Search and Rescue mission, did you save her daughter's life?"

Now they were both in tears as Kate nodded *Yes*!

"Yesterday Michael and I went over to Paula's Bake Shop to order our wedding cake. They are designing something extraordinary, which I'll share with everyone during the luncheon. When I ordered the Groom's Cake, the owner took me into her office and showed me this."

She opened her briefcase and slid out a beautiful scroll made of delicate parchment paper, tied with a satin blue ribbon. Kate unrolled the document inside, to display a blue-ribbon recipe written in calligraphy, her famous Mandarin Truffle Cheesecake.

This recipe represented several years of winning the Blue Ribbon for the state's Best Dessert Contest. Baking was a talent and a successful career business for Paula. Her recipes were famous in Sea Crest, and her Mandarin Truffle Cheesecake was prized above all others.

It's very telling that several large companies have offered her big money, over the years, to buy her recipe. It was never for sale. However, the most valuable gift Paula possessed was freely given away to Kate, in thanks for saving her daughter's life.

Kate and Maggie gazed at the beautiful writing. It described how each of the three layers of the cheesecake was made.

The bottom layer was a chocolate spring cake with mandarin oranges.

The middle layer was a chocolate ganache.

The top layer was a cheesecake with mandarin oranges.

Each layer had to be made with great care and cooled completely. (Preferably overnight).

Finally, Paula had included the instructions to assemble the cake.

Signed: To Kate Walsh-Jensen
With Love,
From Paula
(with the date of Kate's wedding)

Chapter 6

James arrived at the luncheon with Michael and Joe. They waved at Maggie as they mingled and talked with people. Michael saw Kate talking with her mom and made his way over to join them. The couple immediately kissed and remained holding hands as they moved slowly to greet everyone at the luncheon.

Grace and Mary Beth came around the same time and hurried over when they saw their friend. "Hi Maggie," Grace called as they approached her. "What are you going to do after this luncheon today? We're going out to the airport later this afternoon. Mary Beth needs to renew her pilot's license by the end of the month, so we thought she could get that out of the way today. Would you like to join us?"

"That sounds like fun," Maggie replied. "However, I have other plans. It seems like you both have made such a meaningful and positive difference with your volunteer pilot work. I, for one, admire your spirit."

Mary Beth said, "Yes, Grace and I started our flying lessons because of Kate. She was a shining example of learning meaningful skills that could serve others. We were able to get our pilot licenses by the end of high school. Of course, Kate was far, far ahead of us in the flying department. But Grace and I have each been able to help out in many emergency situations."

"Yes," agreed Grace. "We volunteer and fly as needed for several humanitarian organizations such as Aviation Without Borders, Angel Flight, Samaritans Purse, and St Jude's Hospital. Mary Beth and I work together, alternating as a pilot and co-pilot team, to fill in during our free- time."

She spotted Joe and waved back as she showed Mary Beth, "Look, there's Joe. He's saving seats for us. We'll catch up with you later, Maggie."

"Okay, you two have fun," called Maggie as they departed.

Kate and Michael clinked their glasses with their spoons to get everyone's attention. "Welcome! We'd like to thank all of you for coming today."

Everyone clapped and found their seats. "While we're eating, we'd like to share a few ideas for our Wedding Celebration," said Michael. "We plan to have the whole wedding reception here on the beach, between the lighthouse and the restaurant."

Kate added, "We'll have an expansive triple tent combination. Each tent will have a high peak in the middle and feature clear canopy tops. Crystal chandlers will hang from the center of each of the three peaks."

The amazed friends and staff called out, "Wow," "Nice," and other complimentary remarks.

Kate smiled as she happily continued, "Our time for the celebration is planned for late afternoon and lasting on into the night. We plan to take advantage of our beautiful Sea Crest Sunset and, later, let them view the stars overhead.

"Of course, the Sea Crest Lighthouse, where we fell in love and where we were married, generates the perfect ambiance for our Wedding Celebration."

The special events manager gave the signal that the buffet was set up, so Kate announced that they'd finish discussing the plans after they ate. The waiters and waitresses started to file into the outdoor cafe area with the food and drinks.

The outdoor area was arranged to reflect the festive event in a delightful design. Teak tables and matching teak chairs and benches, with comfy pillows, were set up in the large patio area. The matching umbrellas were white canvas, which presented a very upscale and casual elegance.

James awkwardly approached Maggie and sat down next to her. "You look surprisingly lovely today," he said, with an uneasy glance at her.

She just stared at him suspiciously.

James felt the need to explain, "I hardly know anyone. Is it okay if I sit here?"

Maggie was taken aback. It had never even occurred to her that he didn't know anyone. "Of course, excuse my manners. I'd asked you right off if I'd thought of it."

After a moment, she spotted Joe and Grace looking her way, and she had the distinct impression that they were talking about her. "By the way, I didn't know Joe was even coming," Maggie mentioned with surprise."

"Oh, he told me last night that he wouldn't miss it for the world," stated James, but he questioned what that meant.

"You had a chance to talk with him last night?" Maggie wondered if that was before or after the phone call.

"Yes. It was so good of Joe to volunteer to let me stay with him for a few days. He mentioned that the guest wing of the beach house probably wouldn't be ready to stay in yet."

"Yes, that was sure nice of him," replied Maggie. Her suspicions were starting to kick in as she remembered, *This is highly unusual. However, James had stayed with Joe after I had put him in jail, as the prime suspect, and Joe, as his attorney, sprang him out in his custody for the next few days. Just what is my good friend Joe up to?*

"He's been helping me with a few of the wedding customs here at Sea Crest," added James.

"How nice of him," replied Maggie again. Her antenna was going up as she asked, "Just which customs has he shared with you?"

"Oh, you know the one where I, as the best man, will be expected to take part in the celebration, give a toast to the happy couple, and have a dance with the bride," James said. But he didn't complete the rest of this thought, *and probably the maid of honor, too.*

"By the way, that reminds me," he continued. "Joe says my grandmother's beach house has an extensive wine cellar, which is famous in the Sea Crest area. Joe thinks you and I should go up and pick out the best champagne we can find for the toast. Hopefully, we'll run across some bottles of Dom Ruinart Blanc de Blanc, or perhaps Moët & Chandon's prestige cuvée, Dom Perignon.

"Of course," he continued, "I don't have the keys to get into the beach house, but Joe said he has a set at his office. No problem." James paused, then added, "How does that sound to you?"

First of all, Maggie thought, *I should go tell Joe to mind his own business and stop putting ideas into James' head.*

Maggie looked around the patio and saw Joe and Grace as they tipped their punch glasses to her, with a nod. She wondered, *Why are they both smiling at me? Now they're giving me a thumbs-up sign. Of all the nerve!*

"Well, James, I think that's a marvelous idea. I think I'll go ask him for a key right now."

"No, he said he'd give me a whole set of keys to the various doors and entrances tomorrow afternoon. He has a luncheon meeting, but he'll be available after 3 PM. Hey, I can come by, and we can ride over to the beach house in the Bentley if you'd like."

Maggie almost laughed as she imagined*, James opening the front door and falling backward into the bushes when he sees Misha.*

She answered, "That sounds like a splendid idea." She wrote down the address on a napkin for him and said, "I've also got a couple of flashlights. I doubt the electricity is on at the beach house, and I doubt the wine cellar has a window."

Kate and Michael soon came over to join them and sat down. Kate's face radiated with pure joy as she asked, "I wonder if we've ever had a party this exciting before?"

Michael put his arm around her as he answered, "Well, I sure haven't. And I know for a fact that my dear brother here hasn't either."

"Hey, you don't know everything." protested James. Then he laughed and nodded, "But he's right. This is the best yet," as he curiously glanced at Maggie.

After a moment, James continued, "Have you thought about inviting Dad? Does he even know you're married?"

"Yes, we called him while we were on our honeymoon. We talked for quite a while. Of course, he's very happy for us. He's also very shocked that we fell in love and got married at the top of the Sea Crest Lighthouse."

"He was planning to come when we called him to let him know about the Wedding Celebration," said Michael.

"Great. I haven't seen Dad in a while. I brought his Jensen's plaid tartan kilt down with me, as well as our Chambers' plaid tartan kilts. He can stay with me at the guest wing of the

Chambers' beach house if that works out for everyone," he said as he looked at Maggie.

She immediately replied in surprise, "Of course, that's fine as far as I'm concerned. I'm sure the papers and all won't even be signed over to me for a few weeks. You're welcome to stay in your own beach house. Goodness," she laughed. "You don't need to use the guest wing."

"Thanks, we'll take you up on that, if you're sure it's no problem."

James turned to Michael and said, "By the way, since we're giving the toast at the celebration, Maggie and I are going to go up to the beach house tomorrow. We'd like to bring back a couple of exceptional champagnes and wines."

Kate and Michael looked at each other and grinned. "Wow, I didn't even know there was a wine cellar up there," Michael said. "I truly don't remember anything about the beach house, but I've had several 'Deja Vu' experiences since I've been here at Sea Crest."

Kate said, "We have asked Paula's Bake Shop to create our wedding cake. They have designed a one-of-a-kind cake topper for us. It has a little Sea Crest Lighthouse. The little bride is wearing a parachute wedding gown, and the groom is wearing the Chambers' plaid tartan kilt."

Kate whispered with delight to let James know about the special Groom's Cake that she is having made. "It's a prize-winning Mandarin Cheese Cake that Paula has entered at the state fair, multiple years."

Kate's face was beaming as she explained about the delicate parchment scroll tied with the blue satin ribbon. "This is the most precious gift she could give me. She said she could never repay me when I saved her daughter with the Coast Guard Search and

Rescue Team last year. Paula said I could share it with Maggie, but no one else."

James happily responded, "Kate, I'm so impressed with your Coast Guard Search and Rescue career. I guess I never even considered that this beautiful Sea Crest community was so vibrant with patriotic talent and skills. By the way, it's a pleasure to join your family through marriage. I admire you on so many levels.

"I look forward to getting acquainted with the majority of your friends tomorrow."

"The whole Wedding Celebration event will be an elegant affair," Maggie joined in with excitement.

A few minutes later, everyone at the luncheon gathered around as Kate read from the large notebook and explained the plans in detail. "We've made a few changes as we worked through our ideas."

She turned the page to display a drawing she had made. "Look, I've made an outline of the Wedding Celebration layout on this little map of the Seacrest area."

She continued, "Here are the three of enormous clear-topped, entertainment tents with the high peaks in the middle. It's a perfect way to frame the stars, the night sky, and the Sea Crest Lighthouse. That's as good as it gets."

"Inside of each peak of the clear canopy, an exquisite crystal chandelier will hang. Each area will be lit below by the candles in the table centerpieces plus above, by the shimmering chandeliers. The perimeter of the three tents will be outlined by beautiful tiny white lights, and sheer flowing draped material to add to the elegant event."

"Were you able to arrange for the Lighted, Click Together, Dance Floor you wanted?" asked James. "I know you wanted them large and lit with rotating pastel colors. The giant 3' by 3' squares change the dance floor color from white to pink, sky blue, or lavender."

"Yes, they'll be delivered and set them up," for us.

Kate continued as she passed around another drawing, "This sketch shows the backdrop for our elegant Wedding Celebration on the beach. A vast, triple canopy with posts and beams that independently support each of the three peaks. Sheer material drapes into graceful scallops as they flow from peak to peak and then out to the surrounding supporting posts. These are gathered and held back with loose ribbon ties and flowers."

Michael added, "Overhead, the stars and night sky are displayed beneath the canopies. In the unlikely event that we have inclement weather conditions, this entire triple-tent structure's walls can be enclosed."

Next, he smiled as he shared the choice of music for the celebration. "The Four Tenors, who specialize in both Irish and Scottish music, will provide the music."

Everyone cheered as he continued, "They will start the music with the Irish Wedding Song, "Red is the Rose." That song shares its melody with the Scottish Wedding's traditional last dance song, "The Bonnie Banks o'Loch Lomond." Both of these are folk songs that can be traced back well over one hundred years. In fact, Kate told me that "Red is the Rose" was also known as "My Love is Like a Red, Red Rose," and there have been variations on the verses as time has passed."

Kate smiled and explained, "Our Irish wedding receptions traditionally start with the song "Red is the Rose." Michael and I will use it as our first dance. Since it's known and loved by our whole Sea Crest community, we can all join in to sing it. We can run through it once for practice if you'd like."

Everyone happily joined in and sang with heart-warming emotions. It somehow reflected the goodwill that they felt towards this likable young man who had swept their Kate off her feet.

Come over the hills, my bonnie Irish lass
Come over the hills to your darling
You choose the road, love, and I'll make the vow
And I'll be your true love forever
Red is the rose that in yonder garden grows
Fair is the lily of the valley
Clear is the water that flows from the Boyne
But my love is fairer than any
'Twas down by Killarney's green woods that we strayed
When the moon and the stars they were shining
The moon shone its rays on her locks of golden hair
And she swore she'd be my love forever
Red is the rose that in yonder garden grows
Fair is the lily of the valley
Clear is the water that flows from the Boyne
But my love is fairer than any

Kate stepped up and laughingly waved for them to stop singing, "Wow! I must say that was great! Thank you! I think 2 verses are fine for today. Since we'll probably outnumber Michael's attendees, I don't want them to feel overwhelmed, all though it's too late for Michael to get cold feet.

"Now Michael will explain his time-honored Scottish tradition for our last dance of the evening," smiled Kate.

Everyone laughed and cheered Michael on as he stepped forward.

"Thanks, Kate," said Michael as he kissed her. He quickly looked embarrassed, as if he had forgotten that everyone was watching them. He turned red and shrugged as he laughed, "I'm sorry, but I just can't be around her for very long before that happens."

Everyone happily smiled at his kiss as he proceeded to explain, "Scottish weddings usually end with the song, "The Bonnie Banks o'Loch Lomond," performed with a bagpipe."

As an after-thought, he laughed as he added, "It's our version of what you might have seen at Greek weddings. We don't break a lot of dishes, but it's still a lot of fun. Okay, gather around in a large circle and hold hands, and I'll show you how the dance works," he directed.

Maggie and James, who had been sitting together, stood, and nervously looked at each other. "Oh well. When in Rome...," James said uncomfortably, as he held his hand open for hers.

James watched the surprised look register on Maggie's face as she shyly reached towards his hand like it was a snake or something. *Really,* he thought. *I am a gentleman, after all.*

However, he was surprised at how much it meant to him that she accepted his offer. *Oh well, nothing ventured, nothing gained,* he thought as he felt her slender hand slip into his. The slight quiver of electricity he felt at her touch was nothing like her failed karate chops. The spark ignited a glimmer of hope for something much more.

Maggie was equally unprepared for the tremor of pleasure that ran through her whole body when she touched his hand. She almost grabbed it back, but he held it firmly.

Michael continued with his directions. "Now, you all know the melody. It's the same as "Red is the Rose." As the familiar music starts, friends and family start to gather as fragmented couples, and families all begin to form a wide circle with the bride and groom in the middle."

"We can sing the tune while we're practicing today. You're welcome to sing the Irish version if you'd like. Okay, here we go."

By yon bonnie banks and by yon bonnie braes
Where the sun shines bright on Loch Lomond
Where we two have passed so many blithesome days
On the bonnie, bonnie banks of Loch Lomond

Everyone happily joined in and sang with heart-warming emotions that reflected the goodwill that they felt towards this likable young man who had swept their Kate off her feet.

O ye'll take the high road, and I'll take the low road
And I'll be in Scotland afore ye
But me and my true love will never meet again
On the bonnie, bonnie banks of Loch Lomond

Maggie could hardly believe her ears as she heard the rich, mellow tenor voice of the man who was holding her hand. She glanced sideways to verify that James was singing those unlikely notes.

I mind where we parted on yon shady glen
On the steep, steep side o' Ben Lomond
Where in purple hue, the Heiland hills we view
And the moon shinin' out from the gloamin'
O ye'll take the high road, and I'll take the low road
O And I'll be in Scotland afore ye
But me and my true love will never meet again
On the bonnie, bonnie banks of Loch Lomond

Michael continued to lead, “Okay, double clap.” He started to clap his hands over his head as he kept the beat. “The tune is irregular: the first part is two measures of 6/4 time, repeated. Now add the Stomp," he yelled above their singing.

They clapped their hands over their heads and stomped to the compelling music. Michael beamed with genuine delight as he clasped Kate's hand.

"Fine," Michael congratulated them as they followed his pied-piper lead.

"Now, let's try what happens as the song progresses. The outside circle of people will join hands and move the circle in, smaller towards the couple. Then back up to expand the circle into a large, all-inclusive band of guests, as they sing the familiar chant in time to the music."

"The festivities and final song will be drawn-out as everyone gets involved with the increasing rowdy stomping and clapping. The guests and family join in the loud, enthusiastic singing like an Anthem, as they dance around the wedding couple. (That will be Kate and me, by the way)."

They both beamed with love as Michael happily announced, "This Scottish tradition will be joined with the Irish traditions for our new family."

This intimate gathering of family and friends felt a unique, endearing bond with this engaging young Scottish gentleman, who had captured the heart of their Lightkeeper's Daughter, Kate.

Chapter 7

The following afternoon, James went with Joe to have the duplicate keys made. Joe advised the clerk, "Yes, I need a double set of each of these keys."

Then he turned to James and explained, "That would cover the set for Maggie when she takes possession of the beach house."

"Thanks. I'm picking her up in an hour. We want to pick out something special from the wine cellar to toast Michael and Kate. I was telling them yesterday that I didn't know they had a wine cellar. I really can't remember anything much about the house at all."

As an afterthought, he said, "While we're in town, I need to drop off my watch to get it serviced and replace the battery. Do you know which jeweler would be the best one to use?"

"Well, it looks like you have a Rolex, and I didn't think any of them had batteries."

James laughed, "Well, you're mostly right. Only one model of Rolex watch, the Oysterquartz, has ever had a battery. They made them in the 1970s to 2001, I think. I'm not sure if a jeweler here in Sea Crest handles these, but it would sure help me out if I could get this serviced while I'm here."

"The best place in town is right next door. It might take a couple of days, but they do great work," explained Joe.

"Thanks, I think I'll go over and see if they can help me get my watch taken care of while you finish getting the keys made."

"By the way, if you want to do something special for Maggie, why don't you have a little box of fancy dog treats, gift-wrapped next door," advised Joe. "She has the cutest little puppy that she simply adores. That way, you are not showing up at the door with flowers for Maggie, which she might misconstrue as romantic. But she certainly can't object if you present a box of treats for her puppy. Plus, it would make you look chivalrous and kind."

"That's an excellent idea," James said as he headed out the door. "Oh, is the little puppy a female or a male?" he asked.

"The tiny little thing is a female," Joe answered with a smile as he thought about calling Grace and telling her how he'd set up James.

A little while later, Joe and James parted ways, as James started his Bentley, with the gift-wrapped treats on the car's seat. Alongside it was a second little, gift-wrapped box.

When James arrived at Maggie's address and turned into the circular driveway, he was taken aback to see a charming coastal cottage with the white picket fence along the front sidewalk. The yard was overflowing with a collection of some of the most exquisite flowers he'd ever seen.

The covered wrap-around porch had a large bed of hydrangea blossoms facing the street. Boston Ferns were hanging along the perimeter of the palatial sun porch, spaced perfectly to showcase three tranquil tropical ceiling fans. The oversized pillows on the wicker furniture and the porch swing completed this peaceful, comfortable space. The climbing rose-covered trellis behind it gave shade and privacy while lounging.

Large pots overflowing with beautiful flowers lined the steps leading up to the porch. A miniature lemon tree adorned the space next to a tea-cart. Even more potted plants were staggered along the floor, accenting two small tables.

James pulled out the napkin that Maggie had written her address on and rechecked it. *Yes,* he thought, *shockingly enough, this is Maggie's home. Wow, this is unexpected. In fact, her place looks so inviting and so comfortable that I feel like I could take a seat on the side porch and happily stay there all day.*

He gazed at the simple mix that combined the best old-fashioned style with the addition of the best of new. He felt the home and the landscaping looked like a postcard, and James fleetingly realized he longed to be in it.

This warm and tranquil mood fueled James' confusion as he mumbled, "Well, this just doesn't seem like the guns blazing, 'You're our Prime Suspect,' FBI Special Agent, Maggie that I know."

Chapter 8

James parked the Bentley and looked down at the car seat at his two gift-wrapped packages. "I hope the little dog likes them," he said as he opened the car door.

It was sure nice of Joe to come up with this idea, he happily continued silently to himself. *I'll have to thank him again this evening.*

As he exited the vehicle and went up the front steps, he suddenly got anxious. He thought, *What in the world do I need to feel nervous about anyway? I am just taking Maggie to pick out a couple of bottles of champagne, in the middle of the afternoon, for heaven's sake. It's certainly not a date,* he insisted. *He was dismayed when he realized that his palms were sweating.*

Maggie came to the door on the first ring. As she opened the door, she was saying, "Misha, calm down. He's my friend."

What did she say that for? James wondered, as his eyes met eye-level with the eyes of the biggest dog he had ever seen in his life.

Maggie held the collar of a Great Dane, as the colossal dog went directly for the gift-wrapped packages that James was holding.

This was so unexpected that James took a small miss-step backward as Misha continued to investigate, sniff, and finally snatch both packages before James could stop her.

As James teetered precariously on the edge of the top step, Maggie reached out to help him regain his balance. They both grabbed onto each other awkwardly, but James was too heavy for Maggie to hold, as they slowly toppled backward out of the doorway. He naturally shielded her from harmful twigs and branches while he tenderly held her close as they fell. By the time they landed in the bushes, James had protectively carried Maggie right along with him to the end.

Maggie's auburn red hair was flying everywhere as she tried in desperation to get her balance and climb off James. "I'm so sorry," she cried as she struggled to get up. "I don't know what would have caused Misha to go after those beautiful packages," Maggie gasped.

James watched this fascinating exhibition of her stumbling around, apparently humiliated, when he had needed to help her avoid harm, as they fell off the porch. Maggie continued to apologize profusely. "Oh, I'm so sorry. I know you were trying to cushion the fall for me. I hope you weren't hurt... Are you okay, James?"

"Yes," James responded quietly. "Of course, I'm all right. What about you?"

He was thoroughly confused. He tried to recover from the shocking realization that, *I've just been holding my previous arch-enemy in my arms. Still, she felt like the most precious person in the world to me.*

Just then, he saw Misha looking down at both of them, with dog treats, paper scraps, and ribbons sticking out of her mouth, and James just started to laugh.

Maggie looked to see the very guilty but happy dog with the contents of one of the gift boxes in her mouth. She began laughing as she apologetically asked James, "What in the world was in that box?"

"Dog treats," James laughed. "Joe said you had a new PUPPY! Just wait till I see him. Does he know you have a Great Dane?"

They shared a hilarious carefree laugh as they hugged for the sheer delight of being fooled by Joe's joke. James, still laughing, rolled over, but suddenly stopped cold.

He propped himself up on one elbow and carefully looked down at Maggie. She had stopped laughing too, as she whispered, "Thanks for the dog biscuits. That was terribly kind of you."

Misha watched the two of them intently while she finished the first box. She thought Maggie and that guy were having fun, but she sure wanted to find some more treats. When she turned to investigate the other box, she heard James yell, "No, don't let her eat that dog collar!"

Both Maggie and James scrambled up, and Maggie retrieved the beautiful diamond dog collar. "Why James," exclaimed Maggie, "this is gorgeous." She continued to hold it up to the light and admire the collar as she thought, *I've never seen rhinestones sparkle like this before.*

"Well, it's way too small," answered James with a laugh. "Joe is truly in for it now. He said you had a tiny little puppy."

"Yes, we should think up something good, to pull on Dear Old Joe. I think Grace is conspiring with him. We'll have to get them both," laughed Maggie.

"In the meantime, let me exchange this collar for one the correct size. Do you think her neck will get any bigger? I want to have the proper one that will serve her now and well into her adult life."

"I'm not sure," she answered thoughtfully, "but my dad knows everything. I'll ask him."

"If you asked the owners of the breeder that you got her from, they should be aware of stuff like that too."

"That will be a problem," Maggie said sadly. "Misha was abandoned here in Sea Crest a few weeks ago, and no one has reported her lost. We've checked up and down the coast."

"You've got to be kidding. Why would anyone do something like that?" James was appalled.

"The shelter told me that maybe the previous owners didn't know how big a Great Dane would get. They also might have thought that if a dog was this big, it was no longer a puppy but an adult dog. They expected her to be calmer, not running around and acting playful as a puppy does."

"Wow, this is shocking to me," declared James.

Her voice broke as she quietly confessed, "My biggest fear now is that the owners will come back and try to take her away."

She appeared lost in that possibility as she unconsciously touched his hand. Maggie seemed unaware of the outlandish idea that James might remotely symbolize safety to her. As she whispered the heart-wrenching secret, "I don't think I'll be able to stand it."

That's when he heard himself offer, "I promise, I will never let them take her, Maggie."

"Thank you," Maggie was barely audible, as she lifted her teary eyes to his.

He glanced briefly into her shining emerald eyes. This small gesture will prove to be life-changing for James. Every fiber of his being was screaming, *Now you've done it!*

He did not realize that he had just stepped over the line, and his goose was officially cooked.

Chapter 9

Upon further reflection, James believed that he had technically tried to avoid her eyes and had every conscious intention of doing just that. That fact had to account for something. He certainly hoped it meant he had achieved success as he narrowly escaped falling for her because, after all, she started it. No one could have possibly made a choice to ignore her fear of losing Misha.

To change the mood, he announced, “Let’s get ready and go up to the beach house.”

“Yes, that's an excellent idea.”

“I’ve been wondering if we should take anything extra with us?” said James.

“I hate to tell you what an over-preparer I am,” answered Maggie.

“You can’t be any worse than me,” laughed James. “I picked up a few things last night. My list includes extra wine corks, a couple of wine corkscrews, and some little cups, for a start. What have you got?”

“You’ll never believe it, but I looked up a few hints online for wine tasting parties. Are you ready?” asked Maggie.

“Here we go: I asked the Sea Crest Restaurant to make up a batch of Fancy Grissini, which I was told to heat up this morning. It’s one of the things they serve at their wine tastings. They have a slice of prosciutto wrapped around breadsticks, at an angle, slightly overlapping," bragged Maggie. "There, can you beat that, Buddy Boy?"

"No, you had me at Fancy. Nicely done," conceded James. "When we have finished tasting wine and champagne, we can feast on French bread and an elaborate tray, laden with cheeses, grapes, and chocolates. How does that sound, Your Highness?"

"Great," answered Maggie. "Now, I'm going to make a pot of hot coffee. I have a large thermos that I use for stakeouts, and I'm sure it will come in handy in case we are cold."

"And don't forget the flashlights. You promised me a flashlight," added James.

"Oh, I've got that covered," Maggie assured him.

James followed Maggie into the kitchen. James' newest best friend trotted along behind him.

As Maggie finished the preparations and the coffee started to drip, James sat down in an oversized, comfortable wing-backed chair. He laid his head back in the corner and thought about how relaxed he felt here. As he sank into the coziness, a sense of well-being and contentment came over him.

Misha sprawled out on the rug next to his feet.

The phone rang, and Maggie answered on the first ring, "Special Agent, Maggie O'Hara speaking."

After a moment, she cut in to explain, "No, I will not be available to take over this witness protection case until later, next week. Yes, I understand he needs a 24-hour watch and that his status is high alert level. Yes, he is at risk until he testifies at the trial. No, I am not available. I know he's in imminent danger. You may have to move him to a more secure jail for his protection. No, I'm not the only qualified special agent that can protect him."

Maggie walked over to the sink and rinsed out the thermos. "Well, see what you can do until mid-week."

The person on the other end of the line said Good-Bye and hung up. Maggie did not hang up because she noticed that James appeared to be listening in on her conversation, and she thought this would be an ideal time to have a little fun at his expense.

She talked into the dead phone, "See if it's possible to delay this guy's extradition to the United States for a few days. Then, have armed guards and FBI agents accompany him. Keep the shackles and handcuffs on him the entire time. Have him flown by US Coast Guard Helicopter to our landing pad on the Sea Crest Beach. I will have an unmarked car to transfer him to my protection."

James felt a chill of alarm run down his spine. He listened to this conversation and wondered*, Does this mean that Maggie would have this terrible criminal here on the property, alone?*

This is not good; he felt like he was in a nightmare again. *What was she thinking?*

She paused and listened, then restated over the dead telephone line, "I know he drugged me, tied me up, and left me for dead the last time, but I won't let that happen again. In fact, I've taken some additional karate lessons, and I'm sure I'll be able to take him this time."

With that, Maggie hung up. She was calmly rinsing out the thermos parts and laying them aside until the coffee was ready.

James was not calm at all, as he bolted out of the chair and exploded, "Wait just a minute! This is not a good idea!"

"What are you talking about?" she asked innocently.

"Maggie, this is dangerous!" James shouted in frustration. "Don't do it!" James was sick with outright fear for her.

She looked at him with surprise, "Oh, I'm often guarding someone un-chaperoned, if that's what bothering you," she smiled.

James found that absolutely incredible as he tried to get through to her, "Maggie, I'm serious. This guy is a savage criminal. You can't do this."

"Oh, he won't hurt me. I know karate."

"Wait just a minute. I forbid..." he started.

Maggie couldn't keep a straight face any longer, and she burst out laughing, "Oh, James, you are a riot. I'm just kidding you."

"What?" James was a combination of relieved and confused.

"They hung up way back at the beginning of the conversation," she laughed as she swatted at him with the kitchen towel.

"Really? You know you could get in trouble doing that, little girl," answered James as he grabbed the towel.

She let go of her end of the dishtowel and, joking, asked, "Oh yeah? What are you gonna do?"

James laughed as he answered, "Oh, you'd like me to tell you, huh? No. I'm going to lead you into a false sense of security, and when your guard is down, I'm going to scare you to death. See how you like it." She took a step backward and realized she had backed right into the corner.

James was now in charge. He put his hands on his hips and said with a nod towards Misha, who was still lying on the floor with her head resting calmly on her paws, watching this strange behavior. "Now, Misha and I want you to apologize for being so mean to us."

"What?" she laughed.

"You heard us. We want you to promise that you won't scare us like that, ever again."

Maggie laughed as the telephone rang. She quickly escaped past James and answered the phone. "Yes, but hurry, we're almost ready to leave," she responded with a smile.

She started pouring the coffee into the thermos, as James asked if everything was all right.

Maggie explained as they headed for the front door, "Well, Kate's on her way over with Michael because he wants to see our tiny little dog. Kate wants to see his face when he opens the door and sees Misha," she finished as fast as she could. "Oh, they're in the driveway now."

"Joe strikes again," laughed James.

He looked out the window where she was pointing and explained, "By the way, Maggie, you are not off the hook." When he saw that she was ignoring him, he added, "And another thing, You could also get into trouble misleading the FBI by pretending you know karate."

When Kate and Michael came up the front steps, Maggie opened the door, and there stood Misha, expectantly waiting for Kate's treats. Michael took a step back, and Kate caught him.

"Well, Michael, that's not nearly the catastrophe your brother suffered," said Maggie. "I had to fish him out of the bushes."

"You did not," protested James. "I had to rescue you from yourself after you pushed me out the door backward and used one of your failed karate chops to land right on top of me and crush me to death. Oh, and by the way, I was both horrified and utterly shocked by how much you weigh! I couldn't even move. It was awful."

Maggie wasn't going to let that go, unchallenged as she lit into him, "You've got to be kidding. I was trying to help you and keep you from falling off the porch, but you wouldn't let go of my arm." She stopped for a breath and then continued, "And Misha, my great protector, was so busy eating the dog treats, from her new best friend, that she wouldn't even save me from this - this beast."

Misha wagged her tail and looked excited at the laughter and mayhem. In contrast, Kate and Michael looked at each other with knowing smiles as they recognized what was happening right in front of them.

"Well, you'll see, once you're an old married couple, like us, you learn to help each other," stated Michael.

Chapter 10

"We're bringing you the special lights you asked for, Maggie," explained Kate.

"Did you get two pairs? I hope they're not one size fits all. *You-know-who* has an awfully big head," complained Maggie.

"What are you talking about?" asked James.

"Well, they're what we in the trade like to call night vision goggles. This unique headgear includes headbands that hold the upgraded LED headlamps."

As she mentioned each thing, Maggie was demonstrating the feature like she was a flight attendant and enjoying every minute of it. "The white LED lights are adapted for use in combination with goggles that could be used together or separately depending on the agent's needs. They also have fold-down ear flaps for added warmth," smiled Maggie as she whipped them out of the bag. "These are the regulation, high-powered equipment for use in both the Coast Guard, Search and Rescue Missions, and FBI surveillance."

Next, Maggie took on the cocky persona of a lecture by Barney Fife from Mayberry as she continued in a know-it-all manner. "I'm not sure such an inexperienced person, with no training what-so-ever, such as yourself, James, should even be allowed to touch these. To say nothing about actually wearing them. However, since you'll be with a professional, such as myself, we will make a special allowance for you."

"Yeah, right," laughed James. "You honestly think you're something special, don't you?"

"Yes, as a matter of fact, I do. That's exactly why the FBI promoted me to an FBI Special Agent."

"Oh brother," moaned James. "Let's hope your FBI assignments don't involve any karate. You're terrible at it."

Kate and Michael watched this fascinating exchange, both wondering, what on earth had happened to them and what did they do with the real James and Maggie?

Maggie and James were gathering up the thermos and all their supplies, paraphernalia, and wine tasting stuff, as if they were traveling on a month-long trip. They had acted like no one else in the room even existed, as they finished packing their backpacks.

When they got to the door, James turned and said, "Now, we're going up to the beach house and pick out the most expensive champagne we can find. If we are not back by 1900 hours, military time, or 7 pm civilian time, please do not come looking for us. I'm afraid Maggie will have finally gone too far, and she will be the victim of some dreadful, however, well-deserved accident!"

Chapter 11

Maggie and James quickly got into the Bentley before realizing that their dramatic exit out the front door had left Kate, Michael, and Misha, all staring out the window at them.

James was first to react to their ridiculous walkout, as he mischievously suggested, "Let's just wave goodbye." So, as they drove away with carefree waves of their hands, that's precisely what they did.

Maggie couldn't stop smiling. She had seen brief glimpses of James letting his guard down, but she had never seen his sense of humor before.

As they were driving up the winding road to the beach house, James said, "Will Misha be okay while you're gone? We could have brought her with us, you know."

Maggie was shocked by this statement. She assumed, *The proud James would have never let a strange dog, of any size, to say nothing of her huge Great Dane, take a ride in his precious Bentley.*

She answered, "It's very thoughtful of you to think of Misha, but I'm sure she'll be fine while we're gone."

"Okay, maybe next time," he answered.

After a moment, he continued, "I have been thinking and wondering about the beach house quite a bit lately. You know, I haven't been up here in years. I mostly remember Sea Crest because my father and I were taking my first open water dive here. I was hoping to earn my Junior PADI certification the next year when I turned 13. In the United States, that's for ages 13-15 years old."

"My dad knew about the shipwreck offshore, so we were excited to share this adventure. But in real life, this turned into a very traumatic experience, which has never left me. When my father saw that a piece of the wreckage had cut my air hose, he wouldn't leave me. Instead, he shared the air in his tank," James said sadly. "I remember believing there was no hope for us, and we would both surely die."

"That must have been terrifying!" Maggie whispered as she laid a hand on his arm.

"Yes, it was. That's when a miracle happened. We watched another diver, (who we later learned was your father), float slowly into view. He miraculously appeared from above with 2 fresh tanks. First, he helped me exchange a fresh tank with my old one. Next, he helped my dad change his nearly depleted tank for the other fresh tank that your father had used to descend and search for us. Slowly we each surfaced and survived. Your dad saved both of our lives that day. Over the years, I've had numerous nightmares about being underwater and scuba diving with my air hose cut."

Maggie knew the story, but that didn't minimize her thankfulness that her father had gotten to them in time. She soberly said, "I'm so grateful that my dad was fishing in a nearby cove that day. When your brother sent out the S.O.S. for help, Dad was able to get there immediately."

James and Maggie silently reflected on what felt like a new, however unexpected bond, as the Bentley was advancing up the winding road to a higher level of terrain. As the elevation climbed, so did the spectacular view which overlooked the Town of Sea

Crest and the Sea Crest Lighthouse. James entered the circular driveway and pulled up in front of the sprawling Victorian beach house. The casual layout of the property, with its sweeping covered porches, was spectacular.

As they stepped out of the car, James quietly marveled, "I vaguely remember the house now. I don't remember this view at all.

Maggie was also whispering, "Wow, I haven't been here since I was a child. Kate and I had the unforgettable adventure of selling Girl Scout cookies to a woman here, one time. We didn't know who she was, but she was very kind to us." As an after-thought, she smiled and added, "She bought some cookies, so we were happy."

That seemed to lighten the mood, as James turned to look far out toward the Sea Crest Lighthouse and beautiful ocean beyond.

Neither one spoke as they drank in the breathtaking beauty.

Maggie quietly confessed, "Remember when we watched the fireworks display a few weeks ago, after Kate and Michael's wedding? I almost told you the best place to view the fireworks would be from up here. Although, of course, I was only up here that one time."

After a moment, she finished the thought, with a breathtaking whisper, "I'll tell you now, my memory could never do this view justice."

James felt the depth of her feeling and cleared the lump from his throat, "I know what you mean. This site is incredible."

Maggie was realizing, *I've lived in Sea Crest my whole life, and I've never seen things from this perspective before.*

James' thoughts were more along the lines of regret. *I've avoided this beautiful home for many, many years. I missed sharing this with Grandmother Chambers. What a shame. I wish I could make it up to her.*

His melancholy mood disintegrated as soon as he looked over at Maggie. She was gazing with love and emotion, at the inspiring Sea Crest Lighthouse with rolling waves breaking around it, sending sprays of surf crashing onto the beach below.

He thought of a call he needed to make immediately. "Maggie, please excuse me for just a minute. I have an urgent matter to take care of, and I think I'd better do it before our wine tasting endeavor."

"Sure, go right ahead. I'll continue to enjoy this magnificent view."

James retraced his steps back toward the Bentley until he was out of earshot. He placed a call to Jeffrey Williams, his attorney in New York.

"Hi Jeff, I need a favor. I'm down here at Sea Crest, and I need you to look into something for me. Time is critical. Do we have any detectives or investigators who can drop everything else and do some research for me? It will be like a needle in a haystack, but I'll make it worth their while."

"What's this all about, James? Are you trying to find a reason to contest your grandmother's will again?"

"Of course not. I'm okay with Maggie getting the beach house. However, someone abandoned a Great Dane dog, down here in Sea Crest, and Maggie has taken it in."

"A Great Dane? Do you know how big those dogs are?"

"Yes, I've met the dog. Jeff, you should see them together. It's heartwarming. The problem is that she's fallen in love with Misha, and she's afraid someone will return and take her away."

"Well, that sometimes happens if the people feel guilty and go back to retrieve the dog. Sometimes the dog was lost through an honest mistake or misunderstanding. But most often, I believe it is intentional, and the owners feel bad and try to find the dog again," replied Jeff.

"Well, I promised Maggie that I wouldn't let that happen."

"You did what? You're kidding. How are you going to do that?" asked Jeff in desperation.

"She had tears in her eyes. I couldn't stand it!" said a desperate James. "I had no choice."

Now the truth behind this strange promise was beginning to dawn on Jeff. "Listen, I'll get our best guy on it, but it's going to be hard to find the person who dropped the dog off and abandoned her."

"Well, I'm sure Joe Lawrence will do all he can from this end but don't involve Maggie. I said I wouldn't let anyone take Misha from her, and that's a promise, WE are all going to make it happen. I want her to have a legal document that guarantees that in writing. Of course, money is no object. I'll authorize whatever it takes to get this done. The sooner, the better, time is of the essence."

"Okay, James," said Jeff. His next question took James by surprise, "By the way, this Maggie isn't the same Maggie that's an FBI Special Agent, and the same Maggie that put you in jail a few weeks ago, is it?"

"Listen, Jeff," James paused, trying to come up with a logical explanation. He finally admitted as he blasted away, "of course it's the same, Maggie. So, what if it is? It doesn't matter anyway. That was all a big mix-up when she put me in jail, and you know it."

Jeff laughed out loud at this strange turn of events. "You've got to be kidding me. Well, now I've heard everything."

"Never mind! You, Jeffrey Williams, have not heard anything. Just make sure she can keep her precious dog, okay?"

"Sure, I'll be in touch," said Jeff as they hung up. He shook his head as he laughed and exclaimed out loud, "Boy, I never saw that coming."

Jeff chuckled as he leaned back in his chair and thought, *James, James, James, you're playing with fire, my friend. However, your dear grandmother Chambers would be dancing in the streets if she knew how you feel about Maggie.*

Who knows what she'd say about Michael's new wife, Kate.

Chapter 12

Meanwhile, James slowly walked back to the area where Maggie was looking at the Sea Crest coastline. It was late afternoon, and he hoped they'd be able to see the sunset this evening.

The cool breeze was gently feathering through her delicate auburn-red hair as it swished across her shoulders and back. It seemed to wave and glisten in the sunshine hypnotically.

James had to stop himself before he impulsively reached out to touch her hair. He shockingly thought, *Can this be the very same hair that drives me insane when it flies uncontrollably, every which way, untamed and free?*

This very moment, James marveled secretly to himself, *She looks downright angelic and strangely innocent. How can that be?*

He continued to mull the situation over in his bewildered mind as he glanced at Maggie with anxiety and contemplated, *I have a running struggle with who she truly is. Over the past few weeks, while Michael and Kate were on their honeymoon, I went back to New York. I had decided I would not even think about her. I was separating myself from her. The end. No more. Kaput.*

However, my dilemma continued, even in New York, as my thoughts centered on the most perplexing and confusing person I have ever met. The person in question is none other than this enigma, which now stands approximately one foot away from me, and smells positively heavenly when the breeze gently sweeps through her hair.

What if I'm just attracted to her shampoo, for heaven's sake? He asked himself as he shook his head and laughed.

"What's so funny?" asked Maggie.

James looked at her and made up an answer that sounded good to him. "Well, we came up here to find some champagne, and we can't seem to tear ourselves away from this phenomenal view."

Maggie agreed, "It's even more spectacular than I thought it would be." She sighed and added, "I guess we should figure out where the wine cellar is. Where should we start?"

They retrieved all their stuff from the Bentley, and James headed for the house. As he pulled out the keys and said, "I hope I'll remember things better when we get inside. Since the electric hasn't been on for a long time, I assume the wine cellar is below ground, but I'm not sure where or how to get to it."

They walked up to the large covered wrap-around porch with a gazebo on the right-hand corner. The porch flooring had a checkered pattern of large light gray and dark gray marble tiles, each with an identical intricate inlaid design.

Maggie could not resist expressing her appreciation as she whispered, "Wow, this is exquisite."

"James," she marveled as she knelt to trace the design. "The artistry for this entire surface is unbelievably beautiful. I don't think we should even walk on it."

James was almost as surprised by its beauty as she was. He stooped down beside her, and he ran his fingers over the etched design with great care. He felt perplexed as he admitted, "I don't even remember this front entry at all. Do you think I didn't even realize how special this was?"

Then he added, "Well, come to think of it, we mostly used the back door. Yes, Michael and I spent most of our time in the backyard area. It's coming back to me now. It seems like it had extensive flower gardens, and they even had rope swings from a couple of enormous trees. But somehow, this design looks slightly familiar, so I must have seen it before."

After a moment, they decided to go on inside. James used the new key to unlock the beautifully carved mahogany double doors. As they walked through the entryway, they were again surprised and puzzled. The foyer had a beautiful checkered, highly polished marble floor made of large black and white square tiles.

Maggie said, "Look, James. Each tile has the same intricate repeating pattern, which matches the outside inlaid motif. Isn't this amazing? Who would put this level of skilled craftsmanship in a beach house?"

James was way ahead of her on this one. "I'll bet it's the same one who put this kind of extraordinary skill into the Sea Crest Lighthouse."

They gazed around the expansive indoor space. Drop cloths or covers hung draped over all the furniture. The size and flow of the rooms were imposing, but despite the largeness, it felt warm and inviting.

They stepped into what appeared to be a library with a large stone fireplace on one side of the room. It was facing the inside of the home, and beside it was a large mahogany door with black wrought iron designs. It looked exquisite and stunning.

James stepped over to it and tried to open it. It appeared to be locked, so he took out his collection of new keys. Finally, he came to one that opened the door. "Okay," James announced. "This is the wine room."

They both moved inside as Maggie said, "Yes, this sure looks like a wine room. However, there is no wine in it. Not even one bottle."

James exclaimed in alarm, "Wow, this is odd. I know each of these beautiful shelf-lined walls held the best wines available. Many of these shelves were full. I know it."

"Does this seem more like a memory or just familiar to you?" asked Maggie.

"I can't explain why, but I have a strong feeling about it. Wait, I remember my grandfather leaning his arm on the fireplace mantle right here and..." They heard a strange creaking sound as the back of the shelf started to move forward. Then, as the whole panel moved out about six inches, the entire wall groaned and slowly turned sideways.

When it stopped, they both stared at the gaping hole in the wall. It didn't look nice and finished like the rest of the home. A sudden blast of cold, stale air surrounded them as it came rushing into the room.

James took a flashlight from Maggie and pointed the beam of light into the cold dark space, and craned his neck to see further into the isolated area.-"What is this?" he exclaimed as he stepped forward into an earthen, dungeon-like chamber.

When he abruptly stopped, Maggie ran straight into him.

"What did you do that for?" she whispered.

"Well, I'm sure I don't have any idea! Wow! Just look at this place, Maggie."

She took out another flashlight to discovered that several bricks, rocks, and pieces of wood were scattered on the rough, earthen floor. "Careful where you walk. Don't stumble," she warned.

Next, she spotted an old cupboard that contained a few shelves with glass containers and earthenware. “Look, James. These have something in them. Are these jars of pickles?”

Over in one area, they saw an old piano stool with a seat that spun around on top. The legs even have big glass balls under the claw feet. “Hey,” chuckled James, “This reminds me of a stool from my grandmother’s house in New York. I feel like we’ve stepped into another dimension!”

“I know what you mean, but if you get to choose, make it The Fifth Dimension,” she answered. “I love that music.”

They were several feet apart, but they turned towards each other and smiled before they continued to explore.

She bent down to look at a few pieces of rolled-up material that were piled next in the corner. “Hey, look at this! I don’t know if this is a blanket or a rug,” she said as she unrolled a tightly woven red and black designed fabric.

“Wow,” she continued, “this is beautiful, and I’ll bet it’s warm. It must be a blanket. The colors are so bright.”

On the floor next to it, Maggie spotted a piece of clay pottery. She bent to pick it up, and as she dusted it off, she remarked, “This looks like some of the Indian patterns and designs that I’ve seen from around here. This particular vessel has a symbol of an upside-down bowl with a matching, mirror image on top facing upward.”

She smiled as she nodded, “It almost looks like a butterfly dancing sideways. They didn’t add the head or the antenna, but I’m sure that’s what this is.”

James stepped forward and laughed as he disagreed, “I doubt if it’s a butterfly. It looks like an Indian clay pot, and it belongs with the rugs or blankets. They are made by Cherokee Indians. Their designs are geometric and represent serious subject matter.”

"Oh, you mean like, bear claws?" she sarcastically responded. "That's one of the designs that the Cherokee Indians from this area put on various things."

"No, but I've seen it somewhere before."

"Well, James, I know why I've got butterflies on my mind. In fact, the Sea Crest Scouting programs schedule field trips to a nearby Butterfly Pavilion to earn their badges. However, they don't look exactly like this."

"I never heard about anything like that!" he argued. "I was in the Boy Scouts and ended up as an Eagle Scout. We never visited any butterfly parks. Maggie, seriously, how do you come up with this stuff?"

"Really, we try to give the Scouts at Sea Crest our full support. Each spring, Boy Scouts, Cub Scouts, Girl Scouts, and Brownies are invited to the Butterfly for various fun activities. These include animal encounters, outdoor explorations to meet adventure requirements, and more. Girl Scouts attend their Bug Badge Class, and the Boy Scouts attend their Insect Study Badge Class. You can ask Joe tonight when we get back. He knows all about it."

James laughed as he freely gave his opinion. "Maggie, that all sounds like a convenient scenario, but I don't buy it. I'm sticking with my original, well thought out, basic belief that it's an Indian clay pot."

"Hey, I detect that slightly superior attitude that you often display. In fact, you're famous for it," she replied.

"Alright, I was trying to be nice, but let me explain a couple of obvious flaws in your thinking. First of all, Maggie, you don't know everything. Secondly, I'm positive the Scouts weren't even invented yet when this part of the house was closed up."

She just stared at him, trying to think of something great to put him in his place.

His eyes laughed as he finished with satisfaction, "Unless, of course, you were talking about an Indian Scout."

"Okay, we'll see," she retorted as they continued to look around the perplexing area.

They moved around carefully searching every nook and cranny, investigating this strange space that they had stumbled into.

James suddenly whispered, "There, I knew it was Cherokee! Look at this!" He dropped to one knee as he bent to pick up an old tablet board with some strange symbols inscribed on it.

She was at this side in an instant, "What have you found?"

"Imagine that!" James murmured in astonishment. "Maggie, do you have any idea what this is?"

"Not a clue."

"I don't know what it's doing here, but if this is what I think it is, the only place I would expect to find one of these is in a museum. I hope the Cherokee tribe has one like this. However, I'm not sure it would have survived the Cherokee's Trail of Tears. An Indian named Sequoyah wrote the written version of the Cherokee language called a syllabary in the early 1900s."

"Do you now how old this must be?" Maggie whispered as she gently touched the mysterious symbols.

"Over 100 years," he muttered softly.

They each silently pondered the mysterious Twilight Zone sensation that had come over them the minute they entered this strange part of the beach house.

"How do you know all this?" Maggie asked.

"I've briefly studied a little about the Cherokee." he vaguely responded. "If I'm not mistaken," he continued, "The United States issued a new dollar coin to honor Sequoyah around 2017. I think it's one of those smaller sized gold coins."

She just stared at him suspiciously. "No, I don't believe it. You might be right about the coin. That seems familiar. However, you NEVER studied anything about them," she challenged him. "Did your jet-set life in New York City include a course on the Cherokees?"

"Well, Maggie, since you know nothing about MY life, maybe YOU should research a little about the Cherokee Indians when you get home tonight. I'm sure you'll find all the answers on the internet, which will prove that you don't know Everything!" he laughed.

"Okay, wise guy, 90% of my job is reading people, and I'm pretty good at it. And since you know nothing about my life," she laughed, "might I suggest that you study how to behave in the presence of a lady! I don't care how many pairs of alligator shoes you own.

"Excuse me. Do you see a lady around here?" James looked around innocently.

"Well, if you're looking for an appropriate proverb to live by, here's an old Scottish one that seems to fit you to a tee. *You can't make a silk purse out of a sow's ear.*"

They had a good laugh, then they resumed their search of the area.

On the very top shelf of the cupboard, they saw only one book. James stepped forward and carefully picked up and dusted off the Holy Bible. He opened it to a place that held an old card with the photograph of a seated black woman knitting with white yarn on her lap. The printed inscription on the bottom, which James read aloud: *"I Sell the Shadow to Support the Substance - Sojourner Truth."*

James turned to Maggie, "That name sounds familiar."

"Yes," she marveled as she took the card. "It doesn't come to mind, but I've heard it somewhere too."

"Yeah, let's look it up later this evening when we get home," he said. "I can't remember anything about the card, but I think Sojourner Truth was known for something important."

"Wow, James, I've got it! I know what this is, but I never dreamed I'd actually see one," she continued as she studied the picture. "Last year I also spent some time in Paris. Now, let me think. Yes, this is a French carte de visite. [kaʁt də vizit]. It's better known by its abbreviation, CdV."

"Yes," she continued. "She sold these little visiting cards with her picture to raise money for her activist efforts. This woman was an African-American abolitionist and women's rights activist. These cards were traded amongst friends and visitors."

"You mean like trading baseball cards?" James asked in surprise.

"Sort of, however, these were immensely popular and led to the collection of photographs of prominent persons. I'd say the custom is similar to our scrapbooking hobby. They'd make great albums that became a standard fixture in Victorian parlors.

"I remember overhearing an artist discussing this type of small photograph which was patented in Paris by photographer André Disdéri in the mid-1800s."

"What were you doing in Paris?" asked James.

"My work takes me to some interesting places. The FBI was working with the European clothing industry to strengthen worldwide intellectual property (IP) protection for fashion designers. They were experiencing significant losses from counterfeit, knock-off designs that were appearing worldwide. We worked with The European Union Task Force to track down and prosecute the fashion thieves.

"James, do you think it would be okay if I took this Carte de visit card of Sojourner Truth back with me today? I'd love to show it to Grace tonight. I don't think she's ever seen one before."

"Of course, that's a great idea. Could you also have her check and see if there is any connection to the NASA Mars Pathfinder mission. Their robotic rover was named "Sojourner."

"Hey, wouldn't that be wild? I think I'll put it in my back-back for safekeeping."

"Boy, I can't believe the strange things that are in this area of the beach house," stated James. "I wonder why I never saw any of this on our visits before. Who knows what could be down this passageway," he finished, hesitating as he looked into the dark, shadowy, cavern.

Maggie was speechless (for about two seconds). Then she bolted past James as she said, "Come on, James! Let's find out what's back there."

James held her back as he said, "Wait, it's too cold. What did we bring to keep warm?"

Maggie answered, "I'm wrapping this blanket over my shoulders and putting my night vision goggles on, right now. Can you believe what we've discovered? Isn't this exciting."

"Now wait minute. Give me a blanket to wear around my shoulders and hand me my night vision goggles, too," he said.

She handed him his blanket and goggles, then at the last minute, she grabbed his backpack for him.

"Thanks," James said. He took all his stuff and moved on down the passageway as he put on his goggles. He looked back at Maggie and asked her to do one more thing. "Could you pull that entryway shut before the cold, musty air gets inside the main house?"

"Sure, no problem," she answered. However, closing the panel door proved to be both tricky and challenging, as it scraped and dug into the earthen floor. The panel itself was undoubtedly a strange fit for the opening. She struggled to shut the old warped door, as it stuck and jammed a couple of times. She finally used all her strength and forcefully slammed the old, creaky entryway shut. With great satisfaction, Maggie gave it one last, ultimate shove with her full weight behind it. With this final thrust, she heard the doorway clunk into place.

"Finally, I didn't know you were that weak," laughed James.

"Oh, shut up," Maggie laughed.

At last, they were ready for their grand adventure to the outside wall, approximately 20-25 feet away.

James slowly turned around and thoughtfully surveyed his surroundings through his goggles. This search offered no reasonable explanation, as he stated, "This all seems so weird and unusual. I wonder if my grandparents knew about this and if they ever used this to store their wine."

"I sure don't know, but isn't this a lot more exciting than just walking into the type of wine cellar that we were expecting?" she asked as she caught up with him.

"You've got a point there."

"By the way," laughed Maggie. "Speaking of weird and unusual, James, you look ridiculous."

"Yeah, well, you keep that up, and you might be the victim of that dreadful, however, well-deserved accident, after all."

They both laughed as James continued, "Okay, I'm going in first. Don't crowd me, but stay close. This passage should only go to the end of the house on this side. It should go about 20-25 feet, but I wonder why it's so cold."

"Alright, you can go first on the way to the wall, but I'll be first on the way back," she bragged. She reasoned *all I need to do is turn around when we get to the wall on this side of the house.*

"That's fine," answered James. "But if we get to an outside door, I'll still be first."

They made their way a little further, where Maggie asked, "Hey James, have you noticed that the floor seems to be going downhill, a little bit?"

"I guess so, but it doesn't matter. It looks like this part of the house was never finished at all, so I doubt if they ever used it."

"But it just doesn't make sense that this beautiful home would have any part of it, left in this unfinished condition. What conceivable reason could they possibly have for leaving it like this?" asked Maggie.

"Boy, I know what you mean. Why on earth would they leave it like this? The family had both the money and ways to finish it. It's downright unbelievable."

They took a couple more steps, and they could finally see the end of the passageway ahead.

"Wow," shouted James as he almost tripped over something. He stopped short. "What is this?"

Maggie was right behind him, and she bumped into him as she came forward, "What? Let me see." She tried to stand all the way up, and the ceiling was not high enough for her to do it.

James hunched over to get a closer look at what looked like a pile of quilts. "What are these quilts doing here, in the middle of the tunnel, at the edge of the house? It's so strange."

When he turned back to her, he cautiously said, "Maggie? I think maybe this isn't a wine cellar, after all."

This remark startled Maggie. She looked at his face as she asked in her calmest voice, "What do you mean? Where are we?"

James was wondering the same thing, as his foot caught on something metal along the floor. He tripped sideways and tumbled onto the old quilts that were lying across the passageway.

Carolyn Court

"Help!" James yelled as he fell right through the floor.

Chapter 13

Maggie dropped to her knees as she looked through the giant hole in the floor, and fearfully yelled, "James? Are you okay?"

"Yes, I think so. Boy, that surprised me."

He had fallen about five feet straight down and landed on a pile of quilts. He slowly sat up and adjusted his cock-eyed goggles back into place. "It looks like I landed in another tunnel." He marveled at what he saw, and he continued, "Wow, it seems like this tunnel leads to another cavern."

"What?"

"It looks like this opens out into a large cave or grotto. By the way, there is an old rope ladder with little steps made out of tin, I think. It's hanging from the edge of the hole I just fell through."

Maggie immediately yelled, "Lookout, I'm coming down!" as she stepped through the hole.

"Maggie, wait!" James could hardly believe she'd just done that. He clumsily caught her as she landed, half on him and half sliding off the quilts. "You could have fallen on my head!" he yelled as he held her for a brief moment, before dumping her off onto the quilts.

"Oh, come on," she laughed as she adjusted her backpack and straightened her clothes around her.

"What did you do that for?" James asked sharply, but he couldn't help but laugh. "Why didn't you take the rope ladder?"

"Well, you're not going to have all the fun," she said with a careless air. She adjusted her goggles and started to look around.

"Maggie, wait! Seriously, we need to talk."

She ignored him as she whispered in awe, "This is so strange."

"Maggie, how many steps have we taken since we entered the, ah... wine cellar?"

She paused for a moment before she said, "Oh, I don't know for sure, probably 150 steps. Way past the outside wall of the house, right? It's also been going downhill. In fact, it's almost like a tunnel. James, what do you think this is?"

"Another significant clue might be these quilts. Let's spread them out and see what they show?"

They each grabbed a corner of the nearest one and opened it up to see that same familiar pattern was stitched into the quilt. They looked at each other in puzzlement.

Each quilt block or box was one-foot by one-foot square. Within each of the large squares, there were smaller black and white squares and triangles, of black and white material.

"Hey, this quilt's squares show the same design that is in the entryway of the house. The floors were made up of beautiful marble tiles, and they had a high gloss on them. They were beautiful."

"This has got to mean something, and I think I know what it is," said James. "Grab another quilt and see what that pattern looks like."

They opened two more quilts that had the same design as the tile floors.

The next quilt resembled the Big Dipper constellation. The North Star was made up of the brightest cloth pieces.

"What do you think all these quilts are for?" asked Maggie.

"The hidden doorway from the beach house to this tunnel and the simple quilts. I'll bet these patterns mean something," James whispered.

"What on earth is going on? Remember the things in the first room we saw? It might even look like a safe place to stay for a while." Maggie was getting excited as she continued, "James, what were the dates in that Bible? What was going on in America during that time?"

"I'm not at all sure. But remember that journal your friend, Grace, found in the storage unit contents? In what period was it written? What things were going on in the world?"

"Well, we figured it was in 1850-1880 maybe. I can check when we get back," Maggie replied warily.

"That would cover the Civil War period, don't you think?"

"Yes, that's what we were assuming. Why would this tunnel be here during that time period?" Maggie got a spine-chilling feeling as she thought about this country's history.

James and Maggie both stopped in their tracks and looked at each other for a long, solemn moment. They knew what they had stumbled on was almost impossible to believe.

Maggie was so choked up she could hardly breathe, "This might be incredible!"

They both started talking at once, throwing out questions, and answering them all at once.

James asked, "Why would this tunnel be here, during that time-period?"

"Just as important, why hasn't it been used for decades? I don't think my grandmother knew anything about this."

"Yes," James agreed. "What do all those items have in common? Sojourner Truth. Now imagine that the time frame is around the Civil War."

Carolyn Court

Maggie held her breath as she whispered, "Are you thinking what I'm thinking?"

James was so excited he could hardly contain himself, "Well, there's only one piece of history that might fit the clues we've uncovered."

"The Underground Railroad!" they yelled together as they clapped their hands in disbelief. They grabbed each other and twirled around out of sheer exhilaration at the shock of it all.

Chapter 14

There was just enough room to follow the passageway until it opened into an underground cavern. "James, look at that stream of flowing water. It appears to empty into a pool next to that far side of the cave."

Maggie continued, "I wonder if it's safe to drink that water?"

"Well, you're not going to find out," James warned harshly. He immediately followed up with a serious question. "Maggie, would you make a deal with me?"

She looked at him like he'd lost his mind, so he tried again, "Let's agree, neither one of us takes any unnecessary chances, while we're down here today. Okay?"

"Well, what exactly did you have in mind? You're not planning to fall through any more floors again, are you?"

James just shook his head. Maggie continued, "Maybe you think I expect to fall backward off the edge of that rock over there," she said as she ran over and teetered on the edge like she was going to fall.

"Oh, that's right, it was you who fell off the porch steps this morning, wasn't it? And, if I remember correctly, it was you who just fell at least five feet down through the floor. Now you're asking me, to agree, not to take any unnecessary chances?" asked Maggie innocently.

"Cut it out. I'm serious." James wasn't backing down as he continued. "We are in strange surroundings and unfamiliar terrain. We are also underground where the temperatures are much cooler than outside. We need to be respectful of the things around us and be careful. That includes watching out for each other, that neither one of us gets injured or hurt."

"I'm serious too," she said apologetically. "What should we do first?"

"Well, we need to figure out where we are. We can't go down into areas that we can't get back from. As it stands now, we should have no problem getting back up the rope ladder with the tin steps. And we only have one passageway back to the exit door into the wine tasting room in the beach house. We were at the end of the tunnel when I fell through the floor."

Maggie smiled, "Well, I promise to stay safe until we get back out of here."

"Great, now what do you think of this area?"

She joined in the spirit of adventure and, after about 30 seconds, had an idea, "This looks like it might have been a protected area. I'll bet it was a safe room."

"You mean a secure place for the slaves to stay while they were escaping to freedom," said James. "Look around; there were lots of various things meant for survival. They could safely hide in this cavern for days at a time if needed."

"Granted, it feels rather cold," James explained. "But that is the key benefit of subterranean storage and just look at all the wine bottles that have been stored here."

"Wow! This is absolutely amazing," Maggie exclaimed as she surveyed the area.

"Be careful! There must be a few hundred, just in this area. That's exactly why they were placed in this exact spot. It's ideal for wine with a constant year-round average temperature of around 61 degrees Fahrenheit and a natural humidity of about 55 percent."

"Now, how would you even know that?" asked Maggie.

"I live in New York City. Everyone knows about the Brooklyn Bridge, which opened to the public in the 1880s, thereby connecting Manhattan with Brooklyn for the first time."

"Of course, I know about the Brooklyn Bridge. I've even been to it and traveled over it a few times. What does that have to do with wine?" asked Maggie.

"I could repeat this information with my eyes closed," said James.

"It seems as though the anchorages, which are the underground support structures of the bridge, were built with many vaults that were ideal for storage and lots of passageways throughout. Those sizable compartments were rented out by the city to help fund the bridge. Vineyards and various wine companies rented these storage areas to always keep their wines and champagnes at a constant temperature of 55-60 °F, approximately (16 °C)."

"Wow, get a load of the dates on some of these wines." James blew the dust off a bottle and exclaimed in awe, "This is over one hundred years old."

"Are you sure? Here, let me see." Maggie was genuinely astonished as she looked at the bottle James held in his hand. She bent over the bottle to get a closer look. As her head tilted forward, a lock of her auburn red hair gently brushed over his hand. James' reaction was immediate, as the touch felt intimate and almost forbidden. He let go of the bottle so fast; it would have crashed onto the stone and earthen floor if it hadn't been for her quick catch.

One of her hands had been reaching out to turn the bottle when he had let go of the bottle like a hot ember. Her other hand just naturally cupped his hand gently underneath, so that they both held the bottle safely, together. It seemed like the most automatic, innocent motion in the world. However, the combination of the shocking feel of her unruly hair touching his hand, along with the undeniably thrilling caress of his other hand, left James stunned.

He swiftly held back his instinctive reaction, which was loaded with dangerous consequences. In fact, it took all the willpower he could muster, to calm down and put a stop to this right now.

"Here, you take it," was all he could think of to say, as he gave her the offending wine bottle and turned away to pretend to look at another one. James thought desperately, *I'll just change the subject.*

"I hope the wine is still good," he stated. "Well, at least we know they stored the wine at the ideal temperature." That was when he realized he was sweating profusely.

He quickly tried once more to steer the conversation onto safer ground. "Wow, can you believe we found all these fantastic bottles down here?"

"No, this is a real surprise. Boy, I wonder, when the last time was that anyone was down here. Do you think your grandparents knew about this?" asked Maggie.

"I have no idea," he said. "However, I don't think my grandmother would have kept it a secret from me. We spent a lot of time together in New York City."

"When I was here last time, my grandparents did have a wine room on the main floor of the beach house, and wine definitely filled the shelves. I'm sure it was the same room we were in, and I do remember my grandfather with his arm on the mantle of the fireplace. The hidden doorway never came open. I don't know what I touched to make the panel move as it did."

Maggie said, "It didn't look like it had been open for decades. I can't help but wonder if Joe Walsh, the Irish Architect that built the Sea Crest Lighthouse and this beach house, included this tunnel when he built this house."

James had recently learned of the journal entries from the Captain of the Scottish Sea Crest schooner. They discovered that he and his brother Michael were direct descendants of Captain Chambers.

"James, it appears that Sir Michael Chambers was one of the first Scottish Sea Captains to believe in freedom of slaves," said Maggie proudly.

"Now, what would you say to us opening one of these bottles of wine and making our first toast to my great-great-grandfather, Sir Michael Chambers?"

"I would love to. We've got all our wine tasting food in our backpacks."

They spotted some old lanterns and candles. Maggie offered, "I can use my matches and light some candles to save on the batteries of our night vision goggles. There doesn't appear to be any oil left in the lanterns."

"That's an excellent idea," said James. "Did you notice this stack of plates and cups? They must have been used by anyone who was here and then washed in the water over there."

Maggie looked around and noticed all the quilts here in the cavern. "I'll make a pile over here for us to sit on and spread my shawl on top."

James collected several bottles to taste and unpacked his backpack to add to the collection of food they'd brought. Once they had their extravaganza all laid out, they sat down together.

"I wondered if you'd like to see the sunset later," asked James. "We've probably got about an hour before we need to head back to the beach house."

"Sure, that would be great," answered Maggie as she looked at her watch in the candlelight. "That would give us plenty of time. We can take a couple of these bottles of champagne with us and come back for more tomorrow."

They tested the various wines and picked out their choices for the toasts at the Wedding Celebration.

After they got settled, Maggie looked around the candlelit cavern and gratefully observed, "James, I can't imagine a more thrilling adventure. We're so lucky to have made this exciting discovery."

James felt the same way, "I know what you mean. We are walking in the footsteps of courageous people who shaped our country. I can't believe that we never heard about our family's connection to the Underground Railroad."

"I've never heard anything about it from my side of the family either," agreed Maggie. "I don't know a whole lot about it except that the escape network was not literally underground nor a railroad. It was figuratively underground in the sense of being an underground resistance.

"You know," continued Maggie, "Kate and I are cousins, and we both grew up here in Sea Crest. We think our bloodline is from the Irish architect, Joseph Walsh, who shipwrecked with your great-great-grandfather, Captain Michael Chambers."

James said, "Well, yes, I remember when I was here a few weeks ago."

They were silent for a moment while they each seemed to reflect on their first meeting in which they were arch-enemies.

James decided to sidestep that nightmare as he said, "I'm so proud of our amazing ancestors, with deep-seated religious and moral values. They used their resources, at great risk, to help their fellow man. It wasn't an easy decision by any means. Still, they came to America to live here with real independence, and they felt that dream should be for everyone."

"Yes," agreed Maggie, "I'm proud of them, too."

"If I may paraphrase one of your previous reactions to my grandmother Chambers, leaving this beach house to you, in her will. Neither Michael nor I had ever even heard of you. I, for one, was outraged at my grandmother's decision."

"Oh that," said Maggie solemnly. "To be entirely fair, James, I probably would have felt the same if it was my grandma, and I didn't know why, a complete stranger, had inherited the Sea Crest beach house."

"Well," replied James. "That's what was so unexpected to us. You pointed out that you weren't in the habit of stepping on other people to get ahead. Then you went even further to explain your way of thinking, and I quote, '*I do hope you realize that just because a person can legally do something, doesn't mean it is the right thing to do.*' You needed to figure out why our grandmother had given you such a gift when you didn't even know her. You felt that since you weren't a legal heir, then it likely wasn't ethically and morally right to accept the beach house."

Maggie remembered that little sermonette as James was talking about it.

"I'll tell you, Maggie," he said. "I was in complete shock. You were, after all, the most outrageous woman I'd ever run into in my life."

"Oh, thanks a lot. Well, you weren't so charming yourself, Mister."

James answered sincerely, "Now hold on, Maggie; I'm trying to give you a compliment."

"Well, go ahead. I'm listening."

James cleared his throat as he continued, "as I was about to say, you were positively terrible in every possible way."

Maggie was ready to explode, "That is not a compliment!"

"Just be patient. I'm getting to it. Well, it's that you were my worst nightmare, my arch-enemy, and I was at a total disadvantage. My grandmother had left something valuable to you, and it should have been passed down to Michael and me. You had the law on your side. That was eating me up inside.

"Maggie, you had the opportunity to run me through, to slay me, to win. But did you do that? No.

"You let us figure out what we wanted to do with the beach house. You even offered to rent or buy it if we weren't going to use it."

"Well," Maggie replied thoughtfully. "I believe we all try to go through life looking out for each other and try to live by the Golden Rule. Anyway, that's my experience - except for YOU, of course."

"Of course," answered James with a smirk, before he continued. "I want you to know I see the same character and courage as your abolitionist ancestors had. I feel you have the same spirit of helping those in need, of having the best life possible, even if it costs you something to do the right thing - except for ME," James said as he smiled.

"Of course," Maggie agreed with a laugh as if that were a given.

Time flew by, and they suddenly thought they might have missed the sunset. They scrambled to try to make it out of the cavern in time. They packed up their leftovers and made their way back to the rope ladder.

As they climbed onto the first step, they gave one last look over the area. Maggie said with a sigh of regret, "I almost hate to leave. This cavern feels almost sacred. I mean, how astounding to think of all the lives that were saved and changed completely by abolitionists who were part of the Underground Railroad movement. This tunnel was part of history, part of their path to freedom."

James agreed as Maggie started up the steps ahead of him, "I know, I promise we will come back together as soon as we can arrange it. We'll be busy for the next couple of days, but we should research everything we can get our hands on in the meantime."

Maggie was now at the top tunnel and had an idea. "Hey, let's take one of these quilts with the unique design on it. We can do some research on this simple block design to see if it meant anything special."

This whole adventure was so extraordinary, Maggie didn't want it to end, as she promised. "Someday, we'll have to come back and see if we can find our way out of the cavern."

"Great idea." They were now traveling down the tunnel, and they were almost at the hidden doorway into the wine room.

"Well," said Maggie. "I told you I'd be in the front on the way back."

"Yes, you always get your way," he laughed. "Here, let me up there, and I'll get that door open. But, before I do, I want to thank you for one of the best days I've had in a very long time. Thank you."

Maggie was not going to let him get a chance to get the door opened first, and she was pushing on it with all her might. The door wasn't opening one iota.

"Okay," she said without admitting that she couldn't budge it at all.

James stepped forward and tried to dislodge the opening. Nothing. He then rammed his shoulder into it. Still, it didn't budge.

"Well, Maggie, let's both give this door a few karate moves." Nothing.

"What gives with this opening?" demanded James. "It's not moving, at all."

Maggie asked, "James, do you remember any knob or lock on this doorway?"

"No, come to think of it. I don't remember a door handle of any kind. That's funny," said James.

As they continued to try everything and anything they could come up with, James finally conceded, "Maggie, we've been trying to get out for over an hour. I don't think we can do it from this side. Something must have re-locked from the mechanism.

"If I remember correctly, clockwork mechanisms were built in many old lighthouses. Michael is familiar with the precise workings of it all. It's a system of weights and levers that can be combined with rope pulleys to use in trap doors and hidden entryways. I'll bet this entrance hasn't been opened in decades, and that's why we can't reopen the door from this side."

James looked carefully at Maggie, trying to gauge her reaction to being trapped behind this door. "Do you understand what I'm saying?"

Maggie seriously considered for a moment before she smiled and said, "You mean that today is that someday. We'll have to go back and see if we can find our way out of the cavern."

Chapter 15

Meanwhile, Grace was trying to call Maggie and Kate. She had just uncovered some interesting letters from the Chambers' storage unit, which they had bought last month.

Grace left another frustrating message for Maggie, "Hi, it's me again. I know it's getting late, but I need to talk to you as soon as possible. Please call me back or come over as soon as you get this message."

The doorbell was ringing as she hung up and hurried to the front door. "Oh, Kate," she exclaimed excitedly. "You'll never guess what I just found."

"Well, it must be something great by the tone of the message you left me. I thought if you were calling me this late, it must be important. What is it?" Kate asked as she entered.

"It's a packet of correspondence from Edinburgh, Scotland that Captain Michael Chambers carried as he sailed to America. It appears that his journey had a purpose that we never imagined."

Grace lowered her voice as she whispered. "His ship, The Sea Crest, which shipwrecked along our coast, was a particular type of ship, ideal for carrying out his secret agenda."

"You're kidding!" Kate exclaimed with her eyes as wide as saucers. "Was Captain Michael Chambers a spy?"

"Oh, that would depend on whom you ask."

"What did he come here to do?"

"First of all," Grace replied, "please remember that my educational background is in History. I have a Master's Degree in

American History with a minor in Genealogy. I spent several summer vacations at Brigham Young University as an intern.

"I see events and names from a whole different knowledge standpoint than most people. When I see a handwritten letter from a famous person, such as I saw in these letters, this correspondence is viewed historically.

"For example," Grace continued, "I believe I know the heart and viewpoint of each of these historical figures. I recognize the now-famous organizers that fought the courageous fight for freedom. These rare writings," Grace picked up the precious letters, reverently, "by their own, personal hands, frame and articulate, the tireless work they did for this worthy cause."

Kate was on the edge of her seat, as she asked, "What worthy cause? What happened? What does Sea Crest have to do with it?"

"A whole lot, actually," responded Grace. "For instance, this letter is from Eliza Wigham, the head of the Anti-Slavery Society in Edinburgh, Scotland. She had a close friendship with Harriet Tubman and heavily supported her work in America. Eliza's brother, John Richardson Wigham, was a prominent lighthouse engineer.

"Eliza Wigham was a neighbor and also a very close friend of Sir Michael Chambers and his whole family. Her society was financing his Sea Crest schooner ship, for projects similar to Captain Thomas Garrett's work. His freedom schooner took many runaway slaves, north to Canada."

"Do you mean schooner ships similar to the ones that race in America's Cup, today?" asked Kate.

"Yes, very likely. The schooners of that era were used for the Underground Railroad and usually had two sails. They were swift and easy to maneuver. For those reasons, they were also the first choice of most pirates from that period.

"According to this letter, Captain Michael Chambers used his schooner, The Sea Crest, to take runaway slaves south to various Caribbean Islands. Harriet Tubman was trying to reunite families that had been torn apart due to the slave trade. Since she was from Maryland, on the Atlantic coast of America, she led many to safety, south into the Caribbean. Captain Chambers knew the Caribbean well. He often navigated and traded goods within the islands. He had a perfect cover, for helping the runaway slaves."

Kate whispered in awe, "Boy, Grace, did you ever imagine this happening here?"

"Well, the timeline fits perfectly," she answered. "However, I've never seen any visible evidence of it along the Sea Crest coast.

"Nevertheless, I'm genuinely shocked by what this next letter revealed. I know that Harriet Tubman visited Eliza Wigham in Scotland to plan many ideas that would help with the success of the Underground Railroad.

"This envelope contains several detailed designs by Donald MacDonald, a successful leaded-glass window designer in Glasgow. He fabricated his own window designs as well as those of other artists. One of the sketches mentioned is included with this letter. His draft shows how the motif would work on many different materials with slight variations of the same pattern. This proposal is to be carried to a young contemporary of his, in New York City, named Louis Comfort Tiffany. It seems that they were both skilled in designing leaded-glass and stained-glass art."

Kate was shocked, "I can hardly believe this. Are they referring to Tiffany - like in little blue boxes from New York City?"

Grace stepped in with, "I think she's talking about the son of Charles Lewis Tiffany, who founded the jewelry store. Louis Comfort Tiffany was a brilliant artist of Art Nouveau stained-glass. He was the perfect artist to work on this design.

"In this letter, Eliza Wigham asked Captain Michael Chambers to travel to New York City at his earliest opportunity and show these designs to his fellow glass art aficionado. Tiffany had agreed to use the "Shoo Fly" design on leaded-glass windows and doors, to secretly direct the runaway slaves to help along their way to the Underground Railroad. The motif was to be a symbol of safety."

"Wow, I wonder what the Shoo Fly design looks like!" exclaimed Kate.

"I'll have to look up a picture to verify it," said Grace. "But I doubt we have any around here. As a matter of fact, I haven't seen hardly any stained glass in Sea Crest except maybe the church. But this brings us to the next shocking piece of information."

"Wow," Kate responded. "It can't get much more surprising than what you just explained."

"Oh, yes, it can, Kate. Where have we recently discovered several pieces of stained glass?"

"You mean the little windows at the top of the lighthouse?"

"She wrote, *please use the green pieces of glass in the kaleidoscope to help finance all the Shoo Fly leaded glass art for the windows and doors in America. The emeralds were obtained and donated by Sir Michael Chambers, from his trading business in and around the Caribbean and South America. The cut emeralds included are assortments of shapes and sizes, with setting options that fit each stone perfectly. This allows for a myriad of applications for stunning jewelry with creative possibilities.*

"Kate, I believe that Colombia's emeralds are the most sought after in the world because of their rare brilliance and deep color. They are also among the most expensive jewels in the world.

Grace picked up the letter by Eliza Wigham and continued. *I believe that Louis Comfort Tiffany is on the look-out for pure, historical jewels that his father can purchase for Tiffany & Co.*

"Now, listen to this part," said Grace. *Louis Comfort Tiffany plans to make some Scottish stained-glass works of art for Sir Michael Chambers, in appreciation for his gift of the Colombian emeralds.*

"Kate, I think he made the little windows at the top of the lighthouse."

"I think you're right. Isn't that exciting?"

"Yes! And to think Michael was the one to discover them! Now for your next surprise, here is another correspondence from the same packet," explained Grace. "Whose address do you think is written on it?"

"Grace, I have no idea."

"Well, take a wild guess. Who else do we know about from Captain Michael Chambers' journal?"

"No. Can it be my ancestor, the Irish architect, Joseph Walsh?" exclaimed Kate."

"The very same. This letter is from Eliza Wigham's sister in Ireland, Mary Edmundson."

"Wow. Isn't this amazing?" exclaimed Kate.

"Not only that," continued Grace. "But according to this letter, Joseph Walsh's family was heavily supporting Mary Edmundson in the Anti-Slavery movement. They had agreed to send financial help to enable Joseph Walsh to build lighthouse structures in America. The blueprints will also include numerous hidden tunnels and trap doors to help the Underground Railroad.

"We know that Joseph Walsh was on his way to America to work on lighthouses. These plans must show his details for the lower service room of the tower. That is the location of the clockworks, for rotating optics," she finished.

"Therefore," Kate explained "His voyages on the Sea Crest schooner were ideally designed to achieve this mission for the Underground Railroad, without being noticed."

Chapter 16

"Kate, I'm starting to get worried," said Grace. "I've been calling Maggie for the past hour, and she doesn't even pick up. I know she planned to have this whole week off, but I haven't seen or heard from her all day. Has she been called in, at the last minute, to work on an FBI case?"

"No," Kate replied. "I saw her this afternoon. Michael wanted to see her new little puppy that Joe had told him about."

"Oh, that's funny. Joe called me this afternoon and said that he had set James up by telling him that Maggie had a new little puppy. He then suggested James should take the puppy, a gift of some dog treats, as a peace offering, to smooth things over with Maggie."

"Well, Joe's prank worked on both of the Chambers brothers. Misha had the same shocking effect on them both."

"That's so funny," laughed Grace. "Good for Joe!"

"By the time we arrived at Maggie's, James had already fallen backward off the front steps and awkwardly pulled Maggie right along with him," Kate replied.

"What did Misha do?"

"Much to Maggie's dismay, she just kept on tearing off the gift wrap on the boxes and trying to eat the treats that James had brought."

Grace immediately cried, “Oh, no! I hope she didn’t damage the dog collar.”

“I don’t think so. However, James is planning to get a bigger size for an adult dog.”

Grace sat back and looked at Kate, but she had stopped laughing.

“Okay, what?” demanded Kate suspiciously.

“Kate, Joe told me he thinks the dog collar that James bought has real diamonds in it.”

“What?”

“Well, he’s not sure, but Joe went into the store to pick up a couple of things after James had left with the new keys to the beach house. As you know, that store is very upscale, and the manager thanked Joe for directing a new client to it. James had bought a diamond dog collar and a box of dog treats and had both gifts wrapped.”

“Oh, No! Now, why would James do that?”

“I’m not positive, but I think he’s trying to be nice to her,” exclaimed Grace. “Did Maggie seem like she knew James had given Misha a real diamond collar?”

“Of course not,” declared Kate. “However, I’ll tell you, Maggie and James were both acting so bizarre. They packed up their night vision goggles and made their exit to go up to the beach house. James’ last words were something about if they weren’t back by 7 PM civilian time or 1900 military time, then don’t look for them. Something bad would have happened to Maggie.”

“What? It’s almost 9 o’clock, right now. What was going to happen?”

“I believe the exact quote was: ‘I’m afraid, Maggie will have finally gone too far, and she will be the victim of some dreadful, however, well-deserved accident.”

Chapter 17

"He wouldn't dare hurt her, would he?" asked Grace. "Joe and I think James is crazy about Maggie."

Kate cried, "What are you talking about?"

"Well, have you watched them? Think back to his reactions to her the morning after your wedding. Remember when Michael was reading the letter from their grandmother? James was making remarks aimed at her the entire morning. It was almost like he could hardly control himself at times."

Kate nodded, "Now that I think of it, you might be on to something. In fact, remember when he waved a finger at her and said: 'Thought you could keep a secret from our grandma. Well, think again, Sweetie.'"

"Yes, Kate, and we've seen it happening on Maggie's part too," added Grace. Joe and I know that both James and Maggie had previously hated and blamed each other for Michael and your disappearances. They didn't trust each other at all."

"That's an understatement," Kate agreed. "They must have been flabbergasted when they found out that we had been innocently trapped in the Sea Crest Lighthouse by my brother, Connor, and we had fallen in love."

Grace smiled as she added, "I'm sure they had a hard time handling all their pent-up energy, and I'm sure they could not instantly change their hateful feelings towards each other."

Kate thought for a moment and said, "Maybe that was all one-sided, on James' part."

"Oh, really? Kate, did you ever wonder why James showed up for your wedding at the top of the Sea Crest Lighthouse, missing one of his shoes?"

"What are you talking about? I didn't notice anything about his footwear."

"If you had, you would have noticed that he was only wearing one alligator shoe."

"Well, why on earth would he have done that?" asked Kate in surprise.

"Joe and I were watching them argue over which one of you was to blame for this shocking wedding, at the top of the Sea Crest Lighthouse. They kept up their verbal banter, the entire time the Search and Rescue Helicopter was hovering above them. They finally got into the heli-basket with the Coast Guard Chaplain.

"Joe and I heard James over the swishing sound of the helicopter blades, yelling and making fun of Maggie's karate moves. He laughed and told her to be careful; it was a long way down from the top of the lighthouse.

"Maggie looked ready to kill, as she reached down and whisked off one of his $5,000 a pair, alligator shoes and flung it over the side of the rescue basket. As the shoe splashed in the crashing waves below, she looked at James and agreed, 'Wow, it really is a long way down.'

"Joe laughed with delight and said, 'You know, there's a very thin line between love and hate. I can't wait to see what they do next.'"

Kate was taken aback that she hadn't known about the alligator shoe episode. She was also rethinking the way Maggie had been acting since she returned from her honeymoon. "Gee, I wonder what Maggie is feeling now."

"Well, after looking at things through Joe's eyes, I agree with him," Grace admitted. "By the way, he's taken great delight in setting them up, every chance he gets. He thinks they're crazy about each other, but neither of them wants to be attracted to the other. After all, they have invested way too much time and energy plotting against each other to give in and actually like each other."

"By the way," Grace continued. "It was Joe that set up the idea for James to stay in the guest wing at the beach house. He told me that poor Maggie was so stunned, she was speechless.

"Remember when she called us for the emergency Mah Jongg meeting to tell us what the brothers had decided regarding the beach house? The more I thought about it, she was visibly upset. She's usually able to handle actual life and death situations with ease. However, she seemed genuinely troubled. That was very unusual, wasn't it?"

"It sure was," agreed Kate.

"In fact, she appeared so disturbed that I assumed she did not get the beach house," Grace added.

"Grace, I've known Maggie my entire life. I think she's scared to death. She has never really been in serious love before, and she doesn't think it's safe to let her guard down, especially in someone that she's hated so fiercely."

Grace shared one more observation. "Kate, do you think either of them even knows what's happening to them?"

"I'm not sure about James. I hardly know him well enough to judge. He might date frequently and casually fall in and out of love often."

"Kate," mused Grace, "When you and Michael left for your honeymoon, James immediately left for New York City. Joe said something funny to me about his quick exit, to the effect that, 'James was yanking the band-aid off fast and quick, so it doesn't hurt.' At the time, I thought he meant he'd miss his brother, but that didn't fit at all because his brother traveled all over the world and was rarely in New York City.

"Although Joe was in constant communications with him, James didn't step one foot back in Sea Crest until Michael was back. Joe told him he was welcome to stay in his guest room again until the guest wing at the beach house was available."

"I'm going to be looking at his behavior a lot more carefully now that I know all this," Kate declared. "I'm also going to find out from Michael if James is repeatedly dating all the supermodels in New York City."

"We both know Maggie well enough to know she'd probably die before she let him know that she cares for him," continued Kate.

Grace agreed, "Yes, the unknown factor of if he returns the feeling would undoubtedly weigh heavily on her mind."

Chapter 18

Just about this same time, up at the beach house, Maggie and James realized that they could not move the hidden entryway to get out. Maggie turned to look at James, "Well, what should we do now?"

"I think we should go back to the cavern and make a plan. We definitely cannot get out through this opening."

As they gathered up their backpacks and headed back down the tunnel to the pile of quilts, Maggie pointed out that, "No one will even miss us until tomorrow."

"Joe will wonder about me if I don't show up at his house tonight," James replied. "He knows Michael and I were going over our future proposals until very late last night. I didn't get much sleep, and I intended to hit the rack early tonight."

"Oh, that's right," Maggie said. "I forgot you were staying in his guest room until the guest wing at the beach house is ready."

"He probably wonders what happened to me. He knows I don't, in fact, know very many people here in Sea Crest. He also knows I was going to see you this afternoon, but knowing us as he does, I guarantee he doesn't expect us to still be together at this hour."

They were at the rope ladder, and this time they both used the tin steps to get down. "Oh well, I'll just send Joe a text," James concluded.

"Sounds good. Let him know we need help," Maggie suggested. "In the meantime, let's take a couple of extra quilts down to the cavern."

They both got down to the lower tunnel safely and dragged all their stuff over by the pile of quilts.

James sat down and pulled out his mobile phone to call Joe. "Boy, that's strange. I don't get a signal."

Maggie was a little alarmed, but said, "Here, you can use mine," while she dug out her phone. As James joined her, she flipped it on and just stared at it, waiting to get a signal. "Nothing."

James looked at her phone and glanced up at her face. It was evident Maggie was visibly shocked.

He had to think fast as he said confidently, "Okay, Plan B. Since everyone knows we're here at the beach house, they know we're safe. No problem. They won't be worried or looking for us tonight."

Maggie looked at him like he'd just lost his mind. "Could you please back up to Plan B? I don't seem to remember anything about a Plan B."

James was still trying to think logically about what they should do. "Well, it's almost midnight. I certainly don't believe we should try to do anything further tonight. We don't know how to get out of this cavern, but I'm assuming the runaway slaves departed out through this cavern to tunnels and caves. Yes, that's what many, many people have already done."

Maggie joined in hopefully, "Do you really think they stayed here in the safe house area and then left out through the caves and tunnels toward the ocean? I figured they would go back to the beach house to leave.

"Well," she continued, "I now realize they probably moved on through the maze of caves. That would be my best guess, based on the fact that the tunnels led to this area. If they were only going to turn around and go back out through the house, they would never have gone to the hard work of digging the tunnels all the way through to this area. I mean, really, why would they do it?"

"You're right," he agreed. "Now we have to figure out how the runaway slaves got out of here. After a minute, he added, "Maggie, I'm going to ask you a huge favor. Do you trust me?"

"Well, of course, I do," Maggie remarked as if he should have to know that.

"Okay, I'm going to ask that we stop and try to get a couple of hours of sleep. We have everything we need to be safe and warm for the night. I, for one, am exhausted. We can get a fresh start in the morning after we eat some more of our wine tasting extravaganza."

"Well, that's probably the sensible thing to do, but I'll still keep thinking and planning about how to get out of here."

"I hope so. Maggie, with all your FBI experience, you're going to be the one that figures it all out. There's no one else I'd rather be here with than you."

She was stunned. She didn't know what else to say, so she settled on, "You're not so bad yourself, James."

"Wow, that sounded corny, didn't it?" Maggie laughed.

"Yes. I get silly when I'm tired or nervous, so I'm sorry if I say anything stupid," confessed James.

They spread out some more quilts on their wine tasting pile. They were both stacking quilts on the same pile, and they suddenly realized that they hadn't even thought about their sleeping arrangements. They seemed a little embarrassed and confused as they looked at each other.

James said, "Well, for safety and warmth, I vote we just lay down here and get some sleep."

By now, it was very late, and Maggie agreed. "I'm going to put my ear flaps down to keep my ears warm."

"Good idea. I'm going to use my backpack as a pillow. I'll get a couple of more quilts to wrap around them if you want one too."

"Thanks, that's an excellent way to keep our food safe. We don't want to attract animals, you know."

"Gee Maggie, thanks for bringing that up. Now I won't be able to get to sleep."

"Good," she said as she wrapped her pillow up and lay her head on it to check it for comfort.

James deposited his homemade pillow down beside hers. Then he collapsed on top of the quilts, exhausted, as he asked, "What's good about it?"

Maggie looked back at him and giggled, "You look ridiculous. That's priceless."

"Nice, I'm trying to save your life, and here you are making fun of me," he said, pretending to be highly put out with her.

"Oh, James." She laughed as she said, "A month ago, if someone told you we'd be here, in the tunnels and caves below your grandmother's beach house, could you in your wildest dreams, ever believe it? That we'd be laying on a huge pile of Underground Railroad quilts, with our food wrapped up under our heads, looking at each other with these crazy night vision goggles."

Now James was also laughing as he agreed, "No, I wouldn't have believed it a month ago. And I certainly don't believe it now, either."

"Isn't it funny how people behave," she said? "It's like we all have various sides to us. One facade, we show to family and close friends and one we show to everyone else."

"I know what you mean. Each person has two sides. It is like a two-sided coin," agreed James.

They both silently reflected on this for a few minutes.

Then James continued, "Here's a question for you. When someone chooses which side to show to another, does it follow that we only know them by what they decide to show us?"

"Here's another question I wonder about," replied Maggie. "Since I'm an FBI Special Agent, I struggle with this sometimes. Are we all both good and bad? Can we control how good or how bad we are, or does the other person bring out the good or bad, depending on what they see in us? How much does our environment or our companions influence what we do and who we are?

"For instance," she said thoughtfully, "When I first met you, I only knew you as a rich snob who had hurt or possibly killed my best friend."

"Hey, that's a terrible thing to say!"

"That's my point. I saw what I was expecting to see, and it took an effort to reverse my original opinion when I was proven wrong."

"You're the most confounding person I've ever run across," James blurted out. It was pay-back time, and he was going to get a couple of zingers in himself.

"For instance, I'm having a terrible time getting a feel for who you truly are. Between that tough, professional, take no prisoners, FBI Special Agent and the know-it-all, Barney Fife impersonator. Those are the only two different people I see in you."

"What? Thanks, you're really cute." She flounced over and turned her back to him.

"Now calm down, don't get your dander up. Before you know it, your curly red hair will be all wild and chaotic again. You should never let it loose. Now, it's flying all over, every which way again."

She turned back around and looked at him like he'd lost his mind. "Now, you've got an opinion about my hair?"

James looked at her. He wanted to reach out and touch that hair, but instead, he said, "Well, Maggie, I'm glad you brought that up. I'm way too tired to explain it all right now, but it's out of control."

"What?" demanded Maggie.

"What I mean is, and I'll try to put it nicely. It's very hard to be around you with your hair, so ah...raw. Well, that doesn't sound right, not exactly crude or anything, but all-natural, I guess. Well, it's ah, overwhelming. There, that's it. I find it impossible not to watch to see what will happen next to that unruly disaster. You're like a catastrophe waiting to happen."

"James, I want an apology right now!"

"Just hold on and let me explain." James was stalling, trying to put this situation with her hair in terms she'd understand, but not get mad at him.

But apparently, he didn't work very hard as he said, "Well, when you stomp away during one of your tantrums, your hair is always falling and tumbling freely down your back. Swinging around your shoulders like that was a normal, acceptable way for an FBI Special Agent to wear it. I'm sure some beauty parlors have hairdos that would help subdue your hair. But, personally, I've never seen anything so wild and untamed in my whole life.

"Then when your tantrum ends, you stop and turn around, I think, 'Okay, I don't have to watch that exhibition anymore.' But no, now I see something that's even more astounding, and I can't exactly put my finger on why it's so shocking," he stopped to think about it for a second.

Maggie exploded, "Of all the nerve! That's supposed to be NICE? Where do you come off complaining about my hair anyway?"

"Well, I wasn't finished yet. When you turn around, your hair has even more impact. Especially when I see your face, that disheveled auburn mess somehow makes those huge green eyes of yours even bigger and brighter. They look like...," he broke off as he almost nodded off to sleep.

Maggie was ready to let him have it when he finished with, "yeah, ... like LED lights."

"But on the other hand," he sleepily continued, like that explained everything, "when the breeze touches your hair, like when you were looking down at the Sea Crest Lighthouse today, it was unbelievable. I mean, the sun caught it, and the strands of hair changed colors, and your hair almost glistened in the breeze and light. I'm not sure what made it look like that, but you have no idea how pretty that was," he ended quietly.

Maggie couldn't believe he'd noticed her hair this afternoon. She was turning that over in her mind when he continued.

"Well, ... it's just very distracting for any guy to see. I thought the FBI would make you..., you know," he said sleepily, "... tie it back or something." He yawned, and his eyes closed as he lazily added, "I mean, aren't you supposed to wear clips in it or something?"

Maggie's mouth hung open in disbelief. She couldn't think of even one response to that outlandish remark. She asked herself, *does he truly believe he can nonchalantly say this cruel drivel about my hair, and I won't knock his block off? I don't care how sleepy he is; I won't stand for it!*

Before she could react, James pleasantly issued one final statement, which consisted of him peacefully mumbling something about "What kind of shampoo smells THAT GOOD?"

Maggie was taken aback, as she quietly whispered, "What did you say?"

But she was too late. He was out like a light. She was getting no answers from this idiot in the night vision goggles, which now only revealed two sleeping eyes.

Maggie thoughtfully watched James continue sleeping peacefully for three or four more breaths before he stirred slightly. With a sigh, uttered wistfully, "What if I'm just in love with her shampoo?" as he drifted back off to sleep.

Chapter 19

What on earth was that supposed to that mean? Maggie wondered. She immediately sat bolt upright on the stack of quilts and looked at the offending party.

Just who did he think he was, spouting off declarations of love, FOR SHAMPOO, of all things?

She felt like whacking him with her backpack.

Maggie was thoroughly aggravated and hurt over his outburst about her hair. He had come up with a surprising amount of advice concerning a topic; she didn't even know he'd noticed.

Finally, when I hoped we could mean something to each other, he has to open his big mouth and spoil it all. Well, it's better to know his feelings upfront, before it goes any further, Maggie thought as she looked sadly down at James.

She despondently laid her head back down as a forlorn tear rolled down her cheek onto the quilt. She was confused as she lay in the dark wondering, *Why do I feel so miserable? Why am I crying? Now I have to take my goggles off before they get all wet.*

She dug out a napkin and blew her nose and wiped the tears from her eyes. She sadly recalled, *This afternoon was great. I'm glad I had at least one grand day to remember with him. I'll memorize how this feels and remember it.*

As she tearfully fell asleep, she admitted, *I never knew it would hurt so much.*

Chapter 20

James tugged at the straps of his goggles as he pulled them off and readjusted his head to get more comfortable. He vaguely remembered he was in the cavern and then realized that he was on the quilts with Maggie.

In response to this unexpected awareness, he turned onto his side and automatically moved closer to her. He had second thoughts about his night vision goggles and eagerly retrieved them. Now he was able to gaze on Maggie to his heart's content, instead of having to steal glances.

However, he was most pleased since *"I don't have to worry about looking into her emerald green eyes because they are closed."*

She silently slept in complete, almost angelic, innocence. He quietly reached out his hand to touch her hair and carefully moved a strand away from her face.

It made him smile as he placed his hand near her face by the backpack. *What was that?* he thought. *It's all wet. What happened?* He adjusted his night vision goggles and frantically tried to see what had happened. *Is Maggie bleeding?* he wondered. *What happened to her?* Then with relief, he thankfully thought, *Oh good! It's water, not blood. But there is no water bottle anywhere around.*

James searched around until he saw her goggles nearby. When he picked them up, they were also very wet inside.

He suddenly felt the weight of the truth descend on him. *Oh my gosh. Those are tears. What happened to her? The very thought of Maggie crying is very hard to reconcile with my initial introduction to her as an FBI Special Agent. She was a hard-headed force to be reckoned with for sure. She appeared to have no feelings at all, except wanting to torture me with techniques that the regular police weren't allowed to use. I can't think of one thing that could make her cry.*

Then it came to him. *Oh, No. I'll bet it's Misha. She's afraid someone will come back to claim her precious dog. She can't bear the thought of losing Misha.*

He took her cold hand and held it warmly to his chest. He protectively drew the quilt up around her just a little closer, as she slept. James took a deep breath as he vowed, *Whoever made My Maggie cry is going to pay and pay dearly.*

Chapter 21

Shortly after he drifted back to sleep, James had one of his traumatic Sea Crest nightmares. He was scuba diving his first open-water dive at the wreck of the sunken Sea Crest schooner. As usual, he cut his air hose on the sharp jagged metal from the ship. His dad was sharing his oxygen with him. Since his dad wouldn't leave him, and James was frozen with fear, their death was imminent. This terrifying nightmare had never varied.

However, tonight, this dream sequence had taken a major radical turn. In all the years that these memories had haunted and tormented James, it never changed. Tonight, something new and groundbreaking was happening.

Strangely, he found he was no longer on the ocean floor with his air hose cut, but now he was standing on the beach beside the Sea Crest Lighthouse. What James saw was not good, either. "Hey!" He yelled as loud as he could. "What do you think you're doing?"

Right there on the Sea Crest Beach, Maggie O'Hara was in charge of several FBI agents. She was directing them to dismantle his grandmother's Bentley automobile. They had expensive parts laying all over the place. Everyone seemed pleased as punch to have the rare opportunity to work on such a beautiful automobile.

Maggie looked like a million bucks with her bright green, smiling eyes and her wild red hair flying all over the place in the wind. She cheerfully waved and said, "Hi James, I was wondering what it would take to get your attention."

"Maggie, stop that!" he pleaded.

"Well, stop having those awful dreams, and I won't have to show up and distract you."

He awoke with a start, thinking, *Where am I? Why is it pitch-black in here? Why is my bed so hard? And most importantly, why can I smell Maggie's marvelous hair?*

It gradually came to him that he was in the cavern. And he woke up dreaming about Maggie taking apart his grandmother's Bentley automobile. *What a weird thing to dream. Whatever put that outlandish idea in my psyche?*

Maybe in my brain, she represents the very worst kind of female, as a sort of dragon-lady. But, now I know that she indeed has a good side. After all, she proved her selflessness in the case of the beach house. Let's not forget; she let Michael and me decide what to do when she legally could have just taken possession of it.

Psychologically, I seem to have trouble justifying that she's bad at all. He looked over at her innocently sleeping. He had to smile as he thought of an imaginary halo over her head. *This is all too much.*

I seem to be both confused and conflicted by Maggie, but she makes me smile a lot. He laid his head down close enough to her to hear her breathing. With that, he happily drifted off to sleep; Without one thought of the Underwater-Dive Nightmare that had haunted him for years.

Chapter 22

Over the course of the night, they continued to sleep rather peacefully. That is not to say they didn't have occasional periods of sleepily stirring and intermittently awakening to find themselves lying next to the one person who had turned their lives inside out and upside down recently.

For example, James woke up with a sense that something was different. Not exactly wrong, but not normal. Before he opened his eyes, he wondered, W*hat is it?*

Then he realized his eyes were open, and he saw pitch black. *Wow, that's a weird sensation. It's like I'm looking out into a vast dark space. It would feel very lonely if Maggie wasn't here with me,* he thought.

I was exhausted last night, but I remember talking with her.

He searched his memory until it slowly started coming back to him. *Let's see... I think I was trying to give her some advice about her hair. No, maybe it was about her eyes. The shade of emerald green is bright and clear. Sometimes a light sea green. Sometimes almost like an aqua blue/green. I guess it changes depending on what she's wearing. Or what kind of light she's in, I suppose. Maybe it changes when she gets mad.*

After looking over at her and wishing her eyes would open up, he remembered, *I've strictly avoided looking directly into them. There is an old superstition that she'll take my soul or have some power over me, or something. It might be a Scottish fabrication or tale, but I'm not taking any chances.*

I'm not too sure what exactly will happen, but I'll be a goner. So far, I haven't looked at them very much.

Well, I'm not counting the part about a tear rolling down her cheek at the meeting at Joe's office. After all, I'm only human, and being the gentleman that I am, I needed to be sure she was all right. They'd have to make allowances for a situation like that. I'm sure that doesn't count.

Or yesterday when I met Misha. Maggie grabbed me as I fell off the front porch. We both toppled backward into the bushes. I mean, she fell right on top of me.

I could hardly circumvent that situation. I surely didn't intend to let her fall to the ground. Now no one could count that unavoidable glance. It's like when you're fishing, and you catch and release the fish. Well, something along those lines should be exempt, I would think.

At any rate, I feel secure that the rule is something about me needing to gaze directly into her big, emerald green eyes before it would be considered a valid look.

With that strange and sleepy declaration, James nodded off to sleep again.

Chapter 23

Later, Maggie woke up with a vague feeling of strangeness. As she opened her eyes, she saw nothing, but she heard James' steady breathing as he slept beside her. She felt around for her goggles and silently put them on.

Ah, there he is. She felt strangely comforted, as he came into view. *His face is only inches away.* She turned onto her side and studied the man as he lay peacefully sleeping.

What is it about this man? she wondered. *Why has he consumed my thoughts, night and day, since I met him? Now, for some inexplicable reason, we are trapped in this cavern together, and neither of us seems that afraid. I think we're somehow stronger together.*

Maybe it's the excitement we shared about discovering our descendants participating in such a meaningful way in the Underground Railroad here in Sea Crest. It's amazing.

If our ancestors provided a safe place for the runaway slaves to hide along their journey to freedom, that is utterly astounding. I wonder why neither of us has one iota of knowledge about it. The situation that James and I are sharing is forming a special bond between us.

James stirred and turned on his side, facing Maggie as if he had just felt it too. Without waking up, he moved his arm between them on the quilt, and his hand barely touched hers. He instinctively took Maggie's hand in his and possessively held it to him. He continued to sleep without missing a beat.

At that moment in time, Maggie felt something she had never felt before, as she dropped off the sleep again.

Chapter 24

Joe was surprised when he received a call at home from Jeffrey Williams the next morning.

"Oh, hello, Jeff."

"Hi, I'm so sorry to call you at home, but I called your office, and Linda said you have the day off."

"Oh, that's fine. How can I help you?"

"Well, Joe, this is in reference to Maggie's dog. Have you spoken with James about his search for the Great Dane's owners who abandoned the dog?"

"No. I know about the dog, but I don't know about any search," Joe explained.

"Well, I was shocked that this Maggie was the one and only, FBI Special Agent Maggie O'Hara who threw our poor James in jail, not even a month ago."

"I can't believe this. Hold on a second," Joe said as he looked out the window for the Bentley. Next, he went down the hallway to the guest bedroom. James wasn't there, and it didn't look like he'd even slept in his bed.

"Man, Jeff. He's staying with me, but I don't think he came home last night."

"Well, he called me yesterday late afternoon and asked if I had any detectives available to track down this, needle-in-a-haystack, as he put it. He explained that Maggie was upset, fearing that she'd lose her dog if the previous owners came back and took her away."

"What? I didn't know anything about this," said Joe.

"Well, I'm supposed to put every available person on it. He also wanted a legally signed affidavit that we could give Maggie, stating that they would never take that dog away from her."

"You're kidding," exclaimed Joe as he sat down.

"No, I'm not. Of course, James made it clear that money was no problem; whatever it takes was all right with him. He also said I should ask you if we needed any extra help. His final request was that we don't tell Maggie."

"Wow!"

"Double Wow!" said Jeff. "Get a load of this. I asked him if this was the same Maggie that had put him in jail, and he acted like that didn't even matter. He saw tears in her eyes, and WE were going to make it happen. Joe, can you believe it?"

"Well, Jeff, I'll tell you, I think he's head over heels in love with her, and he doesn't even know it. I've been watching this develop since they first laid eyes on each other.

"Thanks for calling," he continued. "I'm going to touch base with Maggie and see if she knows where James is. They were supposed to go up to the beach house yesterday and pick out champagne for the Wedding Celebration toast. I'll see if she knows where he might be this morning."

"Fine," said Jeff with a chuckle. "I just wanted you to know I've got three private detectives working on the case of the abandoned Great Dane. Do you have any leads?"

"Leads?" laughed Joe. "Man, I'm still recovering from the news that James doesn't want to see tears in Maggie's eyes. These guys are a riot to watch."

"I'll tell you, Joe, I've known James a long time, and there are plenty of women here, in New York City, who have tried everything possible to capture the heart and money of this bachelor. So far, all the special treatment and flattery have fallen on deaf ears. No one was able to get close to him.

"Now he meets this she-devil, who throws him in jail and threatens to torture him," Jeff continued. "I thought he hated her. Now he's all torn up because he saw tears in her eyes? It's downright unbelievable."

Joe explained with great authority, "Yes, they are something to see. The confusion the two of them struggle with, trying to figure out what on earth happened, is downright ridiculous. Somehow their hate has crossed the line into love. I don't think they have a clue."

"You know what? I was invited to the Wedding Celebration, and I wasn't planning to come, but I just changed my mind. This, I've got to see."

"Great! I'll make popcorn," Joe laughed.

"Primarily, I'm anxious to know what's so special about these women at Sea Crest. What did you do down there? Put something in the water?"

Joe laughed again, "Yeah, well, you better watch yourself, buddy."

"It will be good to see what all the hubbub is about," said Jeff as he hung up.

Chapter 25

Meanwhile, back at the keeper's cottage beside the Sea Crest Lighthouse, Benjamin Jensen arrived for the Wedding Celebration.

Michael happily greeted his dad with a hug and introduced his beautiful bride, "Dad, I'd like you to meet the love of my life, Kate. These are her parents, John and Katherine Walsh, and Kate's brother Connor.

"I'd like you to meet my father, Benjamin Jensen."

They were all beaming and shook hands and seemed jubilant about the surprising wedding.

"As I told you over the phone, Kate's family has been here at the Sea Crest Lighthouse as Coast Guard Search and Rescue Team and Lighthouse Keepers for three generations. They live here in the keeper's cottage."

Kate was called away to answer the phone. It was Joe checking to see if James was visiting them this morning. "Why no, we haven't seen him, although we expected him to come over last night. He never showed up, so we called him a couple of times and left reminder messages. Oddly enough, he never returned the calls."

"Well," explained Joe, "I don't want to alarm you, but I just found out that he never came home last night. He's been staying in my guest room and kept in touch throughout the day, trying to keep things on schedule. It's very unusual that he wouldn't call if he's spending the night elsewhere."

"Yes, that's so strange," answered Kate. "Grace had some news that she found in the storage unit things, and we called Maggie several times with no answer. She never called back either. That is almost unheard of."

Joe was very cautious as he asked the next question. "When did you last see her?"

"Yesterday late afternoon. I took Michael over to meet her new puppy in hopes that he'd be surprised. Oh, and before I forget, you did a great job setting him up the same as you did, James. He fell off the front porch backward and pulled Maggie with him. The only reason Misha didn't join them in the upheaval was that she was busy tearing open the wrapped gifts that you suggested James take over. Nicely done, Joe."

"Well, I do what I can," he answered. "Now, we need to figure out why James didn't come home last night and why Maggie never answered your calls last night."

"Well, they were heading up to the beach house to look for some champagne to toast Michael and me at our Wedding Celebration. I'll run over to her house and get the full story, and it better be good," she laughed.

"Okay, see if she knows where James was going after they finished."

"Joe," Kate said slowly, "they were acting so strange as they left the house." She relayed the dramatic exit they'd performed and also the final words that James had said.

Joe replied, "I'm sure he was kidding; however, that behavior is unexpected. Call me when you get to Maggie's."

"Sure," Kate said as she hung up.

She turned to look at Michael as she asked, "Have you talked to your brother since last night?"

"No, why?"

"Well, Joe doesn't think he came back to his house last night. His bed doesn't look like he slept in it, and he hasn't seen or heard from him since they parted at the store where they had the keys made for the beach house."

"Wow, I wonder what happened."

"I just told Joe that I'm going over to Maggie's to find out why she didn't return Grace's calls last night."

"I'm going with you. Something's not quite right."

They headed over to Maggie's, and when she didn't answer the door, Kate used her key to let herself in. A very excited dog promptly met them. "Hey, Misha, what's the matter, girl?"

"You stay with her," instructed Michael. "Maggie, are you home?" he called as he went from one end of the house to the other.

No Maggie.

"Joe said to call him as soon as we got here," said Kate. "You call him while I take care of Misha."

"Okay, I'm dialing right now."

"Hey Joe, it's Michael. Kate and I are here at Maggie's, and there is no sign of her anywhere. We don't think she's been home since we closed up late yesterday."

Joe sounded worried as he said, "This is so out of character for both of them. We all agree that they were headed up to the beach house. I'll go over there right now."

"Kate just told me that we will be taking Misha over to the keeper's cottage for Connor to watch. Then we're right behind you."

"Okay."

When Kate and Michael stopped by to drop Misha off, they met Benjamin Jensen and Kate's dad. "Somethings not right," said

Kate's dad. "I called Sean, and he's on his way to meet with us. They haven't heard anything from Maggie either."

Within minutes they had all arrived at the beach house. Joe was looking through the Bentley, which was unlocked.

"I don't see a trace of either Maggie or James," stated Sean.

"When we last saw them," said Kate, "they were loading their backpacks full of all kinds of food for the wine tasting. They also took night vision goggles, headlamps, and flashlights. None of that stuff is here."

"I have my set of keys," said Joe. "Let's go see what's inside."

They stepped onto the beautiful veranda and passed to the artistic etched glass design of the doors. As Joe pulled out his keys to open the doors, he was surprised. "These doors are not even locked."

They went through the dramatic entryway with the black and white marble squares that had the little symbol etched in each one. However, they did not stop to inspect them, as Maggie and James had done.

Instead, they were dreading what they might find ahead. Joe called out, "James! Maggie! Can you hear us?"

They passed from room to room, and the only thing they seemed to notice was some dirt and a damp, musty smell beside one of the fireplaces. "There must be a draft from this fireplace somehow," stated Michael. "See, it even feels peculiar. It has a damp strange moldy smell. See for yourselves; it's different over here."

When they reached the back door of the home, Sean said, "does anyone else think it might be significant that the back door is locked?"

"You mean, they brought all their stuff out of the Bentley, and unlocked the front door and .... What happened?" asked Joe. "Where are Maggie and James, and where is all their stuff?"

Michael walked over to his father, "Something else has come to light that I should ask you about, Dad. Do you remember anything special about the lighthouse clockwork used for lens rotation? We just discovered a letter that revealed the architect, Joseph Walsh, who sailed on the shipwrecked Sea Crest schooner, was very knowledgeable and skillful in using lighthouse clockworks. He was also planning to use his talent to build various trap doors and floors in both the Sea Crest Lighthouse and probably this beach house."

"Yes, come to think of it, there were rumors and stories of such things when your mother and I were visiting here, but I never saw any evidence of it," answered his father. "Why do you ask now? Have you discovered some hidden walls or secret doors?"

"Grace found an old letter in a packet, from the Chambers' storage unit, which was left for James and me. One of the letters was addressed to Joseph Walsh. He was the architect on board, The Sea Crest schooner, which was shipwrecked off our coast. He is also the great-great-grandfather of my Kate."

"You don't say. That's simply amazing. That's the site of the wreck where James and I were diving underwater when Maggie's dad rescued us," exclaimed Benjamin Jensen.

"Yes, that's it, Dad," explained Michael. "According to this letter, Joseph Walsh's family was heavily supporting Mary Edmundson, from Ireland, in the Anti-Slavery movement. They had agreed to send financial help to enable Joseph Walsh to build structures in America. They would include numerous hidden tunnels and trap doors to help the Underground Railroad. It seems he was an expert in a very rare air motor, which was used to pull the weight back up that drives the mechanism somehow."

Benjamin was surprised. "Do you know anything about that, son?"

"Yes, we studied that in college; however, they were initially used to actuate the rotation of the lens in the lighthouse towers."

"Dad, we think there will be many similarities in the construction of the Sea Crest Lighthouse and the beach house. They had the same Architect, Joseph Walsh, and the same Captain of the Sea Crest Ship, Captain Michael Chambers. We think numerous things were built to support the Underground Railroad and the freedom of many runaway slaves."

Benjamin was taken aback as he asked his son, "Wow, you think Sea Crest served as part of the Underground Railroad?"

"Yes. According to the letters found in the packet, Grace is confident that Sea Crest was a station with a safe house hidden somewhere in the area."

"Michael, do you think your mother knew anything about its history? I heard rumors about the strange hidden doors, secret staircases, and trap doors. Still, I assumed they were just fabricated romantic stories. This grand old beach house with all its beautiful touches certainly lends itself to all kinds of fantasies. Still, I never considered they were based on actual history."

Chapter 26

"Where are Maggie and James, and where is all their stuff?" asked Joe in frustration. "I don't like the feel of this one bit. I'm calling the authorities right now."

When his call went through to the Sea Crest Precinct, he answered with a worried voice, "Hi, this is attorney Joe Lawrence. I'm up here at the Chambers' beach house, and it looks like some things are not adding up. We think something might have happened to a couple of people."

"What exactly do you think happened and to whom?" asked the officer on duty.

"Well, both Maggie O'Hara and James Jensen are missing."

"Well, have you checked the top of the Sea Crest Lighthouse?" laughed the officer.

"No, kidding. This is serious. No one has seen or heard from them since late yesterday afternoon," countered Joe sternly.

"Sorry, Joe," he replied. "But are you talking about FBI Special Agent Maggie O'Hara and James Jensen?"

"Yes, I am."

"You mean our Maggie and the guy with the alligator shoes? Gee, I hope they didn't kill each other or something."

"Yes, it's them, but I'm positive they didn't do anything to harm each other," Joe answered with exasperation.

"They came up to the beach house late yesterday afternoon. We see James' Bentley in the circular driveway, unlocked. While nothing looks disturbed," Joe continued, "there is no sign of Maggie or James anywhere. Now, could you PLEASE get someone up here to help find out what happened to them?"

Chapter 27

Meanwhile, well below all that commotion, Maggie and James were in the cavern, slowly stirring and shifting around. Since they didn't have any sunlight to wake them, they slept quite late.

Maggie whispered, "Do you think it's morning yet?"

"Yes, in fact, I think it must be almost noon by now. I left my watch at the jewelers, so I'm not sure," James answered.

"Wow, that late?" said Maggie as she turned her arm, so she could get a to look at her watch.

"Well, we didn't get to sleep until after midnight, so I thought it would be about noon," finished James.

"You're right. My watch says it's 12:15. I guess we should dig into our delicious left-overs and eat brunch," she laughed.

"That sounds good," agreed James as he unwrapped his backpack and laid out the food.

They sat on the quilts and ate while they discussed various ways to get out of the cavern. "I think we need to move toward that water on the far side and investigate that area," Maggie said.

James followed up with, "Great idea. When I was in the Marines, we did some training on how to survive in various conditions."

"You were a Marine?" To say that Maggie was surprised was an understatement. "I didn't know that."

"Maggie, there are a whole lot of things that you don't know about me," he kidded.

"That's certainly true," she answered with a smile. "I forgot you know quite a bit about my day to day life. However, I know very little about yours."

"That's a two-edged sword," replied James. "However, I have decided to change my life and start looking for the good in people, especially here in Sea Crest. You have all shown me that my pretentious attitude is completely lost on you anyway.

"In fact," he continued, "my approach was thoroughly ineffective with all of you."

"Exactly, what do you mean?" laughed Maggie. "When I met you, you looked like the poster boy for the rich and famous."

"What?" protested James, although he knew it was true.

But Maggie ignored him as she pointed out, "You had the whole Sea Crest Police Force giving you special treatment like you were a celebrity or something. They completely abandoned any semblance of normal police procedures. Instead, you had them running around like the Keystone Cops."

"Now, wait just a minute there. I was a basket-case when I arrived at the police station. They were trying to help me find my brother."

"Yeah, Yeah. A basket-case with a three-piece suit and a pair of alligator shoes. Oh, and let's not forget the Bentley parked outside the station." She couldn't help but tease him about that.

"James, you made me so mad," she persisted. "You know you were taking advantage of those poor policemen just because of the way you looked."

"Oh Yeah? Well, what about the way you looked? Do you really want to go down that road? When I first saw you, I thought you were so sweet. I was sure you'd be so intimidated by me that you'd hand me over to your boss or the FBI Commander. You know, somebody that could handle the top, leading cases like mine."

Maggie gasped, "What are you talking about?"

"That's right, Baby. You came sashaying into the room with your red hair flying every which way. You eyed me with such surprise that I figured you were intimidated or overwhelmed by me. You tricked me into thinking you were this lovely little thing that didn't even deal with serious FBI work. I assumed you got your title and promotion to FBI Special Agent just because of the way you look. So don't even go there."

Maggie was so stunned that she couldn't even look at him. She certainly couldn't, for the life of her, think of even one thing to say. She was pretty sure her face was as red as her hair.

James, in turn, felt like an idiot and apologized, "I'm sorry. I yelled at you." It never entered his head that Maggie was shocked by his revelation of how she had looked to him.

Chapter 28

"Okay," demanded Maggie. "Tell me all about how we're supposed to get out of here."

"Well," said James, "I learned that caving, sometimes known as spelunking, can be a fun, exciting hobby and a valuable tool for scientific discovery. However, in our situation, we'll start with the basics that I remember, relating to survival and how to safely find our way out."

"Great. I'm all ears," she replied.

"Well, Maggie, I'm sure you know more than I do about safety from your valuable work with the Red Cross and water safety within the Sea Crest Community. Maybe together we can come up with a plan to have a great adventure as well as find our way out of this maze of tunnels and caves.

"However, we've already failed the first and most important step," he continued. "We're supposed to tell someone that we're in the cave and what time we expect to return."

"Wow," said Maggie. "That's true. No one even knows there is a cave, cavern, or tunnel. Plus, they won't be looking for us mainly because they don't know we're missing."

"Well," he continued. "We're doing great on the second step. It's to have a good flashlight in working order with batteries, in addition to a spare light source. We're way ahead of the game with these night-vision goggles with the headlamp attached in the middle. Thanks to you and Kate, we have the very best."

James looked around as he said, "Being able to see our surroundings is the best way to survive in a cave. So, thanks, Maggie."

"You're quite welcome, James," she replied. "What's the next step?"

"It's critical, although it's often overlooked until it's too late."

"Wow, what is it?" she asked.

"We need to mark our path just like the scouts learn to do. They learn to be aware of their surroundings and note landmarks. They always mark their way out at all intersections. In our case, we can't go out the same way we came into the caves, but we still need to use anything we have to mark where we're going."

"You mean like breadcrumbs to make a trail?"

"Yes, but in our case, we can use things such as rocks to make arrows pointing to the way we've been traveling or scratch an arrow on the cave floor. We don't want to be going in circles or get disoriented and get confused and lost."

He continued with a hopeful message, "There is no reason to get lost; we just have to find our way out. We can leave notes, tie ribbons from the quilts or leave candles or other things to mark where we've been, not to be confused with previous people in the cave."

"I've not thought of that," said Maggie. "All the people using the Underground Railroad have traveled through these caves and tunnels also. They have probably left all kinds of footprints and directional signs, even though they were placed in this passageway well over a hundred years ago."

"Yes, the clues we leave must be unique," agreed James.

"Well, we can unravel my sweater and leave ribbons of yarn as our distinctive markings," offered Maggie.

"That sounds like it might work out fine," said James happily. "And that brings us to our next step: Remain calm. It's much easier to think clearly and more efficiently if you're not in a panic.

"We were also taught to stay together and to hold hands if you must move in the dark. There is safety in numbers.

"In our case, we will need to conserve our light sources. Whichever one of us is in the lead should, of course, have our light turned on to lead the way. Maggie, we can take turns if you'd like. The one behind should turn off their lights to conserve the batteries. When we use our headlamps, we should use the lowest output setting."

"Yes, James," said Maggie. "I agree with you; I just wouldn't have even thought of it. Good job."

"Thanks," he smiled as he continued. "We also need to stay dry. We have water over on the far side of this cavern, so we need to be careful. We may also continue to find water along the way," advised James.

Maggie said, "I agree one hundred percent. Do you have any idea of how far it will be to navigate our way out? I mean, what is your best guess?"

"I'm not sure, but I think we should both try to keep moving and see if we can make it out of the caves, during daylight. If this cave tunnel system ends, out over the ocean or along a rocky cliff, we'll need sunlight to be safe."

Maggie was a little worried by that answer as she asked, "What if we can't get out before dark tonight? Do you think we'll have enough food and drink for another day?"

James thought about that for a minute and tried to avoid any undue anxiety. "Good point. We should be careful with our food. As for our drink, we've got plenty of wine and champagne but no actual water and only a little coffee left."

Maggie had an idea, "what if we fill our backpacks with as many bottles of bubbly as we can carry without making them too heavy? That sounds crazy, but at least we'll have something safe to drink. I do not think we should drink this water in the cavern."

"We have no way to test it, but be aware that it may be contaminated, and we should use it only as a last resort," James agreed. "By the way, we also have to figure out the best way to carry some of these quilts. If we need to spend another night in these caves, we'll need them.

"Now that we've made our plans, I vote we pack up our stuff and try to make our way out of this area," said James.

"Sounds good." Maggie agreed. "I think we need to move toward that water on the far side and investigate that area."

"Yes, it seems like the logical place to pass through to a tunnel or whatever is next. However, there is one more important water-related issue that we need to prepare for."

Maggie had started to trust him and wanted to hear what he was about to share. "Well, so far, your safety ideas have been excellent. I'm not experienced in caving, but I've spent my entire life in and around the water. Let me see if I can guess your One More Thing."

After a minute, she admitted, "I don't have a clue about what you're going to say next."

James smiled and asked, "Does this mean you concede that you don't know everything?"

"No, I admit nothing of the kind," she joked. "But given the circumstances, I'd love to hear anything that will get us safely out of here."

"Well," challenged James, "I'm going to go out on a limb here and ask you if you know about the history of a remarkable body of water named Craighead Caverns. That includes the Lost Sea, plus underground waterfalls and caverns."

"No, but it sounds remarkable!"

"Maggie, is that your final answer?"

"Of course, it is," she laughed.

"Duly noted! I'm going to mark this day down on my calendar. 'Maggie O'Hara freely admits there is something she doesn't know!'"

"Oh, come on now. I'm not that egotistical,... am I?"

"A resounding, YES is heard from the crowd."

"You're hilarious, James."

"Now, I'll explain what I know about this historic cave system. It's deep inside a mountain in Tennessee. It's listed as America's largest underground lake in The Guinness Book of World Records.

"Now, does that sound familiar? Have you ever heard of this before?

As Maggie shrugged her shoulders and shook her head, he cheerfully replied, "No? Well, if it makes you feel better, it's not located anywhere near here.

"That entire area was historically known and used by the Cherokee Indians for generations. In fact, an impressive amount of Cherokee Indian artifacts can still be found there today. Things such as jewelry, arrowheads, and pottery; exactly like the cup we saw yesterday.

"Scientists have documented tracks and bones from a giant Pleistocene jaguar, that are believed to be 20,000 years old. Some of these findings are on display in the American Museum of Natural History in New York.

"To my knowledge, they have never been able to find the entire width or depths of the Lost Sea, even though they have used modern equipment and teams of divers. The area with all its underwater caverns seems endless.

"Now I've shared this information with you for 3 reasons, Maggie.

#1. To prove to you that the cup was truly a Cherokee cup, not your "butterfly" nonsense.

I will accept your apology, in writing, as soon as we get out of here.

#2. To prove to you that you don't know Everything.

#3. To warn you, we must be cautious, in and around this water, that is part of the Underground Railroad. We don't know how deep it may be or what animals might live or hibernate here. Safety must be our first priority."

Maggie was quick to state, "Boy, that was something. I don't know where you discovered that information. I hadn't even thought about this cavern being part of a huge cave and water system. I do see parts that look like they've been dug out by hand, and other walls and rock alignments that are definitely natural formations."

"Yeah," replied James. "It might be difficult to read one-hundred-year-old trail markings. Hopefully, they were not altered or erased by animals. I can't tell if the water levels here are affected by the tides, but that could also be a problem if they were washed away."

Maggie's soberly responded, "Yes. James. I promise to be very careful. I'm sure we can make our way out."

James was also serious when he pledged, "Great! I know between the two of us, working together, we can get out. Now, we should probably pack up and get going."

They folded up quilts, gathered candles from the cavern's floor, and stored their leftover food in the backpacks. Then they filled the rest of the space with wine and champagne bottles.

"We should be sure to take our things with us as we move through the cave and tunnel system," said Maggie. "If the entryway quickly slams shut behind us, which it may well do, it might be sealed, like the entryway from the beach house."

Chapter 29

Maggie and James hauled all their supplies over to the cavern's opening by the running water stream.

“James, before we leave, I’d like to tell you that, so far, this has been quite an adventure. Over the past couple of days, we’ve learned a lot about our ancestors’ values and integrity. I’m so proud of them and what they were able to accomplish here,” Maggie said sincerely. “I’ve lived here beside the Sea Crest Lighthouse my entire life. I never expected to discover that the Underground Railroad was right beneath us the whole time. Finding this is truly one of the most memorable events of my life.”

“Yes,” replied James. “I know what you mean. I realize how extraordinary and meaningful this experience is. What are the odds that we would ever stumble upon this fantastic historical evidence?

“I’ll tell you, Maggie; that’s almost as significant as the discovery that we aren’t so bad, ourselves. We started out as adversaries, and now we’ve become real friends. I’m so glad that you and I were the lucky ones that got to share this.”

“Thanks, James,” Maggie whispered with tears in her eyes. “I feel the same way.”

One look at her and James had that feeling again. She had no idea how much he had grown to care about her, but she didn’t take his head off about his remark that they were friends now.

That was a start. James felt the need to get the conversation back on track before he did something, for which she would like to take his head off.

"Now, I think we've got about three, maybe four hours before nightfall," James started. "That will also bring high tide again, so let's see if we can make our way out of here."

They encountered a colossal stone, blocking the path alongside the stream. They pried the rock loose, and Maggie discovered what resembled a pale arrow, scratched on the floor of the cavern.

"Hey, look, a mark!" cried Maggie.

She immediately dusted off the place to see it more clearly. Sure enough, she uncovered an arrow that pointed to the right side of the rocky wall.

James couldn't have been prouder of her, as he agreed, "This appears to be a marked trail signal. Someone has left a clue for us. Great find."

"Yeah, let's see if we can twist or pull something lose."

They didn't know what would happen, but when Maggie pushed on the right side, the rock creaked, groaned, and slowly moved open.

James said, "Here, I'll put another arrow on the pathway with this sharp rock. If anyone ever gets that door open, up in the wine tasting room, they'll come down here and see this fresh mark beside the old one."

As the giant rock opened, they quickly pulled all their supplies with them and made it through to the other side.

"Now let's make a mark on this side, just in case the entryway closes and locks behind us. We'll keep track of where we've been and how we've marked our way back, like bread crumbs."

No sooner had he finished that remark when the opening closed with a heavy, final, clang shut.

"Wow," James declared in amazement. "That was something. It must have been a clockwork timing or something similar that was rigged up to secure their escape to freedom."

They immediately tested the entryway, but it was unyielding and locked securely back into place.

"Well, there's no turning back now," said Maggie with a nervous laugh as she looked at James through her goggles.

Chapter 30

James and Maggie both stared solemnly at the huge stone that had just sealed off any hope of returning to the cavern where they had spent the last couple of days.

Maggie brightly stated, "Well, if we needed proof that this pathway was man-made construction to lead the way to safety, we may have just seen it. This can only be the work of a trained and skilled person."

"Yes," agreed James. "The intricate design of this stone entryway is fantastic. I believe Michael has studied and worked on similar clockwork type machines in some of the old lighthouses that he's worked on over the years."

"I'll bet this was the work of the Irish Architect, Joseph Walsh," stated Maggie. "He was very creative and was commissioned to build and repair lighthouses here in America."

"Yes," replied James. "This verifies that we're on the right track to exit the tunnels and caves. Now, let's take a look at our new surroundings and plan our next move."

"Good idea," said Maggie as she slowly turned around with her flashlight focused on the floor of the cave. "But we must stay together while we search for our next course of action."

"Let's concentrate on the pathway along this wall of rock. We should probably load up our gear and see where it takes us," he said as he lifted up his backpack and supplies. “You take the lead this time,” he said as he took her hand.

Maggie immediately felt a wave of excitement as his hand sought and held hers.

James felt the same thrill and almost dropped her hand, but he abruptly covered up his reaction to her touch with a joke. “And don’t take me through a bunch of water. I’m putting a whole lot of trust in you, so be nice.”

“Okay, but please try to keep up,” she laughed. “You can’t dawdle and dilly-dally like you normally do.”

“You better be kidding. I’ll put my Marines up against your pathetic FBI guys any day of the week. You name the time and the place, Bab....” He stopped abruptly and felt like a fool. He cleared his throat as if he hadn’t almost said, Baby.

Chapter 31

Meanwhile, on the ground high above, no one in the gathering crowd outside the Sea Crest beach house was kidding around.

Officer Jones and the team from the Sea Crest Police Precinct were all business. They were taking this latest disappearance as a chance to redeem themselves.

"That's right," explained Officer Jones. "Everything is by the book this time," he continued as they all remembered their previous mistakes in acting like a bunch of amateurs in the face of some pretty wealthy out-of-towners.

"We will conduct this investigation exactly the way we've all been trained to do," he pointed out thoughtfully.

"Okay by us, but who is missing, and what happened?" asked one of the men.

"We haven't had two disappearances in the whole history of Sea Crest, and now we have two-inside of a month?" pointed out another police officer.

"That's what we're here to find out," answered Officer Jones. "Oh, there's Joe Lawrence," he said as he waved and walked toward him. "He's the one that called our precinct. Let's see what the problem is."

"Hello, I'm glad you got here so fast," said Joe, with an anxious look on his face.

"Who do you think is missing?" asked Officer Jones. He was hoping that his information was wrong, and he hoped it was some teenager fooling around or playing a joke on his friends.

"Well, the who is my previous client, James Jenson," stated Joe.

"Isn't he the prisoner with the alligator shoes?" asked one of the officers.

"Yes, as a matter of fact, he was," Joe answered. "He was last seen yesterday, late afternoon, with FBI Special Agent Maggie O'Hara, leaving in his Bentley automobile. He was coming up to the Chambers' beach house."

"Oh, No!" groaned the very concerned Officer Jones, as he turned to his team and commanded, "We need someone from homicide up here, immediately."

"Well, no, not so fast," Joe tried to intervene as he saw Benjamin Jensen run up to them.

With a stricken look on his face, Benjamin cried, "What? Homicide?"

Maggie's dad was right behind him, and he didn't look any better as he chokingly asked, "What did they find?"

"Okay, everyone, calm down," Joe pleaded. "They didn't find anything. It's just that the police think Maggie and James,...well, they believe that they dislike each other."

"What?" Benjamin and Sean said together.

"Well, I'm sure he doesn't even know her," stated Benjamin emphatically. "And if he did, he certainly would NEVER use violence against a woman."

Officer Jones carefully replied, "We were thinking the perpetrator of the assault was ... just the reverse."

Sean turned to Benjamin and murmured, "Well, I think James knows her, but, well, everyone loves my daughter Maggie. She wouldn't hurt a fly."

Benjamin thought he'd just entered the twilight zone. He looked at this son, Michael, and helplessly said, "What are they talking about?"

Chapter 32

James and Maggie had been walking for quite a while, when James asked, “Hey, what do you say we sit down for a short break?”

“Yes,” replied Maggie. “How about us having a nourishment break as well?”

“I was hoping you’d say that. For some reason, I’m starved.”

Maggie started to lay down the quilts in a dry place, and they pulled out the food and drink. “Well, this is a fine picnic. I’m sure you’ve never had a normal meal on anything like this before, have you, James?”

This opinion of him made him realize how far off her knowledge of him was. He was going to fix that right now if he could.

“Maggie, remember yesterday when we talked about people having two sides, and do people only know us by the side we show them?”

When she said, “Yes,” between bites of food, he continued.

“I’ve always been very aware of the coin-has-two-sides concept. Over my life, I have played with the idea on many levels.

“You, Maggie, have been the prime example that I’ve thought of most often, lately.”

“I’m sure you’ve only remembered my very best qualities,” Maggie laughed.

"Well, granted, I've seen many of those positive sides to you, most recently. However, at the first meeting, I thought you were the most outrageous woman I'd ever met."

"Thanks a lot."

"Oh, I still think that."

"What?"

"Let me finish," James laughed. "I still think that, but now I recognize the other side of your coin. That gives the complete picture of you. The yin and the yang of you."

"James, you better think of something nice to say, and you better hurry up." Maggie was getting ready to defend both her yin and her yang if need be.

"Well, you don't even know what I'm going to say, and you're already getting all miffed and riled up." He wasn't going to admit how appealing that looked, but her eyes were flashing and downright gorgeous.

"Now, if you'll stop interrupting, I'll explain," James said. "I understand you've been to China. Is that true?"

"Yes. So, what of it? That's where I learned about my favorite game, Mah Jongg," she stated with annoyance.

"Well," he glibly said before he could stop himself. "I'll remember that fact if we ever play The Newlywed Game." James froze. *Where on earth did that come from?* he wondered in panic.

He made a quick recovery with, "I was just testing to see if you were paying attention."

Maggie stared at him in complete silence, which must have been from the other side of her coin.

James smoothly continued, "According to the Chinese philosophy, yin and yang show how contrary powers and strengths, which appear completely opposite, may actually be interconnected and complementary in reality. That's where you really shine, Maggie!

"You are an enigma, but you're well worth looking past the obvious, to discover your true heart. You're very nice and almost caring if one can hang on and try to get past the first impression," he explained. "You should really try to work on that, Maggie."

"You are the enigma, James!" she exploded. "You started to explain what changed for you the day your air hose was cut in the scuba diving accident when my dad rescued you. The next thing you talk about is The Newlywed Game and my two-sides of a coin. Not to mention my yin and yang."

"I guess I got off track, but I wanted to explain something to you," said James softly.

"Well, what is it?" Maggie demanded hotly.

"It's how things aren't always like you originally see them. I wanted you to know that I'm not really the same inside as what you may see on the outside. I'm a conundrum too. Everybody probably is to a certain degree."

"How do you think I see you?" she asked.

"If I was a betting man, I'd have to anticipate that you'd think I'm a rich, spoiled snob who has impeccable taste in clothes," James stated.

"Would that extend to a fondness for alligator shoes, James?"

"Of course," James chuckled. "But the alligator, Brioni Shoes and the Bentley are an enjoyable take away from the best-selling "Dress for Success" book. It describes the New York City Financial Manager lifestyle that I've created. I find it essential in my banking and financial profession to intermingle and form friendships with many rich and famous individuals. It's a large portion of my job, and I'm extremely good at it.

"But Maggie, that's not all that I am. Try to keep that in mind when you judge me."

"James, I'm not judging you."

"I know you have in the past," he said. "Now to be fair, I realize you're more than an FBI Special Agent. You've got an incredible, meaningful life in Sea Crest, which is so far beyond your career that I don't know how you do it. I admire all the wonderful secret projects that you and your friends accomplish to make this community a better place to live in. I know, before you start emphatically protesting; The fact that my grandmother Chambers believed it, is good enough for me. She was as smart as they come, and she was an outstanding judge of character."

"Thanks, James," she said. "You don't know how much that means to me."

"Okay, Maggie, that brings us back to what happened when your dad saved both my dad's and my life that day.

"I was greatly impacted by that diving accident where my hose was cut by the sharp steel edges of the wreckage of the Sea Crest schooner. I have never forgotten the feelings and lessons I learned that day. They served me well later, while I was growing through my teen years and developing into a young man.

"What I felt and saw first-hand that day from both my own father and your father has never left me. The underwater situation was an outright terror for me. I knew that I was going to die. I had recently lost my mother. Now, I realized that my father was not going to leave me down there to die alone. He was sharing the small supply of remaining air out of his tank with me. We would both surely die in a matter of minutes."

"Oh James, I'm so sorry that you had to go through that terrible ordeal," said Maggie, as she reached out and gently laid her hand on his shoulder.

James paused before he continued, "After an unbearable length of time, I saw your dad float into view and approach us with two lifesaving tanks of air. He put the diving regulator in my mouth, and I took a lifesaving full breath of air. He looked straight into my eyes with the calm support that conveyed safety and assurance. He helped my dad with the second fresh tank of air and took my dad's near-empty tank, as he signaled us to ascend up to the boat.

"I learned the true meaning of hope and faith that day. I also felt first-hand the gift of life because your dad had the honor and courage, built through rescue training, at the very core of his being. It was a part of your dad's heart that had permeated through all the Coast Guard generations at the Sea Crest Lighthouse. They each pledged to help all seafaring individuals who needed Search and Rescue or Search and Recovery aid. The idea that they would never leave anyone behind became something of a familial bond.

"It's reminiscent of the Latin phrase, *nemo resideo*, or *leave no one behind*. Even Greek mythology often portrayed heroes who rescued those captured by their enemies.

"That day of my rescue, I was not-left-behind, because two men of that generation, believe in that credo. Your father's 'anonymous act of kindness' saved both my father's life and mine. That had an incredible effect on me going forward.

"Granted, that experience did leave me with reoccurring nightmares in which panic would flood my mind. In these dreams, I relived drowning underwater, scuba diving around a wreck, and watching my father sharing his last few breaths of air with me, knowing we would both die.

"Now, for the most part, I find that I value life with the perspective of someone much older. I try to make the most out of my opportunities, and I'm always grateful for my blessings.

"As a young teen, I suppose my life path could have taken a drastic downward spiral after the death of my mom. I was very close to her, as I think all boys are. I didn't understand why she had to die. It wasn't fair, and I was angry that she was taken from our family.

"During the next few months, I felt too bad to act out too much. I wanted to hide in my room and mourn and cry in private. My dad was all broken up himself, and although he noticed, I don't think he knew what to do about any of us. I'm sure Michael also had lots of questions about why our mother died.

"When I processed the anger, I decided to try to do things that our mother would be proud of, as a way to honor her memory. Most of the time, that proved to make my life better. However, I do remember one huge fight with kids from another high school, when they made fun of my mother. I found out later, after we all ended up in jail, that those kids had no idea that my mom had died. It was just a crude remark they often bantered about to intimidate other kids. In the end, they apologized, we made peace, and the charges were dropped.

"One of the essential things I learned from that experience, was that people would sometimes hurt us. But we need to consider where they are coming from and what their intent is before we validate their action with even more trouble.

"Since then, I've tried my hand at learning various survival skills. I even joined the Scouts to earn as many badges as possible. By the time I was eighteen, I had advanced to an Eagle Scout. Many of the skills I learned may come in handy while we're here in the Underground Railroad.

"Overall, I think I've been able to make good choices."

"James, I'm sure your mom would be very proud of you," said Maggie with a smile.

"Thanks, Maggie. That means a lot to me," he replied as he quietly thought about her comment. He was surprised that it meant so much to him.

After a few minutes, he continued, "Well, I graduated from high school and college with excellent grades. At that point in my journey, I joined the United States Marine Corps because I had respect and admiration for them. I knew it would be hard, but I gave it my best effort, and I excelled in it. Soon after I earned my rank as Captain, I took command of a unit that was sent to Afghanistan."

Maggie strangely felt she would burst with pride at hearing him disclose these personal insights into his past. "What did that feel like? I have visited several countries in my career with the FBI. Still, I imagine that your experience was drastically different."

James took so long to answer that she thought he hadn't heard her. Finally, he said, "Yes. It was sobering to get to know and share that time in my life with these young men and women. They represented the bravest, and the best America had to offer, as they proudly served our country on foreign soil. They faced situations that the normal young adult back home would never witness and probably never be able to handle."

He cleared his throat as he tried to decide about explaining anything further. *After all,* he thought, *I don't talk to anyone about what happened during that time. Why do I feel compelled to tell Maggie anything? Why on earth do I think she, of all people, would even care? Yes, I've seen that she has a kind heart when she let me and Michael decide what to do with our grandmother's will and the Chambers' beach house. Plus, I clearly saw how she loves Misha.*

I'm also aware that I'm safe in the Underground Railroad and no one else can hear me telling of my war experiences. It has helped make me who I am, and it's not all about being a rich snob with alligator shoes; excuse me, one shoe, and a Bentley, which thankfully is still in one piece.

He heard himself talking before he had firmly decided to tell her. "My troops were embedded in Afghanistan for quite a while. We were fighting across the world for the right to live with a small portion of the freedom that we take for granted here, every day. Our training would often lead to a safe return home. But I quickly learned that, in those cases, it did not mean that we could ever forget the horror that we had witnessed or the loss of life of our comrades-in-arms.

"The shocking realities of losing a buddy that was closer to you than any other person on the face of the earth was brutal. Instantly dead beside us or right in front of us. We were supposed to protect each other, yet we weren't able to keep them from being killed. The survivor's guilt was alive and well among the troops. Each and every person will carry these heavy burdens home with them.

"The memories of our closest buddies were usually impossible to erase. That is not to say that we wanted to forget the good stuff. The fighting survivors often cannot collectively separate out the precious reminiscences. They allowed us to put our lives in the other's hands, day after day, in the worst possible conditions.

"We had also shared some of the most laughable behavior and pranks of our lives during our training days. These glimpses of mayhem and joy would never let us forget the fun that was shared with our friend, often at the expense of ourselves or of our unsuspecting buddy. However, remembering these times would prove to bring a very dark sadness. It colored and penetrated our hearts and mind, as we could neither justify nor come to terms with the loss of our friend. Most times, it was the loss of many of our friends. It was hard for the human spirit to cope with it.

"This could hardly prepare us for what lay ahead. In many cases, the repercussions of those memories would continue to disrupt and erupt over our entire life, if not treated. The damage would reappear in the form of night sweats, panic attacks, and nightmares, the likes of which you would never want to experience. Many of us would relive sights and sounds that were so horrific that our minds could not handle them, as they screamed out for relief. At times it would seem that the only way out was to use the most extreme measures to make it finally stop.

"They say that prayer is alive and well, in the foxholes of war. That is my experience. I have lifted our lives up to The Good Lord, countless times.

"The human cost of war is not just tallied with the body count, but with the invisible wounds that they endure," James admitted. After a moment, he solemnly added, "For some reason, I needed to tell you. I guess that's the other side of my coin, Maggie."

Maggie was silently weeping. She had never expected this. However, she did know one thing; *It was tough for him to relive and allow me to learn about these experiences.*

She wiped her eyes and took his hand. The honor was not lost on her, and her voice broke as she whispered, "James, it means a lot that you would share that with me. The currency of your special coin just went through the roof. Thank you."

Neither one talked for the next few minutes. They now shared an intimate bond that felt monumental in their relationship.

Finally, Maggie asked, "James is that when you learned about the Cherokee Indians?"

He gave a little smile as he explained, "Yes, Maggie. I think I learned the value of listening during that part of my life. I will never forget what an unexpected reward I received.

"Did you know that American Indians have served in our military for 3 wars, even though we were still withholding several basic rights?"

"No," she said. "What are you talking about?"

"Apparently, it started with the War of 1812, when the Five Civilized Tribes, helped fight on the side of the United States. Later, the United States broke their treaties with the American Indians Tribes when they illegally seized millions of acres of their land.

"The broken treaties continued after gold was found on land that is now Georgia. The United States passed the illegal Indian Removal Act in 1830. The result of that removal led to The Trail of Tears. Indians were forced to journey by foot to reservations in Oklahoma and Texas. This disgraceful event left 2,500 people dead, including many veterans.

"In World War 1, in 1917, several thousand Native Americans joined the armed forces, even though they had not been granted citizenship yet. Their Indian language was so foreign to the German enemy troops that they found it impossible to figure out. Since they couldn't decipher the messages, the Allies were able to win.

"Code Talkers were even more successful in World War 2. The Cherokee Indians in North Carolina were the first Native American tribe to successfully transmit their messages. Other tribes, such as the Choctaws, followed using their own language.

"This entire time, The United States was trying to purge their language and customs from all of the Native American tribes."

Maggie was shocked, "I've heard about the Code Talkers, but I didn't understand."

James agreed, "I would have never known if I hadn't met several Cherokee in the Marines. We became very good friends, and according to them, their history was not written down, so it was left out. Since their tribes were not literate, they had no voice. Their oral history is so important to them because it's how they communicated. The written word is just oral history written down. Maggie, that brings us back to Sequoyah's Cherokee Symbol tablet that we found in the first room.

"As a young man, he spent a lot of time with people who spoke and wrote English. He was fascinated with their *Talking Leaves,* which he knew could represent information to anyone else that could understand the symbols. Most Cherokees were suspicious of the writing and thought it sorcery.

"However, Sequoyah designed a set of symbols specifically for the Cherokees to read and write, in the early 1820s. By using the syllabary, the Cherokees could now *talk-on-paper*.

"Maggie, do you remember Sequoyah pictured on a Golden Dollar coin that came out a few years back?"

"Yes. I think it was the one with Sacagawea on the other side."

"That's the one."

"Sequoyah traveled to Washington, D.C., in 1828. He was a key Indian delegate who spoke and wrote English. The sovereign Cherokee nation covered a vast area of eastern America. They negotiated a treaty for land in the planned Indian Territory, which guaranteed that Cherokee land would be off-limits to white settlers forever.

"However, within 2 years, in 1830, the United States passed the Indian Removal Act, and the resulting heartbreaking repercussions of that action included the needless loss of over 2,500 Indian lives. They were forcibly led to travel on foot to Indian Territory in Oklahoma and Texas.

Maggie and James both sat silently, trying to make sense of this terrible stain on our country.

"The American Indians felt similar racial mistreatment against them from America as the runaway slaves did. They were sympathetic to the situations that the slaves were suffering. Many slaves were able to hide with various tribes and some actually joined the Indian tribes. As the survival issues continued, many Indians chose to flee to the Caribbean along with the slaves, by way of the Underground Railroad due to the common bond they felt.

"The Indians were extremely helpful to the slaves also. The significant advantage the Native Americans had was the skill to be excellent guides and trackers. This had been their land, and they knew it well.

"The ordinary slave was not allowed to leave their master's property. They didn't know the rivers or how to move around the cities or the countryside. They were not permitted to learn to read: hence, the picture quilts.

"I believe the many Native Americans were crucial to the success of the Underground Railroad, and I think you and I are walking in their footprints also."

Maggie softly uttered, "James, I can't believe it. I never knew about any of this and I feel shocked."

He took her hand and said, "I know what you mean."

Chapter 33

After a few minutes, he said, "What do you say we get going again? I'd like to get through to another cavern if possible."

Maggie continued to lead the cautious exploration of the second cave when she came to an abrupt stop. Of course, James stumbled right into her, and awkwardly tried to steady her.

This isn't the same as pulling her off the porch on top of me, he thought. *This has an entirely new feeling to it. This time it resembles a genuine closeness, more like protection for someone you care for.*

Maggie must have also felt the sensation as she responded, "Well, I guarantee you won't fall through a hole in the floor and fall five feet down onto a new tunnel. But look at this," she laughed.

James steadied them both and put his headlight on as he stepped up beside her and said with wonder, "Well, I'll be. Just what do you think we have here?"

"The only thing I know for sure is that it's another pile of quilts. Right in the middle of the passageway."

James knelt down beside her as he inspected the quilts with amazement. Sure enough, they displayed the identical symbols as the quilts in the other sections of the cavern. "Okay, Maggie, you're a great detective. What on earth does this mean, if anything?"

She sat down on one of them and looked up at him. Then she gave him an enormous smile as she whispered, "James. Look straight up."

James lifted his head with his headlight and viewed an opening at the top of the cave. It looked just like the one he had fallen through, yesterday, on his way down the tunnel.

"Wow! That looks a lot higher than the hole I fell through, and the one you jumped through," laughed James. "This time, the quilts are neatly folded directly beneath, and there appears to be no way to get up to reach the opening. No tell-tale ladder made of a ship's rope and rigging."

Maggie had an inspiration, "Wait. I need to pull a couple of napkins and a pen out of my backpack."

She fumbled around and handed James the napkins and pen, as she explained, "Here. Try to draw a map of the path we have taken today. Include all the turns and twists that you can remember. It doesn't have to be perfect. I want to see if it coincides with my memory."

"You sound excited. Do you think you know where we are?"

"Yes," replied Maggie with glee. "Now, I'm going to impress you."

"Okay, I'm waiting," kidded James.

"Do your map first. I don't want you to be so overwhelmed with admiration that you can't think straight."

"Okay, okay. For your information, I'm not going to need both napkins. I won't be making any mistakes."

She only smiled as she thought, *what I don't know for sure, but I firmly suspect, is that with all his Marine training, he has been marking the same directions that I have. But he doesn't know the Sea Crest area's landmarks, and I do.*

Within a couple of minutes, he was done and proudly proclaimed, "All right, Special Agent O'Hara, what do you think of this?"

She studied it for a full minute, nodding her head and smiling the whole time.

James interrupted her before she could speak. "First, tell me what you think should amaze me so much. I'll be the judge of if it's better than my map."

"Okay, here I go. This map is so great that I'd tell you to sit down first, but we're already both sitting down. My entire family, including my dad, who saved your poor sorry life, I might add, informed me at a very early age, that I could never get lost. My sense of direction is so strong that I always know precisely where I am, at all times."

"And, of course, you have had this scientifically verified by experts?" asked James. "After all, I can't go on the word of your loving father, who would have told you anything to see that look in your eyes."

"No, kidding." insisted Maggie. "That's the truth." She couldn't help but laugh at the absurdity of her statements. She doggedly continued pleading her case, "The FBI has followed my lead on numerous occasions, because of my ability to instinctively know where we were."

"Oh brother, now I've heard everything." James laughed.

Neither one of them seemed to grasp just how much things had changed between them. "Prove it, Big Shot! Where are we?" he demanded with great sarcasm.

"We are exactly below the Sea Crest Church. Founded and built, I might add, around the same time as the Sea Crest Lighthouse and the Chambers' beach house."

Chapter 34

It was now late afternoon at the Chambers' beach house, and the Search and Rescue operation for James and Maggie was coming up empty. They knew little or nothing about where or how the two had disappeared.

Even though it made absolutely no sense at all, Kate's brother, Connor, took Misha to make one more sweep past the Sea Crest Lighthouse and surrounding beach.

"Misha, come on, girl. Help us find Maggie." At the sound of hearing Maggie's name, she looked very excited and whined as if to let him know that Maggie was missing, but she didn't lead Connor anywhere helpful. Afterward, he took the Great Dane back to the keeper's cottage.

Connor was discouraged when he found his mom in the kitchen busy baking. "Mom, what are you making? You know we're all too upset to eat. I'm really scared."

"I know. But we both know that Maggie is great at taking care of herself. It's a huge part of her job. We just have to trust that she'll be back as soon as she can."

"I agree," replied Connor. "But you always bake when you're worried."

"Well, I have to keep busy and guess what I'm making. I'm making your sister's favorite, Raisin Filled Cookies. I need to have them ready so she can have them as soon as she gets here."

"Thanks, Mom, I'm sure she'll enjoy them," Connor said as he went over and hugged her.

"Alright, that's better," she whispered. "Now, why don't you take a few of these cookies, hot out of the oven, and ask Patrick to help you do a complete search inside the lighthouse?"

"Okay, that's a good idea. We can also check the view of the surrounding area."

Connor and Patrick did a systematic inspection of the inside of the lighthouse. Afterward, they ended up doing a wide-range visual search from the top, with the binoculars and the telescope; however, they came up empty-handed.

When they reported their results to Joe at the beach house, Connor sadly added, "Time is rapidly ticking away. Neither Maggie nor James have been seen for 2 days."

Chapter 35

Maggie and James were astounded. They were sure they had just discovered the trap door for an additional safe house area, beneath the Sea Crest Church. The high ceiling in that cavern now appeared to join this tunnel.

"Wow," muttered James. "I can't get over the history that was right under our noses. Why didn't Grandmother Chambers tell us about this significant part of our history?"

"I've just been wondering the very same thing about my family. How much do you think they knew?" Maggie was stunned, to say the least. She continued, "I understand that the whole Underground Railroad had to remain extremely secretive and seriously protected for the safety of all that were involved."

"You have an excellent point there, Maggie. I'm sure it wasn't safe to talk about the help they offered, and I can only imagine the great risk that it took. You might innocently let something slip that could easily cost a human life."

"You're right. This portion of the Underground Railroad may have been a secret from a whole generation of our families."

"Wow, it's hard to believe, isn't it?" he solemnly stated.

After a couple of minutes, with both of them lost in their thoughts, James said, "I'm pretty hungry. This looks and feels like a good place to take a break for some of our bread and cheese. What do you say we stop and rest for a few minutes?"

"Yes, I think it's sobering to realize whose footsteps we're following." She motioned to James, "Let's eat over here next to this section of the cave wall."

Maggie quickly retrieved with a couple of quilts to sit on.

James grabbed a quilt and gave it a quick flip to cover the picnic space. While it was floating in mid-air, the light from his head-gear flashed the image on the wall. As he drew his eyes up to it, his breath caught in his throat and he froze as he felt a tingling sensation crept down his spine.

"Maggie, look!" he almost shouted, as he lit the wall behind her.

She spun around in shock, expecting to see something dangerous. But to her surprise, she watched in amazement, as the stone wall revealed writing and pictures on its surface. "This is incredible," she whispered.

"Wow, look at that," Maggie continued as she pointed to something printed in an arch on the wall. "Can we make out what it says over that cross?"

They read it together as they held their flashlights up to the wall. "Bless Those Who Pass This Way."

Maggie was choked up and almost in tears as she quietly whispered, "It's an old Irish Blessing."

"That's got to be well over one hundred years old," James stated quietly. "The drawings here symbolize events that are undoubtedly related to the Underground Railroad and the runaway slave's escape to freedom."

They both stood staring at the wall, taking it all in as best they could. "It tells their story, but how remarkable is it that these drawings are still here?" James observed. "They seem untouched by time."

He suddenly realized that he was holding Maggie's hand, and he had no recollection of when that happened. *Wow, she didn't even notice that I've taken her hand.*

Then it dawned on him, *We're so used to holding hands while we were following each other, that it's not off-limits or strange anymore. Well, that's certainly fine with me. I'm going to take advantage of this new opportunity as often as I can get away with it.*

Maggie, on the other hand, was wondering, *Did I take James' hand without even knowing it? He must be so stunned by this stone wall of writing that he hasn't even noticed. Well, he didn't yank it away, did he? It feels so good to share this small but somehow overwhelming closeness with him.*

She quickly diverted the subject by remarking, "Look at that cross. The church is located right above it."

"This whole area seems to be related to the church."

"Hey, look at this sketch. It looks like the row of black and white keys on a piano. It looks like a small piano keyboard section that only shows about ten keys, but the black and white keys could still symbolize the piano."

James joined in, "Some of this is hard to decipher, but some music notes are scattered around this area. Wait. Wait. Look at this. Under each of the black keys, they have numbers."

"Yes, I think you're on to something." cried Maggie. "Let's figure this out. Did you ever take music lessons?" She didn't want him to realize that she had heard him sing at the luncheon. She was so impressed that she had looked over to make sure it was him that she heard sing.

"As a matter of fact, I was part of a Scottish tenor quartet in college," said James proudly.

"I don't believe it," laughed Maggie. *There, that should take him down a peg or two.*

"Yes, it's true," defended James. "My senior year, we even visited Scotland and sang in a few Scottish pubs."

"Prove it!" challenged Maggie, with all the sarcasm she could generate.

His incredible tenor voice filled the cavern as he started. "You take the high road, and I'll take the low road, and I'll get to Scotland before you," sang James beautifully. "Don't forget, that's the last wedding song of the night, at a Scottish wedding."

Maggie couldn't have been more surprised if he'd pulled a bouquet of fake flowers out of his jacket. She just stared at him for a second, with her mouth hanging open, and then she smiled at James and sang these words to the same melody:

"Red is the Rose that in yonder garden grows,

Fair is the lily of the valley."

James was astonished by her sweet, perfect pitch. "That was beautiful," he uttered, with a lump in his throat.

"Don't you forget, that "Red is the Rose," and it's the first song at an Irish wedding," said Maggie quietly. "The music for both of these songs is identical, and both Ireland and Scotland share it. Nobody knows who used the tune first, but it's really old."

"Where did you learn to sing like that, Maggie?"

"I can't remember when I didn't love to sing. In fact, as a child, I once told my grandpa that if he was going to keep playing music, I'd have to keep dancing. I was usually singing as I danced every step."

"Boy, you get more interesting every day. Here I thought you were only interested in interrogating innocent prisoners. But in reality, you have a warm, human side to you."

"Now, don't try to sweet-talk me to get on my good side. If you had done one thing to hurt Kate, you would have lived to regret it," she defended herself, with a smile.

They turned back to the graffiti on the wall and looked more closely at the piano drawing again. "Now, let's see what was so important that they etched it on this wall," said James.

"It looks like they have numbers under the black keys."

"Let's start with the first black key in the pair. It has the numbers 1, 9, and 10 below it. The second black key has the number 8," said James.

"Right. That brings us to the triple set of black keys. The first black key has the numbers 2,4,7 space 11, 13. At least that's what I think is written for those notes," said Maggie.

"Yes, I think that's it. Then the middle black key only has the 6 and 15 under it," said James.

"Hey, we haven't said a word about the fact that this song has only black notes. That doesn't make any sense." Maggie paused, "what do you think this is James? What are we missing?"

"I'm not sure, but let's finish the last couple of notes and see what it sounds like."

"Okay, the third black note in this set has 3, 5, 12, and 14. Then, we're on to the next double set. The first black note in this set only has a number 16 below it. That's all I can make out."

Maggie and James looked at each other with excitement. "Okay, Maggie, if we had these on a page of sheet music, can you picture the scale and read where these notes would fall?"

"Here let me write it down on a napkin so it's clear," she said, as she started to jot down the notes. "Yes. Let's see, I believe this white key would be middle C," said Maggie as she pointed to one of the keys. "We should be able to decipher at least what this short melody sounds like."

"This is one of the most extraordinary puzzles I've ever run across," James marveled. "If it didn't represent anything meaningful to the Underground Railroad, then I don't believe it would be here."

"It seems strange, but let's try it out," she said, her eyes shining with anticipation.

All of a sudden, James let out a surprised shout, "I think I remember what this is."

"Really, you think you know something about it?"

"Well, it's common knowledge that the black keys on the piano give us a major pentatonic scale. Beginning on F#: That would mean the keys are F# G# A# C# D# and the second F#, would be an octave higher," James stated with a dash of conceit.

He was waiting for her to respond to his vast knowledge of music, but she just stared at him through her goggles.

Finally, she said, "Very funny, Smarty Pants. Now, can you even sing those notes?"

"Well, not in a row, if that's what you want," he admitted. "However, I think you should be duly impressed with my special musical expertise," he laughed.

"Oh, I'm duly impressed, alright. That's putting it mildly," she admitted sarcastically.

"Hey, at least I'm contributing," he boasted.

"Well, do you think you could help me figure out the C# and D# notes? Then you sing the F#, G#, and A# notes.

With a few false starts, they picked up the first notes. "This sounds familiar," James speculated.

"Yes, it sure does," she smiled. "I know, let's put the notes on a scale like we'd see it on a sheet of music."

She found another napkin and they drew the lines for a scale.

As they agreed on the placement of notes they laughed and started again. "Now, let's see what this sounds like!"

They both started again and as they neared the end, they looked at each other, and both yelled, "It's "AMAZING GRACE!""

Chapter 36

Maggie was deep in thought as she studied the newly uncovered secrets before them. "I'll bet, this cross, along with the precious music of the song, "Amazing Grace" is the signal that marks the spot that the runaway slaves had reached the place beneath the Sea Crest Church."

"Yes, I'm positive this part of the wall is marked exactly under the church. I'm sure it represents an important place in their journey within the maze of passageways. I think it also signifies that they are nearing the end of the caverns and tunnels."

Maggie and James were following in the footsteps of runaway slaves, which had stood here over one hundred years ago. They shared the same feeling as they stood, gazing at the hundred-year-old drawings of the notes on the stone wall.

"This is truly the most powerful moment of my life, James. We know what this message truly meant to the lives and freedom of those many runaway slaves, who had stood here before us," Maggie stated with heartfelt humility.

Yes, this is where the ancestors of Maggie O'Hara and James Jensen had stood up for the rights and freedom of those who passed through Sea Crest, on this section of the Underground Railroad.

Maggie and James quietly blended their voices as they sang the hymn through again, checking the order of the notes on the black keys of the piano drawing on the wall.

"Wow," marveled James. "Can you believe the acoustics in this cavern?"

He suddenly laughed out loud as he said, "I'm going to tell you something hilarious about me that not even my family knows."

"That sounds like a great idea. I can hold it over your head if you ever get out of hand."

"Well, when our quartet was learning songs to sing in Scotland, we didn't have access to a practice room." He chuckled again, "I'm afraid to tell you. It sounds so ridiculous now, but we did it anyway."

"Now you've got to tell me," she laughed too, at the thought of James doing something crazy, and actually sharing it with her.

"Okay, but it turned out great. As I said, we didn't have any place to sing, but we discovered that the ideal sound for our voices was actually achieved while we were riding in the subway. We'd find a near-empty car, jump in, and our practice would begin."

"You mean the New York City Subway?"

"Yes! The echo of our voices brought out the harmony we sought," he laughed.

"In fact," he added, "We got pretty good. One time we were at a party, and they wouldn't let us sing. So, we locked ourselves in the bathroom, which echoed, and we sang a couple of our favorites. It sounded so good that they asked us to come out and sing."

James felt elated and happily gazed at the most incredible historical find of his life.

"You know, it's like we've just stepped into a time capsule," whispered James. "I think an appropriate name for this whole section should be the Wall to Freedom."

"It's hard to comprehend how important this genuinely is," agreed Maggie humbly. "Since the time it was used by the Underground Railroad, I don't think anyone has laid eyes on this."

"I know exactly how you feel. I have the strange feeling that there is something else I'm trying to remember about this. It's been so long since I learned about the Underground Railroad. What seems to be bothering me may not even be important, but I hope I can think of it," James said.

"I almost don't want to leave it. I'm worried that if we run across another opening, it might be rigged with the clockwork device. The mechanism will probably slam shut after we pass through," she stated sadly.

James was surprised, but he agreed. He quickly thought of a possible solution and asked, "Maggie, would you be okay with us staying here tonight? I seriously don't believe that we'll be able to navigate our way through the cave and tunnel maze and reach the cliffs over the Sea Crest shoreline before nightfall."

"Oh Yes, James," Maggie said, happily. Her eyes sparkled in her goggles as she clapped her hands together in excitement. It was as if he had just saved the day. "We don't know if we'll ever be able to pass this way again."

"You're right, I know precisely what you mean," replied James thoughtfully. "We may never recapture the treasure that is displayed here on this wall. I would prefer to use our time here in this area since we can't get out safely tonight."

He paused for a moment as he looked at her and then blurted out, "Oh, Maggie." At which time, he stumbled around like an embarrassed schoolboy, trying to make up something that didn't sound utterly dumb and stupid. "Ah, I appreciate your inspiring willingness to make the most of our situation."

He was thinking, *I don't know any women from New York City (or any women I've known in my travels around the world, for that matter), who would share this experience without totally 'freaking out.' They certainly would not enjoy, nor would they appreciate how special this is."*

"Just look at this, James," Maggie interrupted his contemplation. "Someone was keeping count with four straight lines and an additional fifth line diagonally through them to represent five. This might have been a way to record the number of runaway slaves that passed through here," marveled Maggie. "They appear to be randomly marked on these cave walls, in several areas. With the vast amount of marks still visible on this wall, I imagine that this tunnel must have been used for several years."

"Hey, look at this. Doesn't it look like a simple picture of a baby? Doesn't it look like a little one wrapped in a blanket?"

"It sure does, and doesn't that look like a little manger type bed?"

"Yes, I didn't see it before, but I can make it out now. I'll bet that's a story in itself. What if a baby was born here," Maggie said. "Can you even imagine being pregnant and trying to escape from slavery?"

"Boy," said James thoughtfully. "I've never thought of even one baby being born in a network of the Underground Railway. I'm sure it happened many times during those dangerous times. And as wonderful as we think this tunnel is, we can't lose sight of how desperate these poor people were, to have to run for their life like this."

"Well, I, for one, am glad that someone drew this baby picture for us. I'm glad they drew it right here, under the cross, to signify asking for God's blessing."

"I hope they weren't signifying that the baby died here," said James gently.

Maggie gave a small cry, "Oh no. Please don't let it be that the baby died here."

"Yes, let's hope not," replied James sadly.

After a few minutes, he said, "It seems like they simply drew pictures to document their journey. A sign to show and validate that they were here. A piece of iconic history."

"It reminds me of the hieroglyphics that we studied about in school," she answered. "It's been right here my entire life, and nobody alive at Sea Crest today even knew about it. It's amazing."

James couldn't agree more, "Can you believe how lucky we are to be able to find this? It's a real miracle."

A short time later, while eating their long-forgotten snack, a nostalgic and melancholy feeling came over James. He felt the loss of his mother more than he had thought about it in many years. Along with this profound sense of loss was a new respect for the life that his long-ago ancestors had built. They honestly looked out for their fellow man.

He was touched by the knowledge that those who had settled the Sea Crest area seemed to share this way of life. *This was what my grandmother Chambers had witnessed in Sean O'Hara when he had saved both my life and my dad's life, those many years ago. Sean was a hero, through and through, yet he wanted no attention or praise.*

Yes, he thought. *This man is what living along this coastline beside the Sea Crest Lighthouse has produced. The people are often the silent heroes of the modern age. They are like the good*

Samaritans of old. They look out for strangers as well as help their neighbors. It's also who their daughters and sons become.

The shocking truth finally dawned on James, *This is the type of man I want to be. But, my biggest surprise is the feeling deep inside me that this is where I genuinely want to live.*

Wow, what is happening to me? James thought with astonishment.

He straightened up and tried to clear his mind. His distress was lingering, but he sought to make sense of this feeling. He argued with himself, *Okay, I'm missing my mother, more severely than I have in many years. It is playing tricks on my emotions, and it is making me develop new, strange feelings. After all, I have always wanted to live in New York City.*

Maybe I ate something that's affecting me, and this is the result of food poisoning.

Then he fell back into his old habit of blame; *Maybe it's a result of being too close to Maggie. She had a terrible effect on me last time I was here in Sea Crest. She must be to blame.*

But once again, he felt an overwhelming closeness and presence of his mother guiding his heart at that moment. He felt so close to her that it shook him to the core. He marveled to himself, *Okay, the truth. This is where I want to raise my children.*

This realization was utterly appalling to James. He wasn't prepared for these feelings. In fact, up until this journey into the cave yesterday, he certainly had not felt like Sea Crest was anything but a reoccurring nightmare for him. What was going on? He genuinely wondered why he had entertained this strange, traumatizing insight, involving his future children.

Hey, wait a minute, he shuddered at the ramifications of his feelings. *What children?*

James solemnly looked over at Maggie, who had finished eating and was studying the messages on the wall. He wondered, *What on earth am I going to do?*

Chapter 37

Maggie and James have been increasingly happy and excited with their progress through the maze of tunnels and caverns of the Underground Railroad. However, that was not the case for the massive rescue efforts that were underway by the entire Sea Crest Coastal area.

The combined efforts of the Sea Crest Police Force, the FBI, the Coast Guard along with several Public Service Bulletins, had generated no leads at all.

Joe and several people remained at the Chambers' beach house where he'd been most of the afternoon.

He waved Grace over as she drove up to see if there was any news. She had been called to go to the keeper's cottage to pick up some cupcakes that Kate's mom had just finished baking.

Grace parked the car and pulled out 2 big boxes of chocolate mayonnaise cupcakes. "Hi Joe, I'm supposed to put these on the food table with the coffee. Half of these have cream cheese frosting, the other half have peanut butter frosting. These are one of Maggie's favorite treats, just encase she's been discovered.

"Her poor aunt Katherine cried the whole time she was handing these to me. Any news?"

Joe stated emphatically to Grace, "No! How can this be happening? We don't even have one plausible explanation for their mysterious disappearance." His frustration was overwhelming.

All afternoon, agencies worked at full capacity. Kate insisted on stepping in to conduct the Coast Guard Search and Rescue maneuvers along the coastline. Connor and his friends assisted the police in setting up a lookout at the Sea Crest Lighthouse for anything suspicious along the beach and coastline.

Nevertheless, as the sun slipped slowly below the horizon, the incredibly beautiful sunset contrasted the sinking hope of finding Maggie and James alive. The view from the Sea Crest Lighthouse was indeed bleak, as the rescue efforts continued into the night.

Chapter 38

It seemed as though Maggie and James had not given it a second thought about what their friends and families might be going through.

They had agreed to spend the second night in the caves and couldn't have been more pleased with the prospect. They had found several old candles and were delighted to see that the wicks were still in good working condition. They decided to light quite a few and use the old wine bottles for bases.

They loved the special candlelight effect, which looked truly incredible.

James started to hum one of the Scottish songs that he'd sung with his group in college. Ironically, it was about someone named Maggie. He liked to hear the notes with the beautiful acoustics in the cavern, so he happily hummed the melody as they arranged their quilts. They used their backpacks as headrests on the floor of the cave again.

Maggie commented on James' humming, "That's a familiar Irish melody. It sounds great in here, doesn't it?"

"Yes, the Scottish melody is excellent, but it's the words that are deeply disturbing," he laughed. "We used to sing it with my college quartet, but we should have steered clear of any song that even remotely mentions someone named Maggie."

"What do you mean by that remark?" demanded Maggie.

"Well, in our defense, none of us even knew a Maggie. So, when we innocently sang about our fond memories of someone named Maggie, we were not acquainted with anyone by that name. Certainly, not someone like you," laughed James.

"I'll give you one minute to take that back!" demanded Maggie.

"Not on your life," he continued. "Yes, I'm talking about needing a warning about any Maggie, who might show up later in our life. Specifically, someone with the most outlandish, wild hair and green eyes we could ever imagine. She might even throw us into jail, no less. I mean, really! We had no idea of the potential nightmare that we'd be subjected to and the chaos that we'd get mixed up in."

Maggie replied, "Well if you're going to make fun of my song, I'll start singing a couple that would be appropriate for the likes of you."

"Okay, Smarty," James laughed. "Truce! Truce! I call a truce. Can you calm down a minute? As a mutual peace offering, why don't we both sing in this cavern's super sound system?"

"Okay," Maggie reluctantly agreed. "For the sake of an outstanding opportunity that may never come again, I'll agree."

"Thanks. I just remembered that our group sang at a couple of weddings. They requested favorite music as well as Scottish songs. We did some show tunes, and of course, they wanted some classic love songs to dance to."

"I'll have Kate and Michael keep you in mind for a backup if the tenors she has lined up for their Wedding Celebration don't show up," Maggie replied sarcastically.

"Hey, don't be so fast to laugh, we were pretty good," James smiled. "Ya know, I truly think the acoustics in here are too good to waste. I'll bet, "Hallelujah," with the harmonizing sections, would sound terrific. Do you know it?"

"I think I know part of it. You start."

And so, their enchanted sing-off began.

When they finished, Maggie was near tears as she pronounced, "Wow, that was the best."

James soberly cleared his throat and said, "Thanks." He was thinking, *That song was way too emotional.*

"What other songs do you know?" asked Maggie.

"We did Frank Sinatra's, "The Way You Look Tonight."

"You start it, and I'll follow along," she answered.

Once again, they complemented each other as they harmonized their way through it. It sounded terrific.

James started to sing "Here or When," and it was so poignant and wistful that she did not join in, but she just listened in quiet appreciation.

The relaxed feeling that had come over James must have brought up something that he had buried deep in his mind. He sat up abruptly as he remembered and blurted out, "I've got it. I know why that song is etched on the wall."

"What? You mean, "Amazing Grace?"

"Yes, I think I know. When our quartet was singing in Scotland, we were always making sure we were allowed to sing certain favorites, due to copyright issues."

"Wow. Do you think it's got a copywriter on it nowadays," asked Maggie?

"No, it's public domain, but we checked on it, back in college. In Scotland, it's a very popular song, and it sounds the best when it's played with Scottish bagpipes."

"Yes, you're right, of course."

"Our quartet had the remarkable opportunity to attend the Scottish Tattoo in Edinburgh that summer. We were actually invited to go to the rehearsal. It is a day-long event which photographers and musicians, such as we were, could go and take advantage of various behind the scenes things."

"The formal name is The Royal Edinburgh Military Tattoo. We got to see all the famous Scottish marching bands play and compete. It was wonderful."

"Was the music as great as I've heard," Maggie asked? "I know the Tattoo is supposed to be an outstanding event. I know several people who've got it on their Bucket List."

"Yes, it's wonderful. The marching is also unbelievable to watch. They hold it rain or shine, and they have fireworks every night."

"It seems that every song is outstanding."

"What were your favorites?"

"Well," James said. "Of course, they include: "God Save the Queen," "Auld Lang Syne," "Hallelujah," "Scotland, the Brave," "The Water is Wide," "Amazing Grace," and "The Bonnie Banks of o'Loch Lomond."

"Here is what I just remembered. "Amazing Grace" is often played, everywhere in Scotland. It's usually played with the bagpipes, and it's incredibly emotional."

"I know what you mean, but please go on," Maggie happily agreed.

"Well, we were told the story of "Amazing Grace" while we were attending the Tattoo. One of the photographers was explaining what he thought was the real-life story of John Newton. His mother was a devout Christian woman who was ill. She tried to teach her son everything about the Bible at a young age. When John was about seven, his mother died.

"John became a cabin boy on a sailing ship, which was a hard and cruel life. He was beaten, abused, and flogged. He grew up and led a tough life on a slave ship and later became a captain. He didn't value his mother's teachings anymore. Even his ships' crew members hated him. When he fell overboard, they speared him in the hip with a harpoon and hauled him up. This wound caused him to limp the rest of his life.

"As the story goes, he eventually turned his life around. He wrote "Amazing Grace" in the late 1770s. Some historians claim the music resembled the sound of the chanting of the slaves on the ships. Of course, that would follow, because that's where he'd spent many years of his life. It's also thought that the slaves and black spiritual music used only the black music notes to play their songs down through time. Since most slaves were not allowed to learn to read or write, they had other ways of making marks or signs which had meaning only to them."

"That reminds me of the marks on the wall," Maggie whispered softly.

"Yes. Those could represent the black piano notes," replied James.

Neither one of them realized when they had taken each other's hands. James thought he'd better change the mood to something better before they drifted off to sleep. He didn't want to have nightmares all night.

He suggested, "I think I'll get something to drink before we nod off. Would you like anything?"

"Yes, that sounds good," Maggie agreed. "This journey is surprising in so many ways, isn't it?"

He handed her a drink and took a swallow or two himself, as he reflected on how pleasant it was just to have Maggie for company. He softly hummed, "You take the high road, and I'll take the low road, and I'll get to Scotland afore ye."

"What does that all mean," asked Maggie gently? "Why are they taking separate roads?"

"We'll have to look that up when we get back. Maybe they were arch-enemies and didn't want to share the simple company of a good friend."

"Maybe…, but it's a shame. I'm glad we're friends, James. I'm glad we got to share this."

A moment later, he followed up with a tender nostalgic, "I'll Be Seeing You". The beautiful song brought her to tears.

Maggie could not believe what she had just witnessed, as she confessed, "James, this is one of the best times of my life. Your voice is extraordinary. Thank you."

Maggie was thinking, *What an unexpected treasure to hear James sing these songs. I will never forget it.*

They each had their different thoughts as they settled down for their next and, hopefully, last night in the cavern. They had shared an experience that they would never forget. Their journey in the Underground Railroad, following in the footsteps of the runaway slaves, had peeled back the hidden layers of both James and Maggie. To reveal an inner depth that few had ever witnessed. They had formed an unlikely, however fierce bond, that they didn't even know existed.

Before James started the next song, he flippantly explained, "I just need you to know, Maggie, that I'm dedicating this next song to you." He couldn't hold in the sarcasm as he continued, "I confess that, as hard as it is to believe, I've somehow gotten used to your face."

"What?" Maggie chuckled with mocking disdain. "Now, let me tell you something. I'll never get used to yours. It will always haunt me as I go through life."

"Now wait a minute, I'm not through yet," he laughed.

"Oh, yes, you are."

"No, really," he coughed and almost choked with delight as he carried on the charade. "This is going to be nice. I promise."

"Okay, it better be!" Maggie hadn't laughed this hard in quite a while and certainly not with her arch-enemy.

"Remember that I used to be horrified by your hair flying every which way and totally out of control?"

"James, this better be good, or you're going to pay dearly."

James tried to compose a straight face as he impatiently said, "Now wait. Just WAIT for it!"

He earnestly looked over at her and kindly took her hand to show his sincere intentions, but when he started to speak, he totally lost it again.

They both collapsed onto their quilts, with total abandon and unrestrained hilarity.

James' poor stomach was aching from such hard laughter. "I can't remember laughing this hard for years. See what you do to me?"

"Don't blame me," begged Maggie, as she hugged her painful stomach.

"Well, I'm just trying to think of something nice to say,... so that I could dedicate this song ... to you," he tried to catch his breath between peals of laughter.

Maggie was delighted to see that James had utterly lost it again.

He finally regained a little self-control as he started again, "Maggie, I'd like to dedicate... the song, "I've Grown .... I've Grown." He held his stomach as he rocked back and forth and suddenly stopped. He had rolled very close to her, and they were now face-to-face. Then, with tears in his eyes, he finally eeked out the high-pitched squeaky, "I've Grown Accustomed to Her Face."

This dramatic situation would have been unheard of just a few short days ago. But at this moment in time, it felt so... good! If they had even thought about it, they would have known that, this new, unlikely bond that they shared was based on some kind of trust, safety, and mutual respect.

Maggie collapsed into the quilts as she joyously thanked James for the song. After a few minutes, the mayhem subsided, and their exhaustion kicked in.

James was surprised at the energy that he had expanded in this high-stakes debate.

He stopped laughing as he watched the soft candlelight shimmer through her auburn red hair from the flames flickering beside them. The various shades of color glistened in a vibrant, extravagant display, framing her face and flowing wildly across her shoulders and back. James was captivated by the sheer abundance of it.

He reached out and touched one of the soft curls that were dancing around her face. He whispered, "Maggie, it's unbelievable what you look like after two days of trekking and sleeping underground."

She looked up at him and wondered what that meant. So, she smiled and decided to play it safe as she gently whispered back, "Well, I can't believe this is what you look like after two days of trekking and sleeping underground yourself."

James was sleepily replaying their lively, quick-witted sparring and realized that he had met his match. He smiled as he drifted into a deep, semi-sleepy assessment of their relationship.

Yes, he was still holding Maggie's hand possessively as he turned to look at her.

She silently reached out and moved a wisp of his hair away from his eye. They both felt an immediate rush. This small touch felt incredibly intimate and personal.

James gasped at the powerful electricity shared between them.

"Is that all right?" whispered Maggie.

"Oh, Maggie," James groaned as he tenderly touched her face.

The last thought on his mind as he looked deep into her huge emerald green eyes was, *I'm a goner, and I can't help myself.*

James never took his eyes off hers, as he reached for her and slowly drew her to him, whispering, "Maggie, I'm way over my head here."

Her return gaze reflected open acceptance as she gently nodded agreement. He slowly touched her face tenderly and kissed Maggie with all the passion and pent-up emotions that had been building since the day they'd met.

James immediately woke up with a start. He was sweating profusely, and his heart was pounding hard and fast. He abruptly sat up and shook his head to clear it as he remembered, *That dream had seemed so real. How can I possibly feel so much for her, if it's all one-sided? She must feel something.*

James put his head in his hands and looked over at her.

Maggie was calmly sleeping on her side with her face towards him. She had a quilt wrapped around her, and she looked like an angel.

James finally faced the possibility that he was falling in love with Maggie. As he lay back down beside her, he wondered, *How on earth did this happen?*

Chapter 39

James eventually fell into a deep sleep, which happily didn't involve a nightmare about diving a shipwreck and being trapped under the water with a cut air hose. He did, however, dream about that same day. The focus was now what happened after Maggie's dad had rescued him and his dad.

James and his grandfather Chambers, his dad, and his brother, Michael, along with Sean O'Hara, were returning to the Sea Crest shore. They were all in the Chambers' boat, while they towed Sean's boat behind.

In this dream sequence, the men and the two boys were all exiting the boat. They walked up the sand to the Sea Crest Lighthouse.

As they came up the beach, Sean smiled and waved at a couple of young girls, playing in the sand. When they saw him, they waved at him and squealed with delight as they ran to meet him. The little redhead with long, loosely-braided pigtails came running up with her arms open wide and literally jumped into Sean's arms. The other small girl with blond pigtails jumped around, laughing and pulling at Uncle Sean.

He smiled and hugged her also, as he put the redhead down to continue to play.

This dream was so real that James woke up with a start. *Why did I dream of this? I feel this was a second part of the nightmare, but I had never gotten to it before. However, I somehow know there was an element of truth in the event.*

The implications finally struck him. *Could this little redhead with the pigtails be My Maggie? Did this actually happen in real life?*

He turned his head and gazed at her peaceful sleeping face. James felt a chill as he wondered if he had unearthed an authentic memory after singing, "I'll Be Seeing You," to Maggie tonight. He remembered dreaming about Maggie the night before, as she told him to get over his nightmare.

James reached out to touch a strand of her hair, as he marveled, *Have I been seeing your face, in all the old familiar places?*

It was a long time before James fell back asleep this time. After he did, they both continued to sleep peacefully, wrapped in the blessings of the Underground Railroad quilts.

Chapter 40

The next morning Maggie awoke with a feeling of true happiness. This was immediately replaced with the realization that her journey with James through the Underground Railroad was ending in a few short hours.

She seemed oddly disappointed for someone who had been trying to work her way out of this tunnel for days. She reflected on various ways to justify her confused feelings; W*ell, just because last night's feeling of closeness had been exhilarating and epic to me, that's probably not true for James. As soon as we leave this environment, we might both revert to our previous mindset, and the magic might disappear into thin air*. This only made her feel worse.

As it turned out, James was already awake. He had a head start on worrying about last night; *I wonder if my dream included a real event of what I saw when we came ashore, many years ago. I wonder if that little girl was truly My Maggie as a child. That would have to mean that I've seen her face before, and I saw her as she displayed true happiness and love. The way she jumped into her father's arms with pure abandoned joy.*

Is that who she is when you peel away all the no-nonsense layers of tough FBI training? Is this the person that my grandmother Chambers was writing about in her letter? She met her as a child when she and Kate were selling Girl Scout cookies. Oh, good grief! Was Kate the other little girl with blond pigtails?

Are these two girls, now grown into beautiful women, involved in all the secret projects for taking care of others in the Sea Crest area?

Yes, James had done a whole lot of thinking after his dream.

Chapter 41

Maggie looked around, and when she saw James, she said, "Good morning," with a smile.

He answered with a smile of his own as he said, "Good morning, yourself, sleepyhead."

Maggie laughed and asked, "Do you think we are as close as I do? I think, according to the church location, we should reach the area where the passageway would see daylight soon. I'm puzzled as to the location where this tunnel, or cave, meets the ocean or cliffs after we leave this area."

James agreed, "Yes, that's what I think. I just don't know if we'll have another trap door to figure out. I don't believe anyone has entered this area in well over one hundred years."

"Not that any of the runaway slaves would want to come back, but if it's visible from the outside, it seems unlikely that no one found it."

They were each afraid that as they got out of the Underground Railroad path to freedom, this newfound bond of caring and closeness to each other might dissolve. It seemed ridiculous to try to delay the end of their journey.

James had struggled with the realization that *I have about as good a chance of winning Maggie's heart as catching lightning in a bottle.*

"Well," he said, "I think we should have something to eat before we leave this memorable cavern. It's been one of the most exciting discoveries of my lifetime."

"I agree," said Maggie, as she opened up their few remaining food rations. "We're just about finished with the wine and cheese tray. We still have some grapes, believe it or not."

"I'll check the status of the bottles of wine that we carried from the wine cellar," offered James. "Let's see; I've got three bottles in my backpack. We only opened and re-corked one."

"Great, I've got three also," she answered. "Isn't it comical, we're drinking some of the finest wines in the world, each one over one hundred years old, but we haven't had a hot bath or a change of clothes almost three days."

"Yeah, don't forget, we're eating left-overs," James laughed. "We're high class."

James took a long hard look at Maggie as he added, "But, isn't it amazing how happy we are?"

"Yes, that's true," smiled Maggie.

They ate their picnic breakfast, reflecting on how fortunate they felt to have this incredible historical adventure together.

Maggie said, "When we leave, I think if we navigate to the far side of this stone wall, we'll be going in the right direction."

"Yes, I'm sure that would eventually lead to the outside. I'd love to get into the daylight in the next couple of hours. Do you think that's possible," asked James?

"Judging by where we are, with the church directly above us, we should make it in the next hour or so. We'll have to see if we have another secret entryway to figure out."

They soon gathered up their belongings and lovingly inspected the drawings on the Wall of Freedom, one last time before they headed on down the passageway.

Silently, James took Maggie's hand as they started to leave. He was in the lead for this part of the trek, and he sadly repeated what they were both thinking, "we may never pass this way again."

"That's right," Maggie agreed with a lump in her throat. "It makes me feel so sad to be approaching the end of our epic adventure. In fact, I know it will sound crazy but, I doubt we'll ever have another experience this grand, in our entire lifetime."

"Exactly," James replied. "It's not that I don't look forward to a hot shower and a comfortable bed. However, facing the end of this journey looms almost like a feeling of loss. Are you familiar with the term melancholy?"

"Yes, I think it means, gloomy or down in the dumps about something?"

"Well, Maggie, that's how I feel. I know I should be totally happy about getting back to civilization, but a big part of me doesn't want to lose what we've discovered here. The proof of the quality of the brave souls who built and founded Sea Crest and the secret pathway to freedom. They built and supported this segment of the underground railroad for the brave souls who were running for their lives."

"James, that's exactly what I'm feeling," Maggie said. "I couldn't put it better. Thank you for finding the perfect words."

They continued on, following the various clues and marked directions.

They were not surprised when they approached another barrier. Maggie showed the lights from her headband, while James studied the stone floor for any marks or signs to direct them.

Sure enough, James spotted an arrow. "Look, partway up the wall. It looks like a large crack, which runs floor to ceiling. They have scratched an arrow into the edge of those two slabs."

Maggie asked, "Do you think we can pry it open? I've got a knife we can use as a wedge to move it."

They struggled with it for a few minutes, pulling and pushing on various parts, before they felt it move. A loud creaking noise sounded as the large boulders, securely held in place for over one hundred years, slowly moved out of the way.

When it had completely stopped moving, Maggie and James hurried by and pulled all their things through to the other side. Sure enough, the opening quickly slammed closed again with a loud clanging noise.

They were safely on the other side. Maggie was the first to sadly mention that, "They probably couldn't go back to the Wall of Freedom, from this side."

James said, "We'll mark it as best as we can and bring Michael back to see if he can work the clockwork mechanism to open from this side,"

He had just leaned over to carve a clear mark in the stone when he felt Maggie nuzzle his neck. It felt like an intimate kiss, and he turned his head to reach for her. That's when he saw it!

A colossal snake was hanging from the overhanging slabs of stone above them. It had briefly nuzzled James' neck before slithering down the collar of his shirt. It was slowly headed down his back when James whispered, "Maggie, help me!"

She was astonished when her light moved across him. It revealed his stunned face, as well as the source of his trouble.

They each saw that not only was this enormous snake dangling from the jagged edge above, but it seemed that a whole nest of snakes had been unearthed and disturbed by the movement of the trap door. Most of them were now suspended in midair around them as they slowly moved downward toward the floor.

Maggie let out a terrifying scream as she reached for James. This noisy episode caught the attention of the snake that hung closest to her. It promptly nosed around in front of her looking for a sanctuary in which to take refuge. It finally saw something that resembled a nest, as it slid into her chaotic, red hair. It dropped down the front of her face and seemed to twist as it fell even with her eyes. It slowly turned its coiled head in front of her.

James recognized that the snakes were not poisonous and murmured, "Maggie, these are just harmless rat snakes. They will not hurt us. They're more afraid of us that we are of them."

Maggie's bright green eyes were flashing with sheer terror as she pleaded, "James! Help Me!"

James had never seen her scared before, and he quickly tried to reassure her, "Maggie, it's okay. They only eat bats. Just hold still. There, I've got it now."

He gently took the head of the five-foot snake and lifted it carefully away from her face. Next, he continued to calmly extricate the rest of the offending snake from Maggie's wild disheveled hair.

"There! It's all gone," he assured her. "Now I've got to get this one out of my shirt. It's stopped moving. It must have realized I'm not a bat."

He quickly removed it and let it go. Next, he turned and took Maggie's arm and led her quickly down the trail.

"They're all gone now. I'm surprised those snakes were in this cave. It's not unheard of; however, they are usually tree dwellers and rarely frequent caves."

Maggie was speechless and had now started to tremble. James stopped and turned her toward him. "Maggie, look at me."

She silently looked up at him as he said, "It's okay. They're all gone. They're way back there." As a tear rolled down her cheek, he said, "Come here." He wrapped his arms around her and said soothingly, "Calm down. It's over now. You're just fine, Maggie." Then he stopped talking, and he just held her.

Slowly she stopped shaking and started to breathe normally again. Maggie felt so safe as she thought, *it is hard to believe how much my feelings have changed over a few weeks.*

James asked, "You okay?" When she didn't answer, he thought, *It's nice to just hold her like this, but how long can I get away with this? I've got it! Maybe, I'll take this opportunity to educate her on these snakes.*

"Well, Maggie, these rat snakes are just curious. We've got to be the first humans they've ever come in contact with. Now I don't know how old they must be, but I'm sure they've lived totally undisturbed except for an occasional bat or rodent to eat."

Well, Maggie couldn't think of one appropriate response to this vital information.

James thought this was probably a good sign, so he continued, "As a matter of fact, I'll bet your hair, which sticks out all over the place, looked like the most ideal mess of nesting material they'd ever dreamed of. That snake that dropped down and slithered into your hair was just looking for a convenient place to nest."

He happily announced his last fun-fact about the rat snakes with his thoughtful observation, "When they saw us, it had to be surprising. From out of nowhere, they heard the loud screaking, and suddenly alien creatures appeared! Sort of like, - well, imagine what it would be like if we, all of a sudden, saw Martians!"

Maggie couldn't take it any longer as she laughed, "Okay, okay, James. I feel all better!"

James smiled as he released her. As they straightened out their clothes and bent to gather up all their belongings, he explained, "I guess I wanted to point out the other side of their coins."

He took the lead, reached back for Maggie's hand, and stepped forward on the path. They were both silent for the next hour, until James stopped and pointed down the trail.

"Look," Maggie sighed happily. "I see a small shaft of sunlight up ahead."

"Yes," he joined in, "and smell that salt air?"

They let the reality sink in. "Listen, I think I just heard a seagull," she smiled.

Chapter 42

They carefully made their way along the trail until they arrived at the cave opening. It was situated high on a bluff, ideal for use as a look-out and hidden cave.

The cliffs above the rocky coastline near the Chambers' sprawling Victorian beach house concealed the cave opening. The rock shelters and bluff tops hold many nooks and crannies, which are not visible from the shore. Shades of lavender and purple heather cling to the cliffs.

Hidden among these breathtaking walls of rock is one delicate patch of white heather, which is growing along the vertical folds of the rocks to cover a small opening in the cliff. White heather is closely associated with battles and conflict and is said to bring good luck to whoever wears it.

But it's not only brides who believe that white Scottish heather is a symbol of good luck. The symbolism of planting the white heather, as a right-of-passage to freedom, is especially meaningful. It brings good fortune to all who find it, which was a goodwill blessing for those slaves passing through the security of the safe house to sail to freedom. They were on a journey to a new life with a Scottish blessing and the skilled works of the Scottish captain and the Irish architect who made their dream a reality.

James and Maggie stepped out of the cave, high on the cliff above the ocean. Maggie marveled, "Look, you can see the Sea Crest Lighthouse."

"Wow, how convenient! That looks about a quarter of a mile away? What do you think?" James asked.

"Yes," Maggie was excited, to say the least. "See that window high up, near the top?"

"I sure do."

"Well, it is completely hidden from view from the land. They could signal back and forth for the ships to pick up the runaway slaves for passage to freedom," stated Maggie.

As James stepped back from the cliff's edge, into the shelter of the cave, he observed, "Look at all these things inside the mouth of the cave, Maggie. Here is a rope ladder like the one we saw in the cave."

"They even have the Sea Crest Ship's anchor to secure the rope ladder at the top so they can lower it to the rocky shore below," marveled Maggie.

"They would go down the rope ladder with tin steps and meet them at the bottom or get them in a boat. It's all made out of the schooner's rigging."

Next, they spotted an old wooden sea chest against the wall. "Boy, if this chest could talk. All jokes aside, this is truly something," said Maggie as she ran her hands over the rough surface with great admiration.

They also discovered the Scottish flag that had flown over Captain Michael Chambers' Sea Crest schooner. "Wow, the Flag of Scotland, which is also known as the Saint Andrew's Cross," James said. He carefully ran his hand over the white saltire material that crossed the middle of the flag.

Maggie stepped over, felt the sky-blue triangles of the flag, and whispered, “Captain Michael Chambers actually touched this.”

“Look, they could signal passing ships,” said James. “I’m still amazed by the fact that so many runaway slaves escaped to freedom by ship.”

There was a large basket like the ones made in the Caribbean setting on the floor of the cave. It was full of several lanterns and some candles.

As Maggie was evaluating the location of the cave and the surrounding high sandstone bluff, she had a great idea, “I think this is an ideal look-out. It would be a great hiding place to install my FBI surveillance apparatus.”

James’ mouth opened in surprise as he remembered he was responsible for Maggie’s build-out project at the beach house.

He stepped over to join her at the edge of the opening. They gazed out together at the beautiful Sea Crest water, as he agreed, “Yes, I think you’ve found a perfect spot.”

As they surveyed the coastline, they saw a Coast Guard Helicopter coming up the coast in the distance. “Oh, look!” cried Maggie.

“I wonder if that’s Kate?”

Maggie grabbed her mobile phone while she laughingly told James, “I guess it’s time we give someone a call and let them know we’re up on the cliff overlooking the ocean. Do you think anyone would be looking for us, James?”

“I never gave it a thought, but I doubt it,” James said as he shrugged his shoulders.

“Hey, my cell phone has lost its charge. It’s dead,” she said.

“Well, with this tide rising, maybe we better signal that helicopter and see if they can get us down from here. If not, we’ll get to spend another night here,” laughed James.

"As much as I'd love to spend another night here with you, I wonder how the Wedding Celebration is coming," asked Maggie thoughtfully.

"Wow," James was surprised, to say the least. "It has barely crossed my mind."

"Here, help me get the large cloth napkins out of my backpack," Maggie yelled. They both headed to the opening of the cave and started waving and yelling at the approaching helicopter.

Kate was in charge of the Search and Rescue Mission, and she was piloting the helicopter.

The flight crew saw James and Maggie laughing and waving the napkins around like they were having the time of their lives. They assumed they were delirious or suffering from some other kind of mental breakdown.

Kate was thinking, *this could be brought on by whatever stress, pain, or suffering they had endured over the last couple of days. Who knows what horrors they may have experienced? Possible starvation or well, it could be anything.*

"We need to get down to pick them up immediately," Kate commanded.

"Well, we still have the heli-basket on board," said one of the coast guard team.

"Yes, they're quite familiar with that," She replied, as she maneuvered the helicopter around again for a closer look.

Kate called the keeper's cottage, bursting with joy, and yelling loudly over the sound of the whirling blades, "Hey! Mom, we just located Maggie and James, on the high cliffs above the Sea Crust water! They're both waving and hanging on to an open crevice in that huge rocky ledge!

"We're going in for a rescue right now! Call Aunt Mary and Uncle Sean. We'll land on the helicopter landing pad on the beach! Bye."

Everyone back at the Chambers' beach house was currently vaguely hearing the SARS helicopter in the distance and wondering what that meant. When Sean received the call from his sister, he thanked The Good Lord and told her to repeat the news for everyone as he held his mobile phone up.

Katherine's shouts of joy could be heard by everyone nearby as she rejoiced, "They've seen Maggie and James, hanging on to the cliffs! They think they're okay!"

Kate flew the helicopter closer and the crew members communicated by a loudspeaker with James and Maggie. "We'll swing lower and pick you up."

The SARS unit lowered the heli-basket into place alongside the cave opening. Maggie was busy packing up the large Caribbean basket that was full and over-flowing with the white heather that was growing wild. The Scottish Legend promised it would bring good luck to all who find it.

The rescue worker held the basket steady while they loaded in the backpacks with champagne for the Wedding Celebration toast along with the beautiful basket of white heather.

"Don't forget these quilts," Maggie instructed as she handed James several precious quilts from the Underground Railroad.

Finally, James gave Maggie his hand as she stepped into the heli-basket. "Boy, I don't want to lose you now," he chuckled. Without letting go of her hand, James stepped in and sat down close to her.

Maggie just smiled at him and silently thanked God that *I don't have to throw any of his shoes over the side.*

James had seen her smile as she glanced down at his feet. He laughed as he put his arm around her shoulders and bent close to her ear. She felt his lips on her ear as he tried to be heard over the spinning propellers, and said very firmly, "Maggie, My Dear... Don't even think about it."

Maggie turned her head and laughingly reached up to touch his cheek and draw his head closer. Her lips lightly brushed his ear as she answered innocently, "James, My Dear... Is that supposed to be some kind of a threat?"

Poor James was instantly on fire as he thought, *Wow, no more kidding around with her. I can't take any more of this.* He was almost at his breaking point, and he desperately needed to take her in his arms and kiss her. However, the realization that they had landed on the ground stopped him.

James was smiling as he looked directly into her beautiful, emerald green eyes and took one last shot at her as he warned, "Just a friendly warning. Didn't anyone ever tell you not to play with fire? You might get burned."

"I might..., or might not, even care." was her carefree answer.

They continued laughing and kidding around as they got their things out of the Heli-basket. They were also thinking of how good it felt to play and carry on with each other.

As far as the Search and Rescue team observed: they thought James and Maggie were by far the happiest two people that they had ever saved.

Chapter 43

After Kate landed the Coast Guard Helicopter on the landing pad next to the Sea Crest Lighthouse, she finished her post-flight report and gave the information to her co-pilot. He would fly the SARS Helicopter and the remaining SARS team back to the Coast Guard Base.

Maggie and James were standing on the ground, waiting for her and looking like they had just won the lottery. Next to them was a pile of all their stuff. This collection included their backpacks, the champagne to toast the bride and groom, the night vision goggles, headbands, picnic supplies, a huge basket of beautiful White Heather, and a pile of quilts.

They were beaming as she approached them. Maggie rushed up to Kate and hugged her out of sheer delight. "Kate, I have so much to tell you. We had a wonderful time, and you won't believe what we discovered."

Kate almost told her she could already guess what they'd discovered after seeing how they looked at each other. But she didn't.

Kate interrupted her, "Okay, but first, I want you to know how happy we are that you're both safe. I called ahead that we were picking you up, and all the family and friends from the Chambers' beach house are on their way down to see you."

Maggie and James looked genuinely concerned at once. "Oh No. What happened?" asked Maggie.

Kate just stared at them as she said, "Well, for starters, we thought something awful had happened to you! You both just vanished! The Bentley was left unlocked as well as the front door of the beach house. Your stuff was all gone. We couldn't find you anywhere or reach you on your phones."

Maggie was shocked. "I'm so sorry. I didn't think anyone even knew I was gone."

"Well, Maggie, your mom and dad feared the worst, and James let me include you in this. Your father and your brother were also worried sick that they'd never see you again."

"Wait, What? We didn't know anyone was worried!"

The cars had started arriving with the family running to Maggie and James with arms open wide and tears of joy in their eyes. Grace came in Joe's car with another friend, who turned out to be Jeff from New York. A man who looked enough like Michael and James, that just had to be their father, came in a car with Maggie's dad and mom.

Next came the whole Sea Crest Police Force. "We have a few questions for you, starting with where you've been!" demanded the Police Chief.

Then Connor came out of the keeper's cottage with Misha, who went wild when she saw Maggie. The happy dog broke loose from Connor and ran towards Maggie. Her tail was wagging a mile a minute with excitement as she barked and jumped and licked Maggie with boundless love and affection. Maggie tearfully hugged and kissed her right back.

Connor laughed out loud at the sight of this warm, heartfelt reunion. "Boy, Maggie didn't greet any of us like that!"

Maggie laughed back as she reminded him, "Well, none of you greeted me like Misha did!"

James held his hand up and said, "Okay, let's clear this thing up. First, we'd like to apologize for all the worry and trouble we've put you through. We'd also like to thank every one of you who tried to help find us and care for our loved ones. Thank you all."

"Yes," agreed Maggie. "We are so grateful to all of you."

"Now," she continued, "we'll try to explain where we've been and how we got back here. As most of you know, we went up to the beach house to get champagne for the Wedding Celebration. We took along some hors-d'oeuvres, cheese, and wine;- you know stuff like that for our wine tasting."

James added, "Well, we couldn't find any of the wine that we had heard was supposed to be at the beach house. We couldn't even find a wine cellar. However, when I leaned my arm on the fireplace mantel in one of the rooms to try to figure out where else to look, we heard a loud scraping sound next to the fireplace. Next thing we knew, 'voila,' a secret door slowly opened in the wall."

Maggie added, "that was the beginning of a history lesson that just ended about an hour ago. We got locked behind that wall when the clockwork mechanism, which was common in old lighthouses, clanged shut behind us."

James continued, "that's when we lost all cell phone reception and all contact with the outside world."

Maggie just beamed as she said, "this was the start of one of the greatest adventures of my life. We had our headband lights, and our night-vision goggles that Kate and I had gotten together for a joke. They probably made the difference between life and death for us, though. We also brought enough to eat, so we rationed it over the next couple of days. We had a fascinating puzzle to solve. Where were we, and how could we get out?"

James smiled as he added, "We could see well enough to walk around and realize that we were in an old tunnel. At one point, I fell about five feet down, through the tunnel floor, and landed on a huge pile of quilts."

"Next thing I know, Maggie actually jumped through the hole and said she didn't want to miss all the fun," laughed James, as he shook his head and shrugged his shoulders.

"I was so shocked when I heard her jump!" he stated. "I looked up, and she was airborne! She almost landed right on top of me!" Both Maggie and James were cracking up as though this was exceptionally funny.

James looked at the little group that had gathered and helplessly implored them, with laughing tears in his eyes, "Can you believe all the stuff she does?"

What their family and friends were noticing, however, was how exceptionally odd and out of character, both of them were acting right this minute.

Sean and Mary O'Hara were wondering if they'd seen Maggie behave this way, ...ever. *Like she didn't have a care in the world.*

Ben Jensen was wondering just how much of that champagne his son had consumed. He thought, *James has never acted this relaxed and lighthearted in the company of a woman. I thought Maggie was the FBI Special Agent that had previously thrown him in jail.*

Maggie continued to carry on, as she exclaimed, "Oh, look what we found." She danced over to the pile of old quilts with joy.

Grace and Joe Lawrence had been standing near the pile of quilts. Grace saw the design stitched into the squares of the top one was a simple boat with two sails. She was also able to view part of the design on another quilt near the bottom.

Grace felt goosebumps as she whispered to Joe, "I think I recognize what these quilts are."

"What do you think they are?" Joe asked

That's when Maggie sailed over and gestured to the pile of quilts like it was one of the rarest and most valuable discoveries of all time. She shuffled through them until she found the special one, for which she'd been searching. She opened up the quilt and asked, "Does anyone know what this means?"

She held up the chosen quilt with the square that matched the etched emblem that they'd seen on the floor of the beach house.

Grace was standing right beside her as nodded, "Yes, Maggie, I believe I do."

She first hugged Maggie with tears in her eyes and said, "Oh, Maggie. I'm so glad you're safe."

Then Grace turned to take a closer look at the quilt. She carefully felt the stitching that had lasted well over one hundred years. She marveled in awe as her hands touched the priceless heirloom. The design of the bits and pieces of cloth formed a unique pattern that was unmistakable to Grace.

She sensed the burdens of the historical past and the hope for freedom that this quilt represented. She was so overcome with the significance of these historical treasures, laying on the ground before them, that she only nodded her head, yes, to Maggie.

James overheard the exchange and immediately stepped over to join them.

Maggie asked, "Grace, you know what this means?"

Grace answered, "Yes, It's the Shoo Fly emblem, and it represents "Welcome" or "Safe."

"That's brilliant, Grace. Do you know who used it, and why?"

Grace held on tight to the cherished quilt, as she said proudly, "It's the historic emblem used by the Underground Railroad to symbolize a safe place. A welcome place for runaway slaves on their way to freedom."

James was shocked as he explained to Grace, "Maggie and I saw numerous emblems like this up at the beach house. I have never noticed them before, but they are etched in the marble floor tiles, on the doors, and the symbols seem to be everywhere. I had no idea what they meant anything important."

"Well, it often meant the difference between life and death," Grace said. "None of us in Sea Crest ever imagined that this area was an important part of the Underground Railroad. However, the night that you disappeared, I was trying to contact you all evening with news that I found a letter while looking through the storage unit things."

"According to this letter, Captain Michael Chambers was to use his schooner, The Sea Crest, to take runaway slaves south to various Caribbean Islands. Harriet Tubman was trying to reunite families that had been torn apart due to the slave trade. Since Captain Chambers knew the Caribbean well, he could navigate and trade goods within the islands. He had a perfect cover, for helping the runaway slaves."

"I can hardly believe all that's happened in the last few days," said Maggie.

The discussion of all the new historical pieces of Sea Crest went on for some time when James thought of another question that Grace might be able to answer. "We found some other intriguing items that we hope you can explain."

"Wait," laughed Maggie. "James and I have a difference of opinion on why certain pottery would be in the tunnel. Let's ask Grace about that cup that looks like a sideways butterfly painted on it. It looks like this," stated Maggie as she took a pen and drew it on her hand.

Grace looked at the crude outline and said, "I'll bet you'll be surprised when I tell you because it's not as well known, as you'd think."

James piped up with, "I think it's a Cherokee Indian symbol, but I'm not sure how or why it relates to the Underground Railroad."

Maggie immediately jumped in with, "Well, I think it's from the Scouts. It looks like a butterfly. Our Scouts reserve time each year to go the local Butterfly Pavilion to earn badges. Girl Scouts attend their Bug Badge Class, and the Boy Scouts attend their Insect Study Badge Class."

By now, everyone was gathered around offering their opinions.

Grace explained, "The cup you found is a Cherokee cup with the Freedom symbol on it. Certain Native American tribes had been run off their land and hunting grounds. They often provided the earliest safe havens for runaway slaves. Some of the slaves assimilated, blended in, and some even joined the tribe. Some of the American Indians escaped with the slaves for a new and better life.

"In the case of the Cherokee Indians, they lost their land in what is now the state of Georgia, because gold was found on it. The gold rush that resulted from that discovery prompted President Jackson to transfer the Indians to the reservations by way of The Trail of Tears.

"Many American Indians decided to seek a better life by joining the escaped slaves to use the Underground Railroad. Because of their many talents and life skills, the American Indians were also a great help to the escaping slaves. Their extensive survival skills had been used to live off the land for centuries. Their knowledge of the terrain was also invaluable as they served as guides. These two unlikely partners, made a successful combination when faced with their desperate situations, that enabled them to escape to the northern United States, Canada, or the Caribbean."

James and Maggie told of marks on the Wall of Freedom to count those who had passed through the Sea Crest Underground Railroad. Many were able to meet up with their families and start a new life in the Caribbean.

As the afternoon wore on, James and Maggie humbly shared their adventure of how they had finally come out through the high cliffs, hidden from the beach, but within view of the Sea Crest Lighthouse.

Chapter 44

The Sea Crest Police said they might have some follow-up questions later, but that was all for now. They left the area, and some of the onlookers also moved on.

Several members of the family were still in shock, but they were grateful for the happy return of Maggie and James.

Kate's mom told everyone to walk over to the keeper's cottage; she'd have some food ready in a few minutes.

It seemed like the whole Sea Crest Community had come together and brought all kinds of food to the families. Kate's mom and Maggie's mom had taken charge of food and coffee. They had organized and prepared nourishment around the clock for those helping in the search.

Maggie's mom had confessed, "It helps to have some way to assist or aid in the search. This is something we're good at."

As they walked toward the keeper's cottage, Maggie put her arms around her mother as she told her, "Mom, I'm so sorry I caused you to worry. I know you already fear for my safety with my job as an FBI Special Agent. I truly regret that I caused you added pain."

Mary responded, "Well, I'm glad you're home. You seem like you came through it fine."

She looked at her daughter again as they walked. She couldn't believe that she was actually in such high spirits. "Are you honestly all right, Maggie?"

"Yes, in fact, I feel better than I've felt in a very long time." She paused for a moment and then added, "Isn't that odd?"

Her mother had just witnessed the obvious fact that James and Maggie cared for each other. She also knew that, previously, Maggie and James had fiercely hated each other, which led her to ask, "Maggie, how did you survive being around James? He doesn't seem like the man you described before. Does Michael have another brother? Am I mixing them up?"

Chapter 45

As he watched the strikingly beautiful sunset from the Sea Crest Beach, James quietly contemplated Maggie. It was certainly nice to be above ground to enjoy the everyday essentials of life.

However, he couldn't help but wonder, *Will I ever have the chance to be with Maggie again? I'll admit, I don't plan on having another important discovery like the Underground Railroad tunnels and caves again in my lifetime.*

Even if I'm that lucky, there is no one else with the many qualities that Maggie has. It just wouldn't be the same. He was suddenly feeling a growing sense of loss and despair. He wondered, *How could this be? Everyone is saying how fortunate we are, being out of the Underground Tunnel. Well, it's over. I'll have to shake it off and look forward.*

In fact, he thought, *I'm just going to relax and take a well-deserved break from thinking about that time in the tunnels and caverns with Maggie.*

Moreover, I'm not even going to look at her, he enthusiastically pledged.

After all, I've had three days and two nights to look at her, he insisted to himself. *Now we're back in the real world, I'm just going to unwind and have fun.*

The tranquility that he now experienced was, well, it was not only false, but it proved to be what is more accurately called the-calm-before-the-storm.

James looked over the crowd that was finally dispersing and was very surprised to see Jeff Williams, his attorney from New York. He hurried over and shook hands with him.

"Hey, Jeff, did you find the dog's previous owners? Did they sign an agreement not to take Misha away from Maggie?"

James was so excited he didn't give a second thought to the fact that Jeff might be here for Michael and Kate's Wedding Celebration. "Did you tell Maggie about it yet?"

Jeff couldn't believe he was talking with the same James Jensen that he'd known for years. "As a matter of fact, I did have some luck with that dog thing you asked me to handle, but that's not why I'm down here."

"What gives?" asked Michael as he walked up and joined them.

"Jeff was working on something for me. He came down to tell me about it," explained James impatiently as he turned back to hear what Jeff was saying.

"No, I came down to attend the Wedding Celebration of Michael and Kate," he laughed as he shook his head.

"Oh, I forgot about that." James apologized.

"Jeez, James, what's wrong with you, anyway?" asked his very confused brother.

"Nothing," said James quickly as he brushed him aside.

He impatiently turned back to Jeff and persisted, "Okay, what did you find out about Misha's previous owner? I hope they don't think they can have her back. You can't let that happen."

"Hold on. One of my detectives was able to find the couple. They had only had Misha for a few months when the wife found out she was pregnant. They didn't think they could handle both a new baby and a Great Dane who was still a puppy even though she looked huge. They made a trip up the coast and dropped her off at the Sea Crest Lighthouse."

"Those people are idiots. That's the friendliest dog in the world. Well, did they sign a legal contract that they won't come back and take her from Maggie?" asked James seriously.

Michael and Jeff both stared at him suspiciously, wondering what had happened to the real James, that they knew.

"Well, yes, I'm getting to it," answered Jeff patiently. "The detective noticed that they didn't have much money but seemed like good people who just ended up in a situation where they had to make a hard decision."

"Are you kidding me? Abandoning Misha in a strange place was a horrible decision." James was on the verge of losing it. He ran his hand through his hair and put his other hand on his hip in frustration. He looked like he'd like to put his fist through a wall.

He appeared to be suffering real pain as he murmured, "I can't bear to tell Maggie that they just left her precious dog alone, forsaken and dumped in a strange town. That will break her heart!"

Both Jeff and Michael were so flabbergasted by this whole scenario that neither one of them could think of even one appropriate thing to say. They had never seen James get involved with any human or pet situation with anyone else, period.

James sounded troubled as he gave them one more surprise, "The first night in the cave, Maggie cried herself to sleep, thinking she might lose that dog. I woke up and found her goggles and her blanket, wet with her tears. We can't let that happen again!"

He seemed truly fired up when he stated with conviction, "We need to think up something that won't make her cry!"

Then he stood expectantly, waiting for them to come up with it.

Chapter 46

Later that evening, as night fell over the Sea Crest Beach and Lighthouse, things were progressing nicely at the keeper's cottage. Everyone was well-fed and happy.

Several of the family and friends were gathered out on the wrap-around porch reflecting on the sensational events of the day. The appearance of fireflies somehow made the summer evening feel magical.

The ladies talked back and forth, reminding everyone that they had a full spread of tasty eats and drinks that would be available for the entire morning tomorrow. "Don't forget, Grace's mom sent a couple of her delicious Swedish tea rings."

"Yes, and Mary Beth just called to say they finished the Old-fashioned Crock-Pot Apple Butter this afternoon. Her mom made an entire triple-batch of homemade biscuits to go with it. They'll bring everything over in the morning."

Everyone was happily relaxed and engrossed in their private thoughts about the upcoming events of tomorrow. They felt very blessed and fortunate that Maggie and James had been found and that Kate and Michael were having their Wedding Celebration the next day.

Mary O'Hara was the one who innocently suggested, "Why don't we bring out the photo album with pictures from when the girls were in grade school. Kate and Maggie were practically brought up like twins. They were born within days of each other."

"Yes, we need to get some pictures for the Wedding Celebration display." agreed Katherine.

The two Moms proceeded to sort through the photo albums on the shelf. They finally pulled out the one that covered the girl's younger years.

"Oh no," Kate protested. "Don't let Michael see those. They're terrible!"

It was what she said next that especially got James' attention.

"Oh, Maggie, remember our charming pigtails?" asked Kate.

Maggie and Kate both tried to object, although they were secretly pleased as punch that Michael (and James) would have a chance to see them as adorable little girls.

James felt both excited and afraid at the prospect of seeing if these little girls in the album looked anything like the girls in his dream.

And so, began the extravaganza of childhood pictures, but more important was what the images revealed about these families. The Jensens had rarely shared such warmth and out-and-out teasing with each other. This friendly banter seemed so warm and natural.

James looked over at Maggie. She and Kate were sitting on the sofa with the album laying across their legs.

Kate screamed, "Oh, No! Mom, this picture cannot stay in this album for all the world to see."

That was all Connor needed. He jumped up, laughing, and yelled, "Come on, Michael. This should be good."

Kate pulled the album to her, and with shrieks of hysterics and laughter, she tried to justify the picture, "No, it's too funny. I must have been 1½ or 2 years old. I'm not responsible."

Michael got to Kate first and knelt beside her, laughing. "Oh, this I've got to see," he said as he took the album and sat on the floor.

Connor loved that Michael was going to see the picture. He chimed in with, "Well, if it's the one I'm thinking of, then it's truly a winning baby picture if there ever was one. Personally, I think it should go on the picture display at the Wedding Celebration."

Michael looked down at the picture of Kate and cracked up laughing, as he joined in, explaining to his dad and James, "Of course, this is Classic Kate if I ever saw it. She's on the beach, with the Sea Crest Lighthouse in the background, and she's got quite an attitude for a pint-sized lass."

He smirked as he turned to the very red-faced Kate and teased, "You're standing there like you own the whole beach. However, your authority can only go so far, Dear, when you're just wearing saggy diapers and a pair of big sunglasses."

"By the way, Dad, did I tell you that's where I first met Kate?" asked Michael as he winked at him to signal his needed cooperation.

"Well," continued Michael, "it was right there on that same stretch of beach."

"Yes, I think you mentioned it." answered his dad as he played along.

"Clearly, the only reason I even noticed her was that she appeared to have this same attitude as she has in this picture. You know, like she owned this whole beach."

"What are you talking about?" laughed Kate. She now slid onto the floor beside him.

Michael reached for her and settled with his arm around her happily. "You know, that basic entitlement mentality," he explained.

"That's not true," Kate started to defend herself.

But Michael interrupted, "Oh, Dad, by the way, she was busy bossing around a bunch of surfing students."

"So, which was it? The attitude or the bossiness that first attracted you to her?" asked James as he joined in the fun.

"Well, suffice it to say, her beachwear had improved by leaps and bounds...and she sure grew up nicely." bragged Michael as he kissed her on the nose.

"However, I have to confess; I should have just run. I knew she'd be a hand full with that attitude, you know, and the bossy thing was a potential problem also," he stated sadly.

Kate threatened sweetly, "You better take that back!"

Michael shook his head no slightly as he continued, "Well, even though she was way out of my league, I was way over my head, crazy about her. I just couldn't run away without my heart, and Kate had stolen it."

He concluded with, "After all, how many times does the love-of-your-life, even come around?"

Boy, that's a real question, thought James as he glanced over at Maggie and wished he could read her mind.

Chapter 47

Connor was looking at the album when he exclaimed, "Hey, this is a great picture of Maggie and Kate."

Everyone was busy commenting on it, so James moved over to see what was drawing all the attention.

He was stunned as he glanced at a picture of two little girls and thought, *Yes, that's the same little red-headed girl with pigtails. The exact location on the beach, where my dad, my grandfather, my brother Michael, Maggie's dad, and I had all walked up the sand after the scuba rescue.*

James slowly took the book from Connor and sat down before his legs folded beneath him, as he whispered, "Yes, that was exactly the way Sean was walking up to meet the girls, and one of the girls had jumped into his arms, with unrestrained love."

Ben Jensen was carefully watching James, and as he looked up, his dad moved to sit down next to him. "What is it, James?"

"Look. That's us. All of us coming back after Sean rescued us. Can you believe it, Dad?'

His dad took the photo album and looked closely at the picture. This time he recognized the people, the time frame, and an eerie feeling came over him.

Sean saw that something was happening, and he quickly joined them. He saw the photo they were looking at and studied it carefully. He nodded in shock as he agreed, "Yes, this is unbelievable. I haven't seen that picture for years. I had no idea that the photo was taken on the day of the scuba problem."

James' voice broke as he asked, "Is that My Maggie?"

"Yes, James, it sure is."

Maggie had been watching this from a chair nearby, and she rose to see what they were looking at. She recognized the picture. She had seen it many times. Only now did she look closely at the tourists in the picture. "Wow, James, it's you!"

"James, you look like you've seen a ghost. I'm sorry if this was upsetting to you," added Ben.

"Dad, I've had nightmares for years about the scuba dive, but while I was in the caverns, I've had another, well new dream."

"What do you mean?" asked his dad softly.

"Well, at the beginning of the new dream, Maggie was in it, as an adult, and she told me to stop dreaming about the nightmare."

He seemed to think that over for a minute and then continued, "Well, to tell you the truth, I haven't had that nightmare since then."

Maggie was shocked. She looked at the photo again, while James continued.

"But next, I felt my mom was somehow with me. She felt very close. It was surreal. Then," he continued, "I had a dream like this picture. We were walking on the beach, and Sean walked up by these two children, I mean literally, these two girls. This one ran to Sean and threw herself into his arms with pure love and joy. It was incredible!"

"You're kidding," remarked Ben.

"No, it's real. I never remembered it before," he continued. "I just wondered if that child with the red-haired pigtails was My Maggie. Then earlier this morning, I wondered if the little blond-haired girl was Kate."

"Now, I've seen this picture, this exact thing was in my dream." He turned to Sean, "I know it was years ago, but do you remember that day?"

Sean replied, "Of course, I remember it very well. I can also tell you that Maggie did jump in my arms as I walked up the beach from the water. And that was Kate," as he pointed to the blond-haired girl.

"I don't know how any of these dreams work," said James thoughtfully, "but I'll tell you, it feels like a miracle."

Chapter 48

They all had a lot to think about as the family said their goodnights. So much had happened in the last couple of days.

Katherine started picking up the pictures that had been selected for the poster board.

Maggie and Kate picked up the coffee mugs and various plates that were left around. As they loaded the dishwasher, their discussion turned to how they'd wear their hair for the Celebration.

Maggie confided in Kate, "Well, whatever I do with my hair, James can't stand it."

Kate was immediately alarmed by that statement. "Why on earth would you say a thing like that? Everyone loves your hair."

"No honest. James hates it, and he even said so in the cave the first night."

"Maggie," said Kate. "I'm sure you misunderstood him."

Michael had come around the corner in time to hear the conversation. "Maggie, that can't be right. What on earth would make you believe he doesn't like your hair?"

"Oh, it doesn't matter. It's just all the stuff James said about it. He doesn't like it at all. It truly offends him. I think it almost drives him nuts."

"You're kidding. What did that idiot say!" stormed Michael.

"Oh, Michael, it doesn't even matter." Maggie tried to laugh it off, but Kate could see, she was close to tears.

Michael shook his head as he walked away. But he stopped in his tracks when he overheard Maggie quietly telling Kate, "To be perfectly fair to James, his exact words were; and I quote, 'Unruly disaster, very distracting, like a catastrophe waiting to happen, wild and chaotic. He also thinks that the FBI should have rules against it and make me wear clips in it to hold it down or something.'"

At this time, tears were filling her eyes, and she stopped to compose herself.

Wow, thought Michael. *My crazy brother, has really got it bad.*

He ducked back into the conversation to say, "Hey Kate, I'll be back in a few minutes. I need to ask Joe a couple of things. I didn't get the chance to earlier."

"Sure," called Kate, as she turned back to console Maggie.

Michael came running back to her to kiss her. "By the way," he asked. "What time will you guys be getting your hair done tomorrow?"

"I think our appointments are around 10:00."

"Perfect. I've got a few things to do, and I'll try to get them done during that same time," said Michael as he ran out the door.

Chapter 49

Michael made a beeline over to Joe Lawrence's. "I just heard Maggie telling Kate about what James said about her hair. I'll tell you, Joe, James doesn't know anything about women's hair, but I'm sure that he's obsessed with Maggie. In fact, I'll bet Maggie's hair is driving him nuts because he can't have her."

"Yes. What did I tell you? It's plain as day. Did you hear him refer to her as My Maggie?"

"Yes, and I'll bet he's entirely unaware that he feels possessive about her," explained Michael. "In fact, I think he's in love with her. He didn't even want to like her. He hated her. He couldn't control anything about her, especially something as glorious as her hair. He sure must feel all twisted up inside over her. He couldn't control falling in love with his arch-enemy."

"But the next question is, does Maggie have any feelings for James," asked Joe.

"I think I saw a glimmer of hope a few minutes ago. Maggie cried because James hates her hair."

"I think fate needs to step in and finish shaking them up," Joe volunteered.

"Yes. Bring James over tomorrow morning around 10:15. Let's tell him that Maggie's gone to get her hair all cut off."

"Super." agreed Joe. "Let's turn him upside down. We can add that she's getting it dyed dark black. See how he deals with that."

The next morning, James came over with Joe to discuss some plans with Michael.

Joe innocently asked, "Where is Kate this morning?"

"Oh, she met Maggie at the beauty parlor a little while ago. In fact, they are getting the whole works, hair, manicures, pedicures, etc. They want to look beautiful for the Wedding Celebration," explained Michael with a lighthearted laugh.

"Yeah," James joined in laughing. "It will take a whole team to get them looking top-notch."

"Well, Maggie was a little worried about trying something new and different this time around," said Michael.

James went pale white as he asked, "What are you talking about?"

"Well, I'm not entirely sure. I told her if she gets it cut off that short, you know, military-style, it will take years to grow back out," explained Michael.

"What?" yelled James.

"Well, it's not a true buzz-cut, I guess. I think she'd look beautiful regardless, but why would she ever do it?"

"You're kidding!" yelled James.

Michael continued, "Really, she said she needs it so short that it won't curl and stick out every which way. Like an unruly disaster, like a catastrophe waiting to happen, wild and chaotic. The most disturbing thing she's going to do is get rid of that auburn red color. She's changing to straight black."

Michael was just getting started as he explained, "I was going to say something to her about the fact that I like her hair just like it is, but she was crying. I'll tell you that tear rolling down her cheek broke my heart even tho I've heard she was one tough lady. I don't see it."

Now it was Joe's turn, "Maybe someone said something to her about her hair. You know something mean to hurt her feelings."

Michael continued, "No, Kate says, 'Maggie wouldn't care what anyone said unless he or she was really important to her. You know, like family or someone she cared for'."

James took off out of the door at a dead run. He promptly turned around and almost tore the door off its hinges as he yelled, "Where in the world is this beauty parlor?"

Michael said, "I was going to stop by with coffee. Why? Did you want to come?"

Fifteen minutes later, they arrived at the beauty salon (without the coffee).

James ran in, yelling, "This is an emergency! I need to see Maggie O'Hara!"

The frightened receptionist picked up the telephone to call 911. "I don't understand. Maggie is here."

"Where is she?"

"I'll get her. You stay here, sir."

Michael had parked the car, and he was entering the front door when he heard James angrily demand, "If anyone takes a pair of scissors to one hair of her head, I'll bring a lawsuit against this whole operation!"

Michael had rarely, if ever, seen his brother this furious.

Maggie rushed out of the back with a towel twisted around the top of her head. She ran up to James, frantically asking, "What's the matter? Are you all right, James?"

She looked so pretty, he suddenly didn't care about her hair.

"Of course, I'm okay," he answered. "What are you doing here?"

Maggie smiled a sheepish grin, "Well, Kate, and I thought we'd try to see if we could have our hair done in one of those beautiful braids that wrap around our heads. Of course, we'd have soft feathered tendrils falling out. Hey, what are you doing here? Oh, hello, Michael."

Kate came running out of the back room. She had a towel wrapped around her head too. "What's going on out here?"

James cleared his throat, looked daggers at his brother, as he said, "I think we've had a little mix up here."

He took Maggie aside and whispered, "Maggie? Do you trust me?"

She looked worried as she quietly answered, "Of course, I do."

"Come with me," he said as he led her into an alcove for coats and umbrellas.

"May I?" he asked as he tugged on her towel.

She said, "sure," wondering what was going on.

They both unwrapped the twisted towel, and her wavy, long, auburn-red hair fell to her shoulders and down her back.

James breathed a deep sigh of relief as he gave her a brief hug and muttered, "Maggie, please don't cut your outrageous hair off and dye it black."

"What?"

"Promise me, Maggie."

"Okay, if you promise me that you could get used to it or maybe even like it, James."

James just laughed as he reached out to touch one of her silky curls. He wound it around his finger as he said, "Trust me, Maggie," he paused as he turned serious, before he said, "you have no idea what I think, about you and I don't have time, right now, to go into it. So, if you'll excuse me, it appears I need to pay back my little brother for giving me a heart attack."

Chapter 50

A short while later, James apologized to the front desk receptionist and prepaid for everything that Kate and Maggie planned to have done at the salon.

Then James explained to the salon owner, who had been helping Maggie and Kate find a picture of the way they wanted to have their hair braided, "I'm truly sorry for the mix up this morning. Please accept this check to make up for the disturbance".

"Wow," she answered. "This is very generous."

"Just take good care of them, please."

On the way back to the car, James informed Michael, "By the way, you're going to pay half of that check for setting me up."

Michael broke up laughing, "Oh, James. I've never seen you so worked up."

"That was very mean."

"I'd say I was sorry, but I like this swashbuckling side of you. Our daring Scottish ancestors would be proud of you."

"Yeah, well, now you're going to help me finish something nice for Maggie."

"Hey, I've got several things to do for the Wedding Celebration tonight."

"Well, I see that didn't keep you from taking time out to make a complete fool out of me." James pointed out. "In front of everyone," he added, meaning, (*especially Maggie)*.

"Okay, what do you need me for?" asked Michael.

"I need to get over to the jewelers to pick up my Rolex. The owner was putting a new battery in it, for me."

"You mean the store by the locksmith?" asked Michael. "Kate and I went over there last week.

"Yes, that's where Joe had the extra keys made for the beach house."

A short time later, Joe agreed to meet them at his office. "I have the contract ready for Maggie, stating that the previous owners, who abandoned Misha, are legally relinquishing all rights to the Great Dane."

"I hope they won't cause any harm to Maggie or try to extort money from her," said James thoughtfully.

"No problem," answered Joe. "This will be handled entirely through our office so that Maggie's name will be kept private and sealed from them."

"Thanks, Joe," said James. "I owe you big time for this."

"It's the least I could do. I've known Maggie for a long time, and I wish I had thought of doing this for her."

Of course, I'm not the guy that's in love with her, Joe thought with a smile.

"This contract was agreed to, in exchange for waiving legal prosecution," Joe continued aloud. "It was signed by a circuit court judge this morning. No money will change hands in this agreement."

"By the way, Michael, you asked about the store where James left his watch," said Joe. "Well, I'm headed that way right now, James, and I can take you."

"That sounds fine," answered James. "Then I want to pick up the Bentley over at the keeper's cottage. I have a few errands of my own."

Meanwhile, back at the hair salon, Maggie and Kate were admiring their perfectly arranged hairstyles.

Maggie commented on Kate's classic look, "Your blond hair is stunning, the way it just sweeps back in an elegant loosely braided chignon in the back. You couldn't look more adorable. It's you."

"Well, you're looking more glamorous than I've ever seen you," answered Kate. "I love the way your top hair is gracefully swept back into waves on both sides. They've gathered them together in the back into a loose braid for just a few inches. Then the ends fall into the glorious bottom layers of flowing curls. The design is perfect for you, Maggie."

"I know you're going to wear the parachute wedding gown this evening. The one that Michael and James' grandmother and their mother wore at their weddings. You'll look beautiful in it. I'm so happy for you, Kate."

"Thank you," she replied. "I've never felt so loved or so happy in my entire life."

"Now, what are you going to wear, Maggie?"

"Oh, I've got something exceptional that I picked up in Paris last year. I wanted to celebrate after I closed a tough international case. It involved counterfeit fashion clothing and products being manufactured and sold in the United States as genuine goods."

"Wow," said Kate. "I remember when you worked that case."

"I met many of the designers who had their sketches stolen, and I had an opportunity to see many exquisite fashions. After the investigation was over, one of the grateful designers created a stunning gown just for me, as a personal thank you. I wondered when I'd have a chance to wear it, but now I think I'll wear it tonight to the celebration."

"Oh, Maggie. That will be perfect. I'll bet James will flip."

Maggie was flabbergasted. "Kate. What a crazy thing to say."

"Maggie, you've got to be kidding. I think he likes you."

"No, I'm sure he doesn't," she said sadly.

"Well, he's done something very special for you. I don't know what it was, but it's supposed to be a big secret from you. I overheard Michael and Jeff, his attorney from New York, discussing it last night."

"What?"

"That's just it. I don't know. But Michael was saying he's never known James to do anything like it for anyone else. Jeff made Michael promise not to tell you."

"Hey, is this supposed to be something I would like?"

"I sure thought so. It was done several days ago before you got trapped in the Underground Railroad tunnel. Jeff said when he got the call from James, he thought he was talking about a different Maggie. He couldn't believe James wanted to do something nice for the same Maggie that put him in jail as the prime suspect."

"Well, I thought he had done something to harm you."

"I'm sure he knows that now. Anyway, I asked Michael what he was talking about, and he wouldn't tell me. Then he said I couldn't keep a secret from you."

Maggie smiled, "Well, that's true."

Chapter 51

They were pulling into the keeper's cottage when Katherine came out to greet them, "Oh, both of you look beautiful."

"Thanks, Mom. I'm so excited. We only have a couple of hours to get ready for the Wedding Celebration," said Kate.

"It's going to be the event of the season, and you look fantastic."

"Thanks, I can't wait to see you in your Paris designer creation," added Kate.

"All right. Tonight is probably the only chance I'll ever get to wear it," Maggie said as she waved goodbye.

"No, dear. Wait. Come on inside for a minute. Joe has been waiting for you. He has something to give you," said Katherine.

"I saw his car. I wonder what he has for me," she said as she followed her Aunt Katherine into the house.

"Hey Joe, I hear you're waiting for me." She smiled as she joined him at the table with Michael.

"Yes, I have been. Wow, you look terrific, Maggie."

"Thanks," she laughed. "I'm just dying to see what is so important that you waited for me."

She suddenly became solemn. "Oh, No. What's wrong?"

"Nothing's wrong, Maggie. I have something that you need to see as soon as possible. It's important," stated Joe.

"Okay," Maggie replied, warily. She wondered why Michael didn't move to leave, so she figured it might be about the Chambers' beach house.

Joe picked up his briefcase from the floor and opened it. Kate came into the room and stood silently by her best friend.

Joe said, "Maggie, I know you've been concerned about Misha's previous owners coming back to claim her."

"Oh, NO!" came Maggie's heartbreaking cry. Kate rushed to her as they both burst into tears.

"No. No. No. Maggie, it's okay!" Joe yelled.

Katherine dashed into the room and looked helplessly around. "What's happening?"

"Everything is fine. I'm just trying to let Maggie know that I have a legal affidavit signed by a judge stating that Maggie is now the legal owner of Misha."

"What?" screamed Maggie as she jumped up, laughing and crying and hugging everyone in sight.

Frankly, Michael was amazed by this ecstatic reaction. *James had been right. This really was a big deal to Maggie.*

Maggie was jubilantly asking, "How did you do this? Is it real? What if the previous owners come back and take her away?"

Joe assured her, "That's all been taken care of in this agreement. The previous owners have agreed to relinquish all rights from this day forward. They don't know who has Misha, but they know and agree that Misha is now in the care of her new legal owner, and they agree that they will never try to take her away. All contact has been through Jeff and me, and they don't know whom we represent. Maggie, your identity is unknown to them, and the judge has sealed this record."

Maggie was overcome with emotion, as she said to Joe, "I just can't thank you enough."

"Well, I had nothing to do with it, Maggie. I was only involved on the tail end of it," explained Joe.

"The party who ordered the investigation and resulting contract to ensure that you could keep Misha shall remain nameless according to their precise wishes."

"But who on earth would do this for me?" uttered Maggie with a dazed look on her face.

Kate offered a few ideas, "Maybe it was someone who wanted to do something Nice for you, Maggie. Something Big. Keep it a Secret. Do you know anyone like that?"

Maggie was stunned by the realization that it might be Her James.

Chapter 52

Meanwhile, James was still working on his list of errands.

"Let's see:

Go to the jeweler – pick up Rolex,

Check if they have a large diamond dog collar that will fit Misha

See Sean O'Hara – thank him for saving my life

Dress in my Chambers' Scottish plaid kilt, pack my sporran, which functions as a pocket, and hangs on the front of my kilt.

Don't forget - The Special Gift

Go to Wedding Celebration

Chapter 53

She hadn't even looked at this elegant gown since she returned home from France. Maggie thoughtfully unzipped the protective garment bag. "This is unbelievable. It's the most romantic gown I could have ever dreamed of."

Misha had been following her around, non-stop since they'd gotten home, and she now tilted her head sideways, wondering what was in the large bag. She watched Maggie smile as she unzipped the garment bag and carefully slid the elegant dress out.

"Ah, here it is. My dazzling evening gown!" Maggie exclaimed as she lovingly hugged the luxurious, shimmering fabric to her and twirled around with delight.

"Yes. It's perfect for tonight. It's simple enough not to upstage Kate, but it's classic through and through. The airy sea-mist green material twinkles with glittering tonal jewels with my every movement."

Maggie started remembering about her appointments with the talented designer. *The designer had explained, the sleeveless bodice is edged in shimmering tonal crystals and fits like a glove as it ends in a v-neck. The slender waist features glamorous ruching with a chic twist to create curves.*

This dress cascades to a full-length hem to create the striking clean lines that mold the long, tall silhouette of the gown to my slim figure.

It looks both innocent and stunning at the same time.

At the final fitting, when Maggie looked in the mirror, she was delighted that the bottom would seem to flow when she walked or danced gracefully.

As she tried it on now, Maggie thought, *Yes, I appear extremely tall and incredibly slender in this gown. I look like the complete package, but somehow, a much better version of myself.*

She remembered back to Paris again; *I was genuinely surprised when the dress maker fitted me for this gown. The designer had explained, the sea-mist green shade goes perfectly with my lustrous auburn-red hair. It also causes a special luminous effect from my emerald green eyes and my full dark lashes.*

I had to admit, the gown shows me off as better than I've ever imagined myself before. The designer said that's what fashion is supposed to do for me. This dress was made exclusive to complement me, from head to toe.

Maggie was extremely excited about the Wedding Celebration tonight. *"I wonder if James will seek me out. I wonder if I'll have the opportunity to dance with him. After all, the best man and the maid of honor probably should dance together."* All that being said, she wondered how strong his feelings were for her.

Of course, I have to believe that the person who ordered the investigation of the individuals who had abandoned Misha must genuinely care for me.

Maggie looked directly into Misha's eyes as she said, "Add the fact that it resulted in an affidavit stating that I'm your legal owner, Misha," she said tenderly as she hugged her. "Well, that shows that he understood how much you mean to me.

Maggie continued to dress as she considered James. *At first, I could hardly believe that he cared that much. But I've been trained as an FBI Special Agent, and I'm the best in my field. When I examined all the evidence, I must admit that the pieces all fit together that way.*

I sure can't think of anyone else who would go to all that trouble. I'm sure that James is behind this, and I think it's charming that he wanted to remain nameless.

Wow! James did an 'anonymous act of kindness,' for me!

Of course, James did make quite a scene at the Beauty Salon this morning. She smiled as she remembered the fuss he'd made over her outrageous hair. *He, in fact, likes it. Stranger still, I think he truly cares for me.*

As she finished getting ready, she bragged to Misha, "I must tell you that I've had some experience working with a variety of dogs working with the FBI. You'd be so proud of how important they are in sniffing out drugs and bombs, but they are also experts at alerting their handlers when they pick up the scent of blood. We have come to trust and depend on them. Their keen instincts are unmatched and unparalleled.

"Scientists have also weighed in on some interesting facts about dogs, and I'm going to share a secret with you, Misha. We now know that dogs only have two types of cones that detect color. I'm telling you this because I'd like you to be able to see the absolutely beautiful seafoam green color of this gown. However, I know you don't see red or green colors the same as people do. This looks like a yellowish or possibly gray. I'm so sorry you can't see how this matches my eyes.

"I'm going out to Kate and Michael's Wedding Celebration now, but I'll be home later this evening."

Maggie stared at her reflection in the mirror. She had to admit she looked spectacular. *I sure hope James thinks so,* she thought.

Chapter 54

Well, Maggie would never believe what James thought when he saw her enter the Wedding Celebration tents at the Sea Crest Beach that evening.

However, the following questions are among the things that James was impatiently thinking before she showed up:

Where on earth is she?

Is she helping Kate get ready?

What is taking Maggie so much time to get here?

I can't wait to see her!

Meanwhile, Maggie was slightly delayed due to her qualms about facing James. She knew that he had secretly done something extraordinary for her. In fact, it was so memorable and meaningful that she didn't know how to be around him.

She hesitated as she approached the tents thinking, *James knows me so well that he read my heart and knew how much Misha meant to me. All this, together with my growing feelings for him, are making me scared of his forthcoming rejection. Here I am falling in love with James, totally against my better judgment. To make matters worse, I don't seem to have any control over how much I care for him, and I cannot stop it. He now consumes both my waking hours and my sleeping dreams. I can't seem to be around him without wanting him more.*

Maggie saw James before she came through the entrance. She idiotically ducked behind a potted plant, out of sight. Her excitement reminded her of the anticipation that a child feels on Christmas Eve. However, in this situation, it felt more like the long ride up to the top of the first peak of a giant roller coaster. She was terrified of the free-fall of her heart if James didn't want her in return.

Dress or no dress, how could I possibly compete with all the jet-set models James usually dates? Well, this isn't even a date, so what am I thinking? Oh, No! What if James brought a date?

Oh, for goodness' sake, Maggie admonished herself. *Get ahold of yourself. What's the worst thing that could happen? I'm afraid he doesn't like me, much less love me,* Maggie thought miserably. *I don't think I'll be able to bear it.*

She had seen James earlier in the day at the beauty salon. *He made a huge commotion over my hair,* she remembered. *It sure seemed like he had feelings for me. I'm sure it was James that ensured that I could keep Misha. I've got everything riding on James' feelings for me.*

A few minutes later, a guest recognized her and exclaimed, "Why Maggie. You look gorgeous," as she proceeded to draw her into the view of everyone inside the reception tent.

When she walked in, James was talking with his father and Joe Lawrence. However, he stopped in mid-sentence as he observed what looked like a model with a tall, willowy, runway walk, glide through the arched entryway.

Her magnificent, flowing, red-auburn hair was outstanding as she moved through the room.

The sleeveless bodice fit her perfectly. The gown dropped to the floor with lengthy dramatic lines that complimented Maggie's sleek, alluring figure. James had never in his life felt such an intense attraction for any woman.

Even from across the room, James could see the shimmering, sea mist green shade of that dress, enhance her rich sparkling, emerald, green eyes.

James was immediately stunned at realizing that he had spent the last couple of days in the underground tunnels and caves with this sensational, desirable, fashion-plate. Frankly, James was speechless.

Maggie located the table where her parents were sitting and walked over and greeted both of them.

"Hello, Mom. Isn't this beautiful?" she said as she continued to look around at the beautifully decorated tents.

Her mother turned to her in surprise. "Oh, Maggie, you look beautiful," she whispered. "Is that the gown from Paris?"

"Yes, and Mom, I've never worn it before."

Her mother looked closely into her daughter's eyes and saw something new and exciting. "Well, it's perfect for tonight," she said as she hugged her with tears in her eyes.

Maggie wasn't expecting that, but she knew her mom was emotional and excited about Kate's marriage, which probably explained a lot.

Next, her dad came around and hugged her, also. "We love you so much, Maggie."

Boy, she thought. *Dad too?*

From across the room, James had not taken his eyes from her.

Meanwhile, James' father was still waiting for James to finish his sentence. He had just watched his oldest son go completely off the deep end, so he asked him, "James, how are you doing, son?"

He was slow to answer, "I guess I just realized that I haven't seen Maggie dressed up before Dad."

His father would have laughed out loud if he didn't feel so sorry for him. *This was priceless.*

Carolyn Court

Romantic music played on the stage beneath the main tent at the Wedding Celebration, as the guests started arriving. They marveled at the stunning panoramic views as the sun began to set over the Sea Crest Beach and Lighthouse.

The triple tent setting looked like a fairy tale with ribbons of sheer material and flowers, flowing from each peak to the side pillars. The lighting combination of the elegant chandeliers hanging from the inside peak of each tent, along with the soft candlelight settings on the tables, was spectacular.

The roundtables had white tablecloths with an elegant candle and flower arrangement of white roses, purple thistle, and white heather. White high-backed chairs surrounded the tables with little lavender back pillows. A matching wide lavender ribbon was tied like a sash on the back of each chair with a purple thistle and white rose nosegay attached at the knot.

This setting created a stunning backdrop to Kate and Michael's Wedding Celebration.

Chapter 55

Kate and Michael departed from the keeper's cottage in a horse-drawn carriage. Their ride took a leisurely course, meandering beside the ocean and along the Sea Crest Beach.

The carriage stopped in front of the Sea Crest Lighthouse, where they had taken their vows a few short weeks ago. Michael helped Kate step down from the carriage. She held a bouquet, which included white roses and thistle with sprays of white heather mixed in. Maggie had gathered it from the cliffs for good luck.

Kate and Michael celebrated the adventure that led to their falling in love by posing in front of the majestic Sea Crest Lighthouse. The repairs of the lighthouse were almost complete. With the backdrop of the beautiful blue ocean with the crashing waves, the pictures showed an almost perfect portrayal of their stay.

A photographer took photos to commemorate the wearing of the historic 'Parachute Wedding Gown,' which had been handed down from generation to generation in the Chambers' Family.

Kate and Michael insisted on showing off their famous Kiss, in Times Square on V-J Day, for 'A Picture Worth Taking.'

Kate and Michael's happiness and genuine love were apparent in every frame, making for an authentic storybook wedding.

To depict a more down-to-earth memory of what really took place, Kate and Michael had Connor hold his Irish padlock, ready to lock the entryway from the outside. The photographer took various shots of Connor looking like he was up to mischief and knew his sister was locked inside. The photographer thought it was the most fun he had ever had taking pictures at a wedding.

Soon Kate and Michael continued their carriage ride. They circled the entire Wedding Celebration layout with the three tents on the Sea Crest Beach. They waved to the cheering friends and family as they came to a final stop. Michael retook Kate's hand, kissed it happily, and then helped her down from the carriage.

Their family and friends parted to make a path for them to enter the tent. Everyone was wishing them well and congratulating them, but the main attraction was Kate's parachute wedding gown. By now, everyone had heard the story behind the beautiful dress.

Kate told them, "We've got an expert to reveal the history of this precious dress a little later." That seemed to satisfy them for the time being.

Next, Michael stepped up to one of the band's microphones with Kate in tow. He twirled her around to show her off and began, "As you all know, Kate and I were married at the top of the Sea Crest Lighthouse just over three weeks ago."

Everyone clapped and smiled as he continued. "Thank you all for joining us this evening at our Wedding Celebration.

"Now I have some rather alarming news to share with you. Many of you already know this, but I just found out about it during our 'long' engagement," Michael explained like he was agitated.

Everyone broke up laughing at their decision to marry after only a matter of a couple of days. They loved that he had a sense of humor and had referred to their 'long' engagement.

"Okay, here is the shocking news. Kate is Irish!"

At this, their friends clapped and voiced their happy approval.

"Yes, I even checked with her mom and dad to be sure. Please welcome Kate's wonderful parents, Katherine and Jonathan Walsh." They joined them on the stage and warmly hugged both Kate and Michael.

"Now," continued Michael, "the next shocking thing I have to share with you is something that you might have already figured out from my formal attire, but I'm Scottish!"

Everyone was enjoying this as they laughed again and clapped their hands.

"And I double-checked with my dad," added Michael. "He verified it. This is my father, Benjamin Jensen," he said as his dad came up, laughing good-naturedly. He promptly by-passed and ignored Michael but hugged and kissed Kate on the cheek.

Everyone loved that. Yes, this family was going to fit right in.

"Now, I know you're all familiar with Kate's maid of honor. Well, I'll put it another way; How many of you have been interrogated by FBI Special Agent, Maggie O'Hara?"

That generated even more cheering and enthusiastic clapping.

"No one? Well, I guess the only one that has been interrogated, plus locked up, by her would be my best man and older brother, James."

"Here they are, Maggie and James."

James and Maggie looked at each other from across the floor. James' heart felt like it was going to pound out of his chest as he took a deep breath, repeating to himself, *Well, here goes nothing.* He headed towards her with a smile.

Maggie watched him come nearer. She felt deeply drawn to him as she gracefully moved to meet him.

They converged near the stage, and as they started to step forward, James took her hand, like it was the most natural thing in the world. They stepped onto the stage, but James continued to hold her hand possessively.

As they walked toward Michael and Kate, James suddenly stopped. He turned and smiled at Maggie as he whispered, "May I?" His eyes never left hers as he raised her hand to his lips and gallantly kissed it.

Maggie had never felt a magnetic attraction like this before. James was looking into her eyes as if he could see right into her soul. She felt like an open book, but she made no effort to hide it. *He must feel something.*

When they didn't seem aware of anything or anyone else except themselves, Michael laughed and said, "Boy, what are they teaching them in jail nowadays?

"I just don't know what to say," he shook his head in hopeless confusion.

Then he brightly added, "But a little later, they're going to tell you some great stuff about Kate and me, when they make the toasts."

Michael turned to the guests and said, "We'd like to kick off our music this evening with a special Irish tradition. Our band is The Four Tenors, which sings both Irish and Scottish music."

He turned back towards his brother and Maggie and realized they still hadn't moved. In fact, they looked like they were dazed and somehow, frozen in time, in their own private world.

Michael went over and whispered to them, "Okay, you guys can get off the stage now."

Nothing.

"Hey, James," he said louder.

James looked over at him in surprise, "What?"

Michael repeated, "It's over, you guys can get off the stage now."

James softly said, "Come on, Maggie." He turned and led her down the steps. Everyone smiled and tried to figure out what was going on between the two arch-enemies who were still holding hands as they stepped down from the stage.

Kate joined Michael as they tried to cover the awkward moment by explaining to the guests, "Our Irish wedding receptions traditionally start with the song "Red Is the Rose." Michael and I will use it as our first dance. Since it's known and loved by our whole Sea Crest community, we can all join in."

She continued, "Red Is the Rose," also shares its melody with the Scottish Wedding's last dance, "The Bonnie Banks o' Loch Lomond." We'll be closing with that, and you'll love the dance that includes all of us at the end."

Michael led Kate over to the beautiful lit snap-together floor and took her in his arms. "You look fantastic tonight, Kate. Thank you for marrying me."

They had a lovely time dancing, dipping, and swaying to "Red Is the Rose."

By the end of the dance, many other people had joined them, which was common in the Sea Crest community, when they heard that song.

Michael looked around and felt like he was the luckiest man alive.

His brother, however, was incredibly unnerved by his feelings. He had admitted to himself that he loved Maggie, but this feeling was epic.

Maggie looked up at him and realized how distressed he'd become. She wasn't feeling so normal herself, as she ventured, softly, "James, why did you kiss my hand?"

He looked embarrassed as he said, “You’ll think I’m foolish, and it will ruin everything.”

“I thought it was one of the sweetest things you’ve ever done. I‘d just like to know why you did it.”

James glanced at her and then looked away, as he blurted out the amazing truth, “I didn’t want Michael to kiss you before I did.”

Chapter 56

Maggie was frankly flabbergasted.

"Wow" was all she could seem to get out. *I'm sure that Michael would have only kissed me on the cheek. Was James upset about that? Wow!*

"James, I thought you were charming," she said softly.

"Thank you," he replied. They guardedly smiled at each other, and James added, "You thought I was charming? Well, I guess once we got to know each other, we've come a long way from our original opinions."

Maggie laughed as she explained, "Just so you know James, I never have, and I mean never, hated anyone, as much as I hated you."

"The feeling was mutual, times 1,000," confessed James. "Remember when you threw my alligator shoe over the side of the heli-basket?"

"Vaguely," she muttered innocently.

"That put a small crack in the hate. I couldn't believe you; an FBI Special Agent would allow yourself to care that much. But you were truly as scared about your friend, as I was about my brother. Oh, don't get me wrong, I still hated you, but now I felt you were a worthy adversary."

"Oh, really?" laughed Maggie. "Is that supposed to be a step up or something?"

"Sure," he chuckled. "Big, big difference. For instance, when you came out with Kate for the wedding ceremony at the top of the Sea Crest Lighthouse, and I honestly looked at you. I thought it must have taken a whole team of beauticians and cosmetic make-over geniuses to get you looking that good."

"Thanks."

"No, really, I thought if we'd met under different circumstances like we weren't sworn enemies, that I would like you. You know, like a crush. I won't pretend that you'd give me the time of day, but I thought you looked great. Even when I hated you."

Chapter 57

The band started playing "The Way You Look Tonight."

"That brings me to the brink of totally making a complete and utter fool of myself," admitted James.

"Go ahead, I can't wait," answered Maggie.

"I requested this song from the band tonight."

"This is one of my favorites."

"Mine too," said James.

"Well, I don't want to waste it, James. Is it okay if we dance to it?"

James broke into a smile as he retook her hand and led her to the dance floor. James raised their clasped hands over their heads as he twirled her gracefully around just for the sheer fun of it. When their smiling faces met again, he gazed into her beautiful eyes as he lowered one of his arms and slipped his hand around her slender waist. He held her other hand as he drew it up to his chest and hugged it to him.

They swayed to the music as he said, "Maggie since you so kindly asked me to dance, I'm asking you to listen carefully to the words."

"Maggie, The Way You Look Tonight," he shook his head as he held her back at arm's length and took a long sweeping look at her. "Well, believe me, I will never get this picture out of my head."

James possessively drew her a little closer, as he confessed softly in her ear, "Maggie, I saw your entrance tonight. But I wasn't prepared for how strikingly beautiful you are."

"Thanks. However, if the picture of me that you carry around in the back of your mind is along the lines of how I looked while we spent two nights and three days in an underground tunnel and maze of caverns, then that certainly isn't very flattering!" Maggie protested.

"Oh, on the contrary," corrected James. "During that time, I recognized what a beautiful and kind human being you are on the inside."

"That is what I kept discovering about you too, James," replied Maggie.

"By the way," he continued. "Please keep your dance card open for me for."

"That's not fair; what if I meet some other handsome guy?"

"Then, of course, I'll have to cut in."

Chapter 58

The music continued with a combination of traditional Irish and Scottish selections, along with often requested, favorite wedding songs.

The elegant candle-lit dinner was served, accompanied by some of their favorite musical selections.

Kate and Michael were seated at the head table. Maggie sat beside Kate, with Kate's mom and dad next. James was next to Michael with his dad seated next to him.

While the guests were finishing the meal, Michael thought this would be an ideal time to have Grace share her information on the parachute wedding gown.

One of the band members handed Michael a microphone. He asked, "Grace, could you join us here for a few moments to help explain the historical journey of Kate's beautiful wedding gown?"

Grace had been sitting with Joe, and she happily excused herself to go to the stage area.

She stepped forward to share her knowledge of Kate's wedding gown. As she took the microphone, she said, "I'd be honored to give you all the brief story of this beautiful silk dress."

She smiled and began, "It's a miracle to trace where this gown originated and where it's ended up.

"Many of you remember Mrs. Chambers, who owned the beach house up on the hill overlooking the Sea Crest Beach and

Lighthouse. We remember her as one of 'The Summer People' because, in our lifetime, that's when she was here at Sea Crest."

"We have recently discovered that she has historical roots in our area, which date back to the shipwreck off our coast and the founders of the Town of Sea Crest.

"There is an incredible family history connected with Kate's dress. Michael Jensen's grandfather was a paratrooper stationed in Europe during World War II. He planned to marry Michael's grandmother as soon as he returned home, about one month later.

"As was the case for many brides during the war, Michael's grandmother was unable to buy a wedding gown or find any material to make one. Silk and nylon were among the items that were scarce and had to rationed and saved for the war effort. Consequently, they were unavailable to the public.

"On his last parachute jump, his grandfather had an accident. Although he was injured, his parachute had saved his life. He went to a hospital in Europe to recuperate. Since that was his last mission, he sent his parachute home in the mail.

"I can only imagine Michael's grandmother's surprise when she opened the package and saw the white parachute silk. She had several friends and family help her make a wedding gown out of the material. His grandmother Chambers married his grandfather in a wedding dress made from the parachute that had saved his life. During the remainder of the war, his grandmother let many other brides wear her parachute wedding gown to get married in.

"In fact, Michael's mother was the last bride to wear it when she married his father.

"Michael's grandmother saved the parachute wedding gown in a specific storage unit, with instructions for the grandsons to retrieve it. However, it was mistakenly sold at public auction.

"As the town's historian, I usually buy all estate sale items or storage lockers with potential clues to the history of Sea Crest.

"As fate would have it, on the date of the sale, I was not able to go due to an illness. Kate offered to go in my place. She just happened to be the interested party that bought the units, on behalf of our Sea Crest Historical Society.

"We soon found out someone named Michael Jensen was planning to meet with Kate regarding the storage unit contents.

"Within 24 hours, both Kate and Michael turned up missing. Well, as we all know, they had both been locked in the Sea Crest Lighthouse, where they proceeded to fall in love.

"They asked Maggie to see if I had found his grandmother's wedding dress in the storage unit stuff. If I found it, they asked Maggie to bring it so Kate could wear it.

"Well, luckily, I did find the parachute wedding gown. So, Kate was able to wear it, and she looks lovely in the elegant gown," Grace finished.

Everyone was delighted to hear Kate and Michael's incredible story, which included how they met. The music started again, and the friends and family began to dance again.

As Grace headed back to her table, Jeff Williams from New York, met her halfway and asked if he could have this dance.

"Oh, of course, Jeff," she replied with a smile. He was a friend of Joe's, and she'd been introduced to him recently. She wanted to be sure he felt welcome here in Sea Crest.

As they started to dance, he commented, "That was very insightful, Grace. I can appreciate your efforts to reconstruct the history of Sea Crest. That's very admirable."

"Thank you, Jeff," Grace smiled and blushed at his compliments as they continued to dance. It was so pleasant to have someone genuinely take an interest in her work. "A few years ago, we had a severe hurricane, which damaged much of the Sea Crest Courthouse. Many of our records were lost or destroyed beyond repair."

"Grace, please let me know if I can help you in any way. Aside from my law degree, I have a degree in American History," Jeff offered. They seemed to hit it off, as he added, "I've always been greatly interested in our country and how it was founded."

"Well, thank you..." started Grace when she was rudely interrupted by a very annoying voice.

"May I please cut in?" insisted Joe Lawrence, as he nudged Jeff out of the way.

"What? Oh, Joe," laughed Jeff. "Hi, I was just telling Grace that I might be able to help her with...."

"Never mind, I'll talk with you later," answered Joe abruptly.

He turned to Grace and asked, "Would you like to dance?"

"Joe, what on earth is wrong?" she asked.

"Nothing, do you want to dance?"

"Why, yes, but are you okay? You seem upset," said the very confused Grace.

Joe proceeded to dance off with Grace while Jeff just shook his head in puzzlement.

James and Maggie looked over at Joe from the head table. As they caught his eye, they raised their glasses to toast him and smiled. "It's true, Maggie," said James. "Paybacks are great, aren't they?"

"Yes, let's see how HE likes it." agreed Maggie with a laugh.

Chapter 59

The cutting of the five-tiered wedding cake with the Sea Crest Lighthouse topper would be legendary for decades to come.

The little figures of the Groom in the Chambers' Tartan Kilt and the Bride in her parachute wedding gown beside the Sea Crest Lighthouse were created with incredible, refined artistry.

As Michael and Kate cut the first pieces of wedding cake, they reflected the happiness of the most romantic wedding couple that you could imagine. They laughed as they happily fed each other the customary pieces of cake. The top layer of cake, with the Sea Crest Lighthouse topper, was set aside. The restaurant staff took over performing the long-standing tradition for the bride and groom to save the top tier to share on their first anniversary.

As the waiters began serving the cake to the guests, Kate took Michael's hand. She proudly led him over to the nearby Groom's Mandarin Truffle Cheesecake. The display was decorated with the topper centered in the middle with a small bouquet of good luck white heather and a Scottish Thistle Flower. Flowing from the flowers was a beautiful Chambers' tartan plaid ribbon, which swirled around as it cascaded down layer after layer. It was absolutely stunning.

As the cake was distributed, the toasts began.

James stood and raised his glass. To show his respect for Kate and her family, he recited the Irish Blessing.

"Kate and Michael: *May the road rise to meet you."*

After the first line, the entire gathering of family and friends stood and joined James in offering the Irish Blessing to the couple.

"May the wind be always at your back.
May the sun shine warm upon your face;
The rain fall soft upon your fields.
And until we meet again,
May God hold you in the palm of his hand."

James toasted the couple with the champagne from the Underground Railroad wine cellar cave.

Kate's mom wiped a tear from her eye as she thanked God that this wonderful man had come into their lives and swept their Kate off her feet.

The guests clinked their spoons to their glasses to signal that they wanted to see them kiss. Well, they were going to get more than they bargained for.

Michael stood as he took Kate's hand to help her up. Then with her eyes twinkling, he gently tilted back her head and just like the iconic couple in the Times Square Photo, on VJ Day..., They Kissed. They held the elegant kiss and embraced for a full minute while numerous guests and the wedding photographer took 'A Picture Worth Taking.'

As the kiss ended, everyone happily clapped at this magical display of their love.

James' glance was drawn like a magnet over to Maggie. He was surprised but pleased to find her looking thoughtfully back at him. No words were needed.

Benjamin watched this exchange with increasing interest. He speculated, *Everyone is looking at the couple perform one of the most 'iconic' kisses of the century. But my eldest son is looking longingly at Maggie, wishing he could kiss her like that. She feels the same as she looks back at James, and the final proof rolled silently down her cheek.*

Chapter 60

The soft music of "I've Grown Accustomed to Her Face," started and James couldn't take it anymore.

He approached Maggie and said, "May I please have this dance?"

"Of course, I'd be delighted," she smiled as he took her arm and led her to the dance floor.

James took Maggie in his arms and danced to one of the most romantic songs ever.

He whispered softly in her ear, "Maggie, I really need to talk with you."

"Okay, is something wrong?"

"No, but this can't wait," he pleaded. They had stopped dancing but were still holding each other in an embrace.

"Maggie, please come with me," he said, as he led her outside onto the beach.

When he came to a stop, he turned to her, "Maggie, do you have any idea what you've done to me?"

"I'm not sure, James," she whispered.

"Well, let me try to explain. Believe me, I'm as surprised as you are... Wait, before I go further, you look ... that gown, Well," he stammered, at a loss for words.

"In my wildest dreams, I never imagined...That gown is you, Maggie," James said as he stepped back and quietly looked at her.

"Thank you." Maggie was so glad he liked it. "A grateful Paris fashion designer made it special for me. This is the first time I've worn it."

"Maggie, when you walked in tonight, you took my breath away." He helplessly confessed, "I'm still not recovered."

"I had this all prepared, and I've been rehearsing all day for the right way to explain this to you," he continued."

"Whatever it is, James, it's okay. I might already know about it," she said, smiling and thinking of Misha and what James had secretly done for her.

"How could you possibly know? I didn't even know."

"Well, today, after our exciting hair salon appointment, I dropped Kate back at the keeper's cottage, and her Mom ran out and told me Joe was inside, and he'd been waiting for me."

"Joe doesn't know anything. I never told him anything," exclaimed James in frustration.

"He gave me the affidavit, which says that I can keep Misha," beamed Maggie. "Kate and I figured you were responsible for it. Thank you, James," said Maggie as she stepped forward and hugged him.

"You're welcome, Maggie, but that's not what I need to tell you," he said. He tenderly drew her face gently up to him as he bent to touch his lips to hers in a precious first kiss. This first taste soon intensified into an enhanced, full out electrical surge, the likes of which they had never imagined before.

Neither one wanted the amazing kiss to end as they clung to each other, sharing the profound emotional love they felt for each other.

Finally, James drew his head back and looked into Maggie's eyes again; he cleared his throat and tried to find the words, "That's what I need to tell you. I'm in love with you, Maggie. I don't know how it could happen, but I can't help it or control it."

Maggie was trying to follow that when she said, "James, I've got something just as improbable to confess. I'm in love with you, too!"

"Oh, Thank God! I was so afraid it was just me. You are the one person on earth who could truly break my heart, Maggie."

They kissed again, and the intense love they unveiled this time around should have terrified both of them.

James leaned back slightly and looked at Maggie in her elegant gown again. He was not a big risk-taker, so he was worried about his next step. It was too important to mess up.

He searched her beautiful face, and knew he couldn't live without her, as he said, "Maggie, I've got something important to ask you."

"Well, James, it can't top what you just told me, so ask away," she smiled.

James knelt to one knee and pleaded, "Maggie, would you please marry me?"

"What?" she whispered as she dropped to one knee beside him.

"I love you to the ends of the earth, Maggie. I can't live without you. Please marry me!"

"Then, Yes, times 1,000, but only if you'll marry me back!"

James took her hand and helped Maggie back up as he took a ring from his sporran. "This ring was my mother's engagement ring. My father gave us his blessing, and we'd be honored for you to have this as our engagement ring."

"James, your father knows you love me? He knows you want to marry me?"

"Yes, he's the one who offered my mother's ring. Tonight, after we saw you in this spectacular gown," James continued. "We both agreed I better get a ring on your finger as soon as possible. He threatened to marry you if I didn't ask you," laughed James.

"It's beautiful, and it's the most precious ring I could imagine, James."

"Well, your mother said it was your ring size, so she thought it would fit."

"What? My mother? She saw this? She knows?" Maggie was genuinely astonished.

"Well, I had to talk with your dad. It's a Scottish custom, and I thought out of respect for your father, I needed to make sure he knew that I'm in love with you. Not just for now, but this is a Forever Love."

"You're kidding. They never mentioned it to me. However, earlier tonight, my mother said I looked perfect, and she cried. Then Dad told me how much they loved me. I thought it was about Kate."

"I can't believe you talked to my dad," she continued. "Thank you, that means a lot."

"Well, it was especially important for me too. Your dad did save my life, and he needed to know what I feel. That I don't deserve you, but I can't live without you."

The band was playing "Truly" as Maggie and James stepped back onto the dance floor.

James took her in his arms and held her close as they danced. Maggie could scarcely believe she was lucky enough to have this incredible man.

James started to sing "Truly" to Maggie. He would have given Lionel Richie competition on this one.

In the second verse, Maggie started to harmonize and sing along to James, just like they'd done on their last night in the Underground Railroad tunnel.

Chapter 61

The Four Tenors started the music for the time-honored Scottish tradition for the last dance of the evening.

Michael came forward to explain again, "Scottish weddings and celebrations usually end with the song, "The Bonnie Banks o'Loch Lomond." It has the same melody as the Irish, "Red Is the Rose."

He added, "It's our version of what you might have seen at Greek weddings. The only thing different is that we had to promise The Sea Crest Restaurant that we won't break any of their dishes. But it's still a lot of fun."

"Okay, please join us. A few of the celebration planners practiced with us a couple of days ago, and they did just fine.

"Please gather around in a large circle and hold hands and we'll show you how the dance works," he directed.

"It's a double clap and then one long hold.

As the music started, it looked like everyone wanted to join in the festive tradition. Even a couple of waiters and waitresses got into the action with broad smiles on their faces.

"We all sing, and you're welcome to sing the Irish version if you'd like."

Friends and family joined in and happily sang the song, and the double clapping picked up and intensified.

James held Maggie's hand, and as he sang this meaningful ballad to her, except when it got to the part of the lovers, he kissed her hand that bore his mother's beautiful engagement ring.

"Maggie," he had to shout to be heard. "This is the best day of my life!"

The circle closed in around Michael and Kate. It then swelled back out again, losing some dancers and dividing into separate strings of well-wishers and friends, that almost imitated conga lines.

James looked at Maggie as she danced beside him. She felt his eyes on her as she turned to look at him with so much love that she thought she would burst.

James drank in the vision of her with that gorgeous sea-mist green gown. Her beautiful, outrageous hair, and most importantly, he saw the endless love in her stunning emerald eyes. James reached for her and drew his hand up to tenderly caress her sweet face with one hand while he asked her, "Maggie, I don't mean to rush things, but do you know anyone here, who can marry us tonight?"

"Well, I think I saw the Coast Guard Chaplain, that married Kate and Michael."

"Our families are here, and I honestly can't bear to wait another hour."

James took her in his arms and kissed her soundly. Well, it would have been more soundly, except for the fact that everyone had stopped singing and clapping. It appears they were now staring in surprise; some even stood with their mouth open.

The guys were nudging each other and giving high fives.

The women were very emotional and remarking 'Oh, how romantic,' and other sentimental things. A few were covering their mouths with their hankies and holding their chest with their hands in weepy delight. Maggie's mom and Kate's mom had heartfelt tears in their eyes as they saw their Maggie, in love with her arch-enemy.

Joe and Grace hugged each other in triumphant pride in their successful accomplishment. Joe saw Jeffrey looking at him with interest, which resulted in Joe keeping his arm planted possessively right where it was, around Grace.

Maggie searched for Kate, who was running towards her with tears in her eyes.

Kate hugged her best friend as she asked breathlessly, "Did you say, Yes?"

Maggie was so emotional; she could hardly get out the, "Yes. Can you believe it? James loves me! Kate, did you know?"

"Michael wouldn't tell me anything until you guys got up to dance and then went outside." Kate laughed, "I thought something was wrong, and I was going after you to see what he said to you. Michael stopped me and said he was proposing."

"I was happy, but I still wanted to go outside, just to be sure you were saying yes.

"Let me see your ring, Maggie."

"It's gorgeous. Did you set a date?" asked Kate seriously.

"Well, to tell you the truth, we were hoping that Coast Guard Chaplain was still around."

"You're in luck. Michael said that he and his dad saw how wound-up James was, that they were afraid you'd elope."

"Your folks and Benjamin decided we'd like to be there when you marry. Dad and Uncle Sean invited the Coast Guard Chaplain to come to our Wedding Celebration with a marriage license, just in case. I guess he's waiting in the backroom to see what happened."

"Benjamin said he's never seen James so stirred up, and if you turn James down, he'd be so overwrought that he'd positively need the Chaplain."

"Maggie, nobody told me anything, because they thought I'd tell you," laughed Kate.

Chapter 62

The Chaplain stepped forward with this hand, outstretched towards James.

"Captain Jensen, it is an absolute honor to meet you again, Sir. I had no idea who you were last time. When I saw your signature as a witness on your brother's marriage license, I couldn't believe it was really you."

Everyone just stood around looking clueless about what he was talking about.

"Oh, that's okay," said James quietly, like he was embarrassed.

"Are you going to wear your Marine Corp uniform with all your medals?" asked the star-struck Chaplain.

"No, I'm going to wear the Chambers' kilt."

"I, for one, would like to know what you did to get a medal," stated Michael. "I knew you were in the Marines for a couple of years. What did you do?"

"I'm his father," demanded Benjamin as he stepped forward. "I think I have a right to know."

The proud Chaplain didn't need any encouragement to continue, "Well, I checked around, and sure enough, you're the real hero, Captain James Jensen. I didn't recognize you from the previous pictures that came over the wires of you and your troops. It looked like most of them were just hanging on by a thread, but you didn't lose even one of them."

"I visited many of them while they were recovering from that mission in the hospital. Captain Jensen, they each said the same thing (to a man), that they survived solely because of your faith and strength. You said, 'none of them were going to give up on themselves or each other.' They feel that they owe you their lives.

"I have to laugh when I remember getting into that Heli-basket with you and this lovely young lady. I still crack up laughing at the memory. When she threw your snazzy shoe over the side, I thought, now that gal has spunk! Now that I know who you are, Captain Jensen, I think she's exactly who you need to marry. It would be my honor to perform this ceremony."

"Great," declared the very impatient and embarrassed James.

Kate was enthusiastically directing her friends and family how to rearrange the decorations for Maggie's wedding. "Let's move those flowers. We can design an entryway from that arch and interweave the white heather around and through it. Beautiful! Now, why don't we light the whole area by intimate candlelight?"

The Chaplain asked who the witnesses were going to be. Maggie and James laughed as they answered together, "Kate and Michael."

Next, Maggie asked her mom and dad and Benjamin to stand up with them also.

Kate ran up to the head table and picked up her beautiful bouquet. She brought it down to Maggie and laid it in her arms, as she said with teary eyes, "Aren't we the two luckiest people in the whole world?"

The photographer was now busy setting up for the surprise wedding of James and Maggie. He never had a situation where an additional wedding developed during the celebration of the first wedding.

The photographer took numerous pictures of the new happy couple along with the *original* happy couple.

The pictures of the new wedding party and family, included the same people, only rearranged.

"What a picture we make," said Maggie's mother, as she beamed with pride. "Maggie is in her beautiful Paris Designer Gown, and Kate is in the Chambers' parachute wedding gown. James and Michael are in their Chambers' Plaid Kilts, and Benjamin is in his Jensen Plaid Kilt. Your dad in his tux while I'm in the dress I bought, especially for your wedding, in the hope that you, my dear, wouldn't run off and elope."

Most of the Wedding Celebration friends and family were excitedly helping them arrange things for the wedding of Maggie and James. They all gathered around this thrilled family and stood up for their friends also. It was indeed one of the most memorable events of their lives.

The ceremony was exceptionally moving, yet very simple, at James' request.

Believe it or not, both Maggie and James had some touching remarks to include. The Chaplain then asked if they had rings to exchange, but it was only a formality.

James reached into his sporran and withdrew a small box with a wedding ring, which perfectly complemented his mother's engagement ring.

Sean smiled and stepped over to Maggie as he handed her a little box with the groom's matching wedding ring. "We went to the jeweler with James to help pick out the rings. If you'd like something different, it's fine," he said as he kissed his daughter.

"Dad, this is fantastic, thanks," she answered. Then she turned to her mom and said, "Thank you, Mom. It's perfect."

The Chaplain watched as James placed the ring on Maggie's finger, and then Maggie placed the ring on his finger.

"With great pleasure, I now pronounce you husband and wife."

There wasn't a dry eye in the house as he finished the ceremony and said, "You may now kiss your bride."

Keep reading for an excerpt from

The Key to the Lighthouse Cornerstone

The third book in
The Sea Crest Lighthouse Series.

By Carolyn Court

A chilling flood of distress washed over her as the sharp edge slashed her finger. She felt pure agony as she watched the timeworn bottle slip from her hand and fall toward the jagged rocks below.

"Please don't break," Grace pleaded fearfully while she quickly drew her bloody, cut finger to her mouth. "Oh, no! What have I done?" she cried as she leaned to look over the railing.

She watched, transfixed, as the glass container smashed to smithereens! Her legs rushed down the broken walkway from the Sea Crest Lighthouse to the rocky shoreline, but her eyes never left the shattered antique.

Before she could reach it, she spotted a delicately wrapped roll of paper, tumbling from the crushed fragments of glass.

At last, free of the wreckage, the pale parchment was caught by a gust of wind and proceeded to dance along the sand beneath the Sea Crest Lighthouse.

"This message is over one hundred years old! I can't lose it," she cried as she flew along the beach and raced after it.

Finally, she caught up with the sandy, crumpled paper. She bent to touch it, cautiously raised it, and softly whispered, "Now, let's see what was so important that they put you into the cornerstone of our Sea Crest Lighthouse."

Grace carefully unwrapped the old twine from the spiral scroll, as the binding practically fell apart in her hands. However, it revealed a wax seal, which was still set as firmly as the day it was stamped. Her eyes fell on the beautiful interwoven letters, RLS. Grace's hands trembled as she recognized the seal showed the *stamp* of the most famous Scottish Lighthouse family of the mid-1800s.

"Wow!" Grace could hardly believe their good fortune, as she whispered, "RLS – Robert Louis Stevenson!"

She was elated as she unfurled the delicate parchment and read, *My Scottish grandfather, George Stevenson, drew up the plans to build the Tahiti Lighthouse. He specifically chose the site of Captain James Cook's observation conservatory. Our Stevenson family has close ties with his father's Scottish family. I still have my grandfather's correspondence with Captain James Cook, the great English Explorer.*

Grace was shocked. Her own father was named James Cook, and it was whispered that she was also a descendant of Captain James Cook. Once in a while, they questioned whether it was true or not. Still, it had always been terrific to pretend with each other, and anyone else who would believe them. She had once tried to connect their bloodlines, but the time constraints were too much at the time. Grace hadn't gotten back to the project yet.

Grace knew that her father had wanted to travel to Tahiti to view the 2014 phenomenon of the transit of Venus across the sun. This rare event is still most visible from Tahiti, French Polynesia, and the viewing was a huge special occasion. This trip would have been a once in a lifetime opportunity for her father. Sadly, he could not actually make that trip. Still, they continued to research both Captain James Cook's voyages and The Islands of French Polynesia.

Her previous investigation had uncovered that although Captain James Cook had several children, there had been 'no issue' to descend down through a bloodline. She was happy to see that in Captain Cook's ancestry, there were other siblings whose lineage had passed down to present-day ancestors. She also noted that many ancestors, including Captain James Cook's mother, were named Grace.

She picked up the cherished letter again and continued to read.

My grandfather placed a unique locket inside the hollowed-out cornerstone of The Pointe Venus Lighthouse, located on the northern tip of Tahiti in the Society Islands of French Polynesia. It was built in 1868.

In the future, when the cornerstone is recovered, the locket will be found. However, it can only be opened with a special ancestor's key.

Grace was stunned, as she vaguely wondered about an old Victorian key that had been handed down from her paternal grandmother. *I haven't even thought about that key in ages. It's funny, but we never did discover what that key opened.*

~ ♥ ~

Three hours later, Grace stepped aboard a flight to Tahiti. However, she did leave a message for Joe, clarifying in terms that were clear as mud, that she'd explain everything later if he'd please call her at the resort where she planned to stay.

Joe was surprised, but no problem. He placed the call. He wasn't genuinely alarmed until the resort manager stammered uncomfortably, "Grace Cook said she'd be back in time for this call. They must have been delayed."

"Wait a minute, where did she go?"

"Well," he hesitated. "I'm not sure exactly. They flew off in his little yellow seaplane around two o'clock. Ms. Cook was very excited and asked Philip if he'd take her up for a ride in it."

"What? Who is Philip?" Joe demanded. "Does he take guests up for sight-seeing tours?"

"Ah, no!" answered the manager. "This is the first-time-ever that anyone has agreed to go up in what we jokingly call, 'his flying bucket of bolts, that floats!'"

"Oh, no!"

"Oh, yes!" continued the manager. "Ms. Cook stopped in her tracks when we heard him tinkering with one of the pontoons, he was working on, down by the beach. She was delighted to tell me that she was signed-up for flying lessons on a seaplane back home."

"She already has a pilot's license for small fixed-wing planes," added Joe.

"Well, that makes me feel a little better," explained the manager slowly. "When we heard Philip fire up the engine, she clasped her hands together in delight. Then she practically ran down to the water's edge.

"After a few minutes, she returned and told me she asked him if she could ride around the islands with him. She wanted to verify that her French was good enough for him to understand that she wanted to come back here. I listened to what she'd told him and agreed that he definitely should have understood. She happily hurried back to the seaplane and off they went. However, they were supposed to have returned hours ago!"

"Wow, how many islands are there?" Joe choked in disbelief.

"That's just the problem. French Polynesia is a collection of 118 islands and atolls, many of which are uninhabited."

Recipes
Made by the characters

The Lightkeeper's Secret

Mandarin Truffle Cheesecake

Pastry Chef Paula Graziano

Bottom Layer Truffle Cake

12oz dark chocolate
8 oz butter
1 ½ cup sugar
6 eggs
1 can mandarins, drained or
Fresh segments
325 ° oven 9" springform pan, prepped
Melt chocolate, butter over a double boiler.
Add ½ cup sugar, dissolve. Cool slightly.
Separate eggs.
Whip yolks with ½ cup sugar until pale and
triple in volume.
In a separate bowl, whip whites
with ½ cup of sugar until stiff peaks form.
Fold yolks into chocolate mixture, then fold whites.
Combine completely. Pour into prepared pan.
Poke mandarins randomly into the cake.
Bake for 40 minutes or until set.
Cool overnight.

Ganache

10oz good dark chocolate
8 oz heavy cream

Carolyn Court

Make ganache. Cool completely
Needed at room temperature to hold layers together.

Top Layer – Cheesecake

Use 9" cake pan lined completely with foil.
3 – 8oz cream cheese bricks, softened
3 eggs
1 cup sugar
1 tsp vanilla
1 can mandarins, drained

Mix cream cheese until softened, add sugar. Then eggs, one at a time, then vanilla. Scrape well - no lumps. Pour into pan. Arrange mandarins decoratively on top.

Bake 40-50 minutes at 325° until set. Cool overnight.

Assemble cake

Truffle cake on bottom

Spread ganache next - All cakes must be cool and firm, (partially frozen even),
(save some for decorating cake)

Cheesecake is the top layer.

Decorate with remaining ganache and fresh mandarins.

Aunt Helen's Raisin Filled Cookies

Helen Courtright and her daughter, Erma Courtright-Stackhouse

Raisin Filled Cookies

3 cups of brown sugar
1 cup of shortening
2 eggs
1 cup sweet milk
1 tsp vanilla
3 tsp of baking soda
3 tsp of cream of tarter
Flour to stiffen, about 7 to 8 cups

Raisin Filling:

2 cups raisins chopped
2/3 cup sugar
2/3 cup boiling water
1 tbsp vanilla
1 tbsp butter

Cook raisins, sugar & water 6 to 8 minutes or until thick
Add vanilla and butter
Cool before placing by spoonful on the bottom half of rolled out cookie dough
Place on top of each cookie and pinch together with fingers or fork to seal edges
Bake 10-15 minutes at 375

Carolyn Court

Old-Fashioned Crock-Pot Apple Butter

Joan Brown

24-28 apples (preferably Jonathan or Winesap)
4 cups apple juice
Sugar
Cinnamon
Allspice
Cloves

Wash, core, and quarter apples (do not peel). Combine apples and apple juice in lightly oiled Crock-Pot. Cover and cook on low setting for 10-18 hours or on high setting for 2 to 4 hours. (I do this part on the stovetop in a large pot as apples fit better and time is shorter.)

When fruit is tender, put through a food mill to remove the peel. Measure cooked fruit and return to Crock-Pot. For each pint of sieved cooked fruit, add 1 cup of sugar, 1 teaspoon cinnamon, ½ teaspoon allspice, and ½ teaspoon cloves, stir well. Cover and cook on high setting for 6 to 8 hours, stirring about every 2 hours. Remove cover after 3 hours to allow fruit and juice to cook down. Spoon into hot sterilized jars and process in boiling water bath, seal.

Makes about five pint jars.

Chocolate Mayonaise Cake

Jeanette Embrey and Sheila Embrey Martin

2 cups all-purpose flour
2/3 cup unsweetened cocoa powder
1 1/4 tsp. baking soda
1/4 tsp. baking powder
3 eggs
1 2/3 cups sugar
1 tsp. vanilla extract
1 cup mayonnaise
1 1/3 cups water

Directions

1 Preheat oven to 350°. Grease and lightly flour two 9-inch round cake pans; set aside.

2 In a medium bowl, combine flour, cocoa, baking soda, and baking powder; set aside.

3 In a large bowl, with an electric mixer at high speed, beat eggs, sugar, and vanilla for 3 minutes or until light and fluffy. Beat in mayonnaise at low speed until blended. Alternately beat in flour mixture with water, beginning and ending with flour mixture. Pour into prepared pans.

Bake 30 minutes or until a toothpick inserted in centers comes out clean. On wire racks, cool 10 minutes; remove from pans and cool completely. Frost, if desired, or sprinkle with confectioners sugar.

Cream Cheese Frosting

8 ounces cream cheese, room temperature

8 tablespoons (1 stick) unsalted butter, cut into pieces, room temperature

1 cup confectioners sugar

1 teaspoon pure vanilla extract

Soften cream cheese and butter. Combine in mixing bowl and beat until smooth. Sift in confectioners sugar, and continue beating until well blended. Add vanilla, and stir to combine.

Peanut Butter Frosting

1 cup butter, softened

1 cup peanut butter

4 cups confectioners sugar

1/4 cup 2% milk

2 teaspoons vanilla extract

Swedish Tea Ring

Myrle Burnside

Yeast dough:
½ cup scalded milk
½ cup shortening
½ cup sugar, ½ teaspoon salt
1 package active dry yeast
¼ cup warm water (not hot)
3 to 3 ½ cups of sifted enriched flour
2 eggs, beaten

Filling:
Melted butter or margarine
2/3 cup firmly packed brown sugar
2 teaspoons cinnamon

Powdered Sugar Icing

1 cup powdered sugar
1 to 2 tablespoons warm water, milk or cream
½ teaspoon vanilla

Scald milk. Add to shortening, sugar, and salt. Stir until sugar dissolves; cool to lukewarm. Dissolve yeast in water; combine with milk mixture. Stir in half the flour; add eggs; beat well. Add enough of the remaining flour to make a soft dough. Turn out on lightly floured board; knead until smooth and elastic.

Carolyn Court

Put in a greased bowl; brush with shortening; cover; let it rise in a warm place (80 to 85 degrees) until it doubles in size (about 2 hours).

Turn out on a floured board. Roll into a rectangle 8 by 12 inches. Brush with butter and sprinkle with brown sugar and cinnamon. Roll up like a jelly roll; shape into a ring on a greased baking sheet; pinch ends.

From outside, cut through the ring toward center almost all the way through in 1-inch slices. Fan out slices to side. Brush with shortening; cover; let rise 45 minutes or until dough doubles in size.

Meanwhile, set the oven to 325 degrees

Bake 25 to 30 minutes.

While warm, spread with confectioner's sugar icing.

Delicious Variations:

Add raisins to the cinnamon mixture.

Sprinkle with walnuts, pecans, or candied fruit.

Raspberries cream cheese (regular or light) filling.

Roll into two portions to make 2 smaller tea rings.

Acknowledgments

Special thanks to our daughter, Pastry Chef Paula Graziano, for letting us feature her Prize-Winning Mandarin Truffle Cheesecake recipe for the Groom's Cake in this book. She is the former owner of Paula's Bake Shop in California and has won numerous awards for this particular recipe.

A warm thank you to my Aunt Helen for her Raisin Filled Cookie recipe. I suspect her mother, Grandma Twinning, might have initially baked them. My aunt made a huge tin of these cookies ahead of time for camping trips. They were enormous, and I loved them. I'll always cherish the memory.

Growing up, I shared memorable vacation camping adventures with my wonderful cousin Erma Jane Courtright-Stackhouse. They often camped at Robert H. Treman State Park, Ithaca, New York. The park is in the beautiful Finger Lakes area. Erma Jane and I were loyal friends. What one of us didn't think up, the other one did.

One summer, due to our good behavior (ha, ha), we were allowed to rent a tandem bike while camping. (A bicycle built for two.) Double-trouble, but no surprise as our dads were twins!

Thanks to Jeanette Embrey and Sheila Embrey-Martin for the delicious Chocolate-Mayonnaise Cake recipe. This cake has been in the lives of these two sisters-in-law for more years than they'll ever admit. They tell me that Sheila's mother, Jeanette's mother-in-law, made this cake numerous times for special occasions.

I've also enjoyed their company for Mah Jongg, shopping, and lunches. I feel blessed to have them in my life. They've both been a great help with proofreading this second book.

A special thanks to Myrle Burnside for her Swedish Tea Ring recipe. I've had the good fortune of having Myrle as my next-door neighbor since we moved here. She is famous for her Swedish Tea Rings, and she makes them for holidays and many special occasions. I'm honored that she let me put her recipe in my book. She's been a great support for my writing.

Joan Brown's recipe for Old-Fashioned Crock-Pot Apple Butter is delicious. She usually picks the apples locally and generously shares the delicious apple butter with us every year. I'm so lucky to have Joan as a beta reader as well as a close neighbor. She's a wonderful, caring friend to all who are fortunate enough to know her. We are blessed to have her in our lives.

Thanks to another one of my extraordinary Mah Jongg friends, Sandy Wemmerus. She's a dear friend and valued beta reader. I love and respect her refreshing point of view on life. She's known in our community for her generosity and her wonderful sense of humor.

Special thanks to my invaluable friends, Jeanette Embrey, Linda Harrington, and Mary Szadvari. They dropped everything and cheerfully volunteered for the road trip to The Michigan Lighthouse Festival for my two-day book signing. Of course, then we had to explain to our husbands exactly why we needed to overnight in Cleveland, Ohio, (Rock'n'Roll Hall of Fame), on the way out. And naturally, it was an absolute necessity for us to stay at Niagara Falls, Canada, on the return. Our dinner at the revolving restaurant at the top of the Skylon Tower overlooking the Niagara Falls and the Horseshoe Falls was wonderful. (I briefly hoped our husbands were not eating TV dinners at home that evening.)

I've been blessed to have these dear friends help make my books a success. Thank you!

My special thanks and appreciation go to those who shared their expertise and time to ensure this novel's accuracy. If errors exist in this book, they are my mistakes alone.

Research and Resources

The characters and events in this novel are entirely fictional. Any resemblance to living persons or events is purely coincidental. However, I have woven historical events and known people into the storyline along with references to document the research. The subjects and events about lighthouses and shipwrecks are from my imagination, not a specific lighthouse.

I am a current member of the United States Lighthouse Society. The subjects and events about lighthouses and shipwrecks are from my imagination, not a specific lighthouse. My book reflects my knowledge that I have obtained from my visits to numerous lighthouses in Asia, Europe, The Caribbean, Bermuda, Tahiti, and The Galapagos Islands. Canada, Central, and South America, and the United States, including Alaska and Hawaii.

The United States Lighthouse Society www.uslhs.com Please consider joining this wonderful non-profit historical & educational society.

U.S. Lighthouse Society's podcast "Light-Hearted," is hosted by Jeremy D'Entremont. He is a fellow lighthouse lover and educator who interviews the staff and volunteers at various lighthouses each week.

National Mah Jongg League, Inc: nationalmahjonggleague.org

Information on 'A Picture Worth Taking' references: A SAILOR KISSES A COMPLETE STRANGER, a Nurse, in Times Square in New York City on V-J Day Aug 14, 1945. A picture of, The Kiss appeared on the front page of the New York Times the next day.

Information about The Parachute Wedding Gowns in World War II can be found at; en.wikipedia.org/wiki/ - parachute wedding gowns and scroll down through the options.

Information related to the wedding celebration
Groom's cake - https://en.wikipedia.org/wiki/Groom_cake
Flowers - http://www.scottish-at-heart.com/scottish-heather.html
The Scottish people are big on superstition, good (and bad) 'omens,' legends, luck
White Scottish Heather – good luck, https://www.scottish-at-heart.com/scottish-thistle.html
Sporran - https://en.wikipedia.org/wiki/Sporran, The traditional part of the male Scottish Highland dress, is a pouch that performs the same function as pockets on the kilt.

https://www.liveabout.com/minimum-age-for-scuba-diving-2963215
Aviation Without Borders USA – Integrated Humanitarian ...https://www.awb-usa.org
https://en.wikipedia.org/wiki/Brooklyn_Bridge - 324k - Cached - Similar pages
https://en.wikipedia.org/wiki/History_of_Champagne
http://www.wikihow.com/Survive-in-a-Cave

Scouts Information: https://cheslights.org/education/scout-patch-program/
https://butterflies.org/learn/children-and-family-programs/scout-classes

The clockwork of lighthouse lens:
http://www.lighthouselens.com/items/index
The lower SERVICE ROOM = the location of the clockworks (for rotating optics)
http://www.seathelights.com/other/anatomy

The Underground Railroad

http://www.historicsoduspoint.com/2011/08/underground-railroad
Aug 26, 2011, Captain George Garlock (1829 – 1906) ran a freight schooner (sail only) out of Sodus Point, NY, named "Free Trader" in the mid-1800s. Several safehouses were used to harbor "Freedom Seekers."
To find several informational connections of Harriet Tubman to the work of Scotland's Abolitionist, Eliza Wigham, Google: Harriet Tubman-Eliza Wigham.

www.harriet-tubman.org/letter-by-thomas-garrett
To find the information and pictures connecting the Scottish Abolitionist Eliza Wigham to her sister, Mary Edmundson, in Ireland, Google: Eliza Wigham-Mary Edmundson.

https://en.wikipedia.org/wiki/File:Wigham_eliza_and_sister_mary_edmundson.jpg
https://en.wikipedia.org/wiki/Eliza_Wigham - 102k. The family members were Quakers.

https://www.tripsavvy.com/emeralds-of-colombia-
https://en.wikipedia.org/wiki/Tiffany_and_Company_Buildin
g
https://en.wikipedia.org/wiki/Louis_Comfort_Tiffany

Nellie Bly Kaleidoscopes and Art Glass,136 Main St, Jerome, Arizona 86331

www.nbscopes.com Beautiful scopes

Information on Native American Timeline

https://www.bing.com/images/search?q=Native+American+Symbol+Freedom+and+Emancipation&form

America's largest underground lake, according to Guinness Book of Records Known and used since the days of Cherokee Indians https://thelostsea.com/history

https://en.wikipedia.org/wiki/Carte_de_visite#GallerySojourner Truth (/soʊˈdʒɜːrnər ˈtruːθ/; born Isabella [Belle] Baumfree; c. 1797 – November 26, 1883) was an African-American abolitionist and women's rights activist.

https://en.wikipedia.org/wiki/Sojourner-Truth

On the shelves in the 1st Safe room, Carte de visite of Sojourner Truth.
https://en.wikipedia.org/wiki/Carte_de_visite#Gallery

The carte de visite[1] (French: [kaʁt də vizit], visiting card), abbreviated CdV, was a type of small photograph which was patented in Paris by photographer André Adolphe Eugène Disdéri in 1854,

https://www.history.com/news/trail-of-tears-conditions-cherokee

Carolyn Court

Ttp://nativeamericansofdelawarestate.com/Delmarva_Indians_&_Underground_Railroad.

https://www.eiu.edu/eiutps/underground_railroad.php

https://ufdc.ufl.edu/UF00101148/0000

https://www.history.com/topics/native-american-history

https://www.britannica.com/event/Trail-of-Tears

https://en.wikipedia.org/wiki/Trail_of_Tears

https://www.wcu.edu/library/DigitalCollections/CherokeeTraditions/ArtsAndCrafts/rivercanebaskets.html

https://en.wikipedia.org/wiki/Sequoyah

https://www.encyclopedia.com/people/history/us-history-biographies/sequoyah

https://en.wikipedia.org/wiki/Cherokee_syllabary - 336k - Cached - Similar pages

https://en.wikipedia.org/wiki/File:Cherokee_orig_Syllabary.jpghttps://www.usmint.gov/coins/coin-medal-programs/native-american-dollar-coins/2017-sequoyah

https://www.britannica.com/biography/Sequoyah

https://en.wikipedia.org/wiki/Code_talker

https://www.history.com/news/world-war-is-native-american-code-talkers

Information about the piano playing of runaway slaves and all-black notes:

http://www.aaregistry.org/historic_events/view/blind-boone-musical-prodigy

www.maineantiquedigest.com/events/ambrotype-of-runaway-slave-and.../5076

https://pjcockrell.wordpress.com/2007/11/22/amazing-grace-just-the-black-notes/

https://en.wikipedia.org/wiki/The_Water_Is_Wide_(song)
Public Domain – English origin, written in the 1600s. Claimed by both Scottish and Irish as a folk song with slight variations.

Irish Wedding Song, First Dance: "Red is the Rose"
https://en.wikipedia.org/wiki/Tommy_Makem - 102
Scottish Wedding Song, Last Dance:
https://en.wikipedia.org/wiki/The/Bonnie/Banks/o'LochLomond/189k

The yellow-red rat snake (Pseudelaphe flavirufa)
http://www.atlasobscura.com/places/cave-of-the-hanging-snakes
http://www.rescuediver.org/tips/res-rec.htm

To view pictures of quilts from the 1800s
https://www.pinterest.com/vickie720/old-whig-rose-quilts
To learn more about the National Quilt Collection, by the Smithsonian, visit https://americanhistory.si.edu/collections/object-groups/national-quilt-collection

https://www.livescience.com/46565-are-dogs-colorblind.html

ABOUT THE AUTHOR

Carolyn Court is a writer of romantic suspense novels and is a member of The Romance Writers of America and the Faith, Hope, and Love Chapter. She's a member of the United States Lighthouse Society as well as the Chesapeake Lights Chapter.

The subjects and events about lighthouses and shipwrecks are from my imagination, not a specific lighthouse. Her books reflect her knowledge that she has obtained from her visits to numerous lighthouses in Asia, Europe, The Caribbean, Bermuda, Tahiti, and The Galapagos Islands. Canada, Central, and South America, and the United States, including Alaska and Hawaii. She was a longtime member of the Caribbean Tourist Board in Washington, D.C. Her travel memories from Scotland and Ireland are woven throughout this book.

The Lightkeeper's Secret is the second book in The Sea Crest Lighthouse Series. The first book is *The Heart of the Lightkeeper's Daughter.*

Made in the USA
Middletown, DE
27 September 2022